# PETS, PENS & MURDER

A Dickens & Christie Mystery
Book VII

## Kathy Manos Penn

# Also By Kathy Manos Penn

**Dickens & Christie Mystery Series**

Bells, Tails & Murder
Pumpkins, Paws & Murder
Whiskers, Wreaths & Murder
Collectors, Cats & Murder
Castles, Catnip & Murder
Bicycles, Barking & Murder
Pets, Pens & Murder
Candy Canes, Canines & Crime (2022)

*ON AMAZON*

*To Linda Jordan Genovese and Katie Scarborough Wills, my long-time readaholic friends, who have been dedicated Beta readers from the beginning. My books are better because of you.*

*Never tell all you know—not even to the person you know best.*


— AGATHA CHRISTIE

# Contents

# Cast of Characters

## The Americans

**Leta "Leta" Petkas Parker**—A retired American banker, Leta lives in the village of Astonbury in the Cotswolds with Dickens the dog and Christie the cat. Nicknamed Tuppence.

**Henry Parker**—Handsome blue-eyed Henry was Leta's husband.

**Dickens**—Leta's white dog, a dwarf Great Pyrenees, is a tad sensitive about his size.

**Christie**—Leta's black cat Christie is sassy, opinionated, and uppity.

**Anna Metaxas**—Leta's youngest sister lives in Atlanta with her husband Andrew, five cats, and a Great Dane.

**Sophia Smyth**—Leta's younger sister is married to Jeremy and lives in New Orleans.

**Bev Hunter**—Bev is Leta's Atlanta friend who fosters dogs.

**Dave Prentiss**—A journalist from NYC, he and Leta met when he stayed at the Olde Mill Inn in Astonbury. Nicknamed Tommy.

**Scarlett Callahan**—A graduate of Clemson, Scarlett now resides in London and assists Emily Paget-Ford with the Poison Pens Literary Festival schedule and other details.

## The Brits

**Gemma Taylor**—A Detective Inspector at the Stow-on-the-Wold police station, she's the daughter of Libby and Gavin and lives in the guest cottage behind the inn.

**Wendy Davies**—The retired English teacher from North Carolina returned to Astonbury to look after her mum and has become good friends with Leta.

**Peter Davies**—Wendy's twin and owner of the local garage, Peter is a cyclist and cricketer.

**Belle Davies**—Mother to Wendy and Peter, Belle lives at Sunshine Cottage with Wendy.

**Rhiannon Smith**—Rhiannon owns the Let It Be yoga studio where Leta and Wendy take classes.

**Ellie, the Dowager Countess of Stow**—Ellie lives in Astonbury Manor and is active in village affairs.

**Jake Nancarrow**—A Detective Inspector from Truro, the Astonbury group met him when they were on holiday in Tintagel.

**Gilbert Ward**—Gilbert is a collector of Sherlock Holmes memorabilia and a member of the Sherlock Holmes Society.

**Daisy Owens**—The Event Coordinator at The Grand Hotel, she oversees the Poison Pens event for the Golden Age Literary Association.

**Sue Fairchild**—The little old ladies met this Dartmouth English teacher at a yoga retreat in Tintagel.

**Emily Paget-Ford**—The founder of the Golden Age Literary

Association—the GALAs—she is the host of the literary festival.
**Oliver Fletcher**—The elderly gentleman is a participant at the festival and also the tour guide for the Agatha Christie Mile.
**Rhys Ford**—A presenter at the festival.
**Felicity Jenkins**—Detective Sergeant Jenkins recently transferred from Exeter to the police station in Torquay and is delighted to be attending the Poison Pens Literary Festival.

# Chapter One

WENDY WAS THE PERKIEST passenger in my London taxi this morning. Dickens snored softly in the back seat, and I hadn't heard a peep out of Christie since I placed her in the backpack and strapped her in next to her canine brother. While Wendy chattered, I mainlined another mug of coffee in an attempt to shake off my morning stupor. Staying up late to finish a book was never a good idea the night before a trip.

My friend pulled out her sunglasses. "Leta, can you believe what a beautiful day it is?"

Once again, Wendy and I were taking a road trip, one of our favorite pastimes. Travel wasn't on my radar when I moved to Astonbury eighteen months ago. Instead, my number one task was updating my 1840s Schoolhouse Cottage. Painting the drab walls, ripping out the brown carpet to reveal the flagstone floors, framing the wood-burning stove with built-in bookcases, and adding cheerful splashes of red and green made a huge difference. Those changes transformed the atmosphere from austere and somber to cheerful and welcoming.

There was no need to touch the exterior where the original schoolhouse bell still flanked the front door. Built of the luminescent golden stone the Cotswolds were famous for, my new home was picture-perfect—except for the garden, where my brown thumb was no help. Thankfully, I hadn't killed anything yet and had even managed to add a bit of color with the help of the local gardener. Time would tell.

Only then was I ready for Dickens and Christie to join me. Last year's arrival of my happy-go-lucky dog and sassy cat was all it took to make the house a home.

After we three had settled in, Wendy and I took a short trip to Oxford and discovered we were excellent travel companions. The fact we'd both taught English, Wendy for thirty years and me for four, and our love of shopping, books, good food, and good wine meant there was never a dull moment when we were together. For the Oxford trip, I left Dickens behind, but he accompanied us on our subsequent travel adventures to Dartmouth and Tintagel.

The morning clouds giving way to sunshine was a welcome sight, especially since the weather in our Cotswolds village had been cloudy and damp for what seemed like a month. The forecast for Torquay, today's destination, was a week of sunshine with moderate temps—a miracle for England at any time, much less in late October.

"No, and I'm crossing my fingers the weather holds." I glanced at Wendy as she fiddled with the radio. "I still can't believe I let Gilbert talk me into bringing Christie on this trip."

"Well, I admit I was surprised to see her in the back seat when you pulled up. I mean, taking her to a yoga retreat is one thing. A literary festival? I'm not so sure. Explain to me again why Gilbert wanted you to bring her."

I sighed. "He was a bit cagey about it. Something about her being the perfect prop for the presentation he's making. He was his usual charming self, and I just couldn't say no. As for Christie, she was amenable, so here we are."

"You crack me up. Christie was amenable. Sure she was. What did she do? Meow sweetly and smile at the prospect?"

Little did my friend know that I was serious about Christie's reaction—that I had asked my cat whether she'd like to accompany me. No one knew that I *did* talk to my four-legged friends—as in carried on conversations with them. I'd had this strange talent since I was a child and learned pretty quickly to keep it under wraps. I could understand dogs and cats, and vice-versa, though I seemed unable to converse with other animals. Perhaps that was a good thing. If I could understand the chatter of songbirds, horses, donkeys, and foxes, I would never have a moment's rest.

"Why yes, Wendy, I had a long conversation with her. Her only hesitation was that she didn't want to miss yoga with Rhiannon and Snowball."

When a stray cat gave birth in the donkey barn in September, our yoga instructor Rhiannon adopted the white kitten, so Christie now had a fellow feline yogi in Astonbury.

Wendy laughed. "I can imagine that. She seems to be showing Snowball the ropes at the yoga studio, and they make a cute pair—your sleek black cat and the tiny, fluffy white one. Has she made friends with Spot yet? Or is she being snooty?"

Timmy, my young next-door neighbor, had convinced his parents to let him choose one of the kittens as his first-ever pet, and the calico was his choice. He gave her what I'm sure seemed like a logical name to him. "She hasn't taken to Spot yet. I'm not sure why."

Dickens perked up and yawned at the talk of kittens. "I still want a kitten."

Laughing, I glanced in the mirror at my boy. "No, Dickens, our little family is quite complete with you and Christie." I didn't get a chance to seriously consider a kitten before Christie put her paw down and said no way.

Wendy gave me a playful nudge. "Your family is quite complete as far as furbabies, but there's room for a two-legged addition, right?" She was alluding to Dave's recent decision to relocate to Astonbury from New York City—a move that made me ecstatic and, if I was honest, a bit apprehensive.

"I'm still pinching myself. I was trying hard to take it one day at a time and not worry about how our long-distance relationship might wind up. I keep thinking I'll wake up and find it was all a dream—that there's no way Dave will give up his life in NYC to move here."

She shook her head. "Ye of little faith. The man's smitten—has been from the get-go—and seeing you only every few months was never going to work for him. I'm so happy for you both." With a sideways glance, she added, "But I'm still waiting for you and Peter to work things out."

Eyes focused on the road, I reflected on the happenings of the past few weeks. It was looking more and more as though I would have to take the bull by the horns and have a heart-to-heart with Wendy's brother. I refused to let myself believe that this awkwardness between us was permanent.

I kept thinking the tension would dissipate, but it had been several weeks, and nothing had changed. True, my concussion had put a temporary halt to our Sunday bicycle rides, and Dave's visit meant I wasn't as available as I usually was, but I knew none of that was the problem. When I asked Peter to cycle last weekend while Dave was in Carlisle for a literary festival, he brushed me off with a terse text—something he'd never done before.

Shaking myself, I glanced at Wendy. "I know I'm the one who will have to bring it up. He's gone out of his way to avoid me, and I *will* make him talk about it, but for now, I'm playing my Scarlett O'Hara card. I'll think about it *tomorrow*—or at least after Dave returns to New York City."

"I get it. When I brought up the flowers he sent you, he turned beet red and made noises about it being a simple thank you for the Little Old Ladies solving his friend's murder. Except he couldn't explain why Mum and I didn't get flowers too. He's embarrassed, and he's taking the easy way out."

*This too shall pass.* "On a brighter note, I can't wait to see Dave. It's funny that I can adjust to not seeing him when he's in New York, but when he's here, I miss him after only a few days. And it's been a week now."

"Personally, I can't wait to see Gilbert. I didn't get to spend nearly enough time with him when he was here last time."

Dave met Gilbert Ward at a Sherlock Holmes Society meeting in London. He was there working on an Arthur Conan Doyle article for Strand Magazine, and Gilbert was generous with his time. Though he claimed he was neither a serious collector nor scholar, he was a wealth of information, and we both enjoyed his company.

I laughed. "There's no doubt the man's entertaining, and he's sure to provide a running commentary on the festival presentations. Whenever I'm around him, I can't help but see him as a character in a BBC series set in the 1940s."

"You're right! Perhaps a compatriot of Lord Peter Wimsey."

"I wonder what persona he'll take on this week. You know, it's hard to believe I never attended a literary festival until I met Dave, and now we're booked for the Poison Pens Literary Festival on the English Riveria. I can't wait for the session comparing Dorothy Sayers to Agatha Christie. Sayers is the author who first hooked me on British mysteries with her Lord Peter Wimsey tales. When Gilbert adds his Arthur Conan Doyle perspective, there'll be no end to the literary trivia we'll hear."

Wendy twisted in her seat to look at our hanging bags. "Plus we get to dress up—always one of my favorite activities. You'll look marvelous in your burgundy velvet dress, and I can't wait to wear my turquoise sheath again."

Glancing at the bags in the rearview mirror, I pictured the two of us in our fascinators. Wendy's was topped with a peacock feather with a blue middle that set off her short platinum blonde hair and blue eyes. And then I thought of Dave in his tux.

"What are you grinning about, Leta?"

"Oh, Dave escorting the two of us into the ballroom. With his dark hair and eyes, the man does look dashing in a tux."

Wendy laughed. "That he does. I can still see him swooping into your costume party last year with his top hat and white silk scarf."

"Does your mum plan to wear the blue velvet dress she wore to Ellie's birthday dinner?"

Wendy grinned. "Oh yes, and I'm so glad she's feeling better. With her new trainer and Ellie's encouragement, she's been a lot more mobile lately. She even mentioned tackling the stairs at Greenway so she can see the second-floor exhibits. She hated missing those when we visited last year."

A private tour of Agatha Christie's summer home was one of the activities on the festival schedule. It was billed as including more intimate details of the author's life than the usual tour.

When we pulled up to The Grand Hotel, we were suitably impressed. The elegant Victorian structure may have opened over a hundred years ago in 1881, but its grandeur hadn't faded. Perusing the pictures ahead of time, Wendy and I had admired the rooms and open areas, not to mention the stunning views of the waterfront.

After a short break for Dickens, we followed the porter to the front desk, where we got the usual comments about Dickens looking like a miniature version of a Great Pyrenees.

Wendy had booked a two-bedroom sea-view suite to share with Belle and Ellie, who planned to join us in time for dinner. Tomorrow, Dave would arrive with Gilbert on the morning train from London. I chuckled as I signed for the suite Dave and I would share with Dickens and Christie.

"Leta, what are you laughing at?"

"I wonder what Gilbert would say if I suggested Christie share *his* room. After all, she's his prop cat."

That elicited an indignant squeak from Christie. "I'm not a prop cat, and I'm not sharing a room with anyone but you. Well, maybe Wendy and Belle, but no one else."

"Just teasing," I murmured as I reached back to tickle her chin. "You and Dickens are with me."

It was Christie's squeak that caught the attention of the desk clerk. Reaching over the desk, she stroked Christie's head. "A cat? In a backpack?" She spoke to a woman standing at the end of the desk. "Daisy, look! Isn't this the cutest thing?"

Looking up from her clipboard, the tall blonde grinned at the sight of Christie stretching out her paw to the clerk. Once again, my four-legged friends were stealing the show. "I'll say. And this must be the cat Gilbert Ward called me about."

"Oh, you know about that?"

"Yes." She held out her hand. "I'm Daisy Owens, Events Co-ordinator, and I try to keep track of all the guest speakers. In this case, I guess it's a guest cat! Who knows? Gilbert's session may be the most popular one this week."

Her comments prompted me to explain that I was looking forward to this event because I *wasn't* hosting it. "It's people like you, Daisy, who kept me from going gray at a much younger age." We laughed together as I shared my memory of a particularly stressful corporate event in NYC at the Waldorf.

Dickens and Christie weren't welcome in the restaurant, so I served their dinner in the living room of our suite and assured them I'd be back to take them for a stroll. Dickens chowed down, while Christie did her usual finicky act.

She sniffed her dish, sat back, and meowed, "Excuse me. Aren't you forgetting something?"

That was her way of telling me I needed to fluff her food with a fork and center the small dab in her little plastic dish—several times. When it finally met with her approval, she deigned to eat it.

Walking through the lobby, I caught sight of our friend Sue chatting with Wendy. "Sue," I called, "you must have been able to get that extra day off. So good to see you again." The members of the Little Old Ladies' Detective Agency—Belle, Ellie, Wendy, and I—had met Sue and her sister when we attended a yoga retreat in Tintagel in August. The sisters were teachers who hailed from Dartmouth. "Is Penny with you?"

Sue grinned. "Are you kidding? She reads the book of the month selection for our local book club, but a weekend about Golden Age authors? No way. That would be more than her math teacher brain could take. But I'm in heaven. I still can't believe the festival dates coincided with this year's October break."

"Why don't you join us for dinner?" I looked at Wendy. "Is it safe to assume that your mum and Ellie made it?"

"Yes, they'll be down momentarily, and I know they'd love to catch up with Sue." That settled it. Sue picked up her bags and said she'd change clothes and be back.

The hostess seated us by the window, and Wendy and I ordered a bottle of sauvignon blanc for the table as we waited for the others. We alternated between admiring the view of the pool surrounded by twinkling white lights and perusing our copies of the festival brochure. All of the sessions were enticing.

As I read aloud the names of the speakers, I noticed Kate Ellis, one of my favorite authors, was the host for the Archaeology & Agatha session. Later in the week, I noted Gilbert's segment comparing Arthur Conan Doyle and Agatha Christie.

"I didn't realize Gilbert had a co-presenter for his Conan Doyle and Christie session. I wonder who Rhys Ford is."

Wendy didn't respond right away. "Hmmm. Rhys Ford? That name sounds familiar, but I can't think from when or where. Oh well, maybe it will come to me. I hoped we might hear from a representative of Agatha Christie Limited, but it doesn't look like we will."

I smiled. "Attending a festival in the hotel where Dame Agatha honeymooned with her first husband isn't enough for you? And rambling along the Agatha Christie Mile with a tour guide? I've got cold chills just thinking about walking in her footsteps."

Ellie, Belle, and Sue came in together, and we quickly called for a second bottle of wine. Sue inquired about Gemma and Rhiannon, whom she'd also met at our yoga retreat, and was delighted to hear that Detective Inspector Nancarrow, whom we had dubbed the dishy DI, had spent his two-week holiday in Astonbury with Gemma.

Her eyes twinkled. "I knew there was a romance brewing there. I can't wait to tell Penny."

"Speaking of romance," interjected Belle, "Leta's charming boyfriend arrives tomorrow."

I blushed. No matter that Dave and I had been dating for a year, the term boyfriend always seemed strange to me. I quickly glossed over that comment. "And he's coming with our friend Gilbert, who, believe it or not, asked me to bring Christie."

I pointed to a Wednesday spot on the festival program. "He's co-presenting 'The King of Detectives vs. the Queen of Crime—Conan Doyle vs. Christie.' I still don't know why a black cat is needed for this topic, but I guess I'll find out soon enough."

Smiling, Ellie took a sip of wine. "With Gilbert, there's no telling, but I'm sure it will be entertaining. Sue, you're in for a treat." She went on to give a brief description of our friend and how he had helped us solve a literary crime in Chipping Camden. Sue clapped her hands. "It sounds like it. I can't wait to meet this character."

The combination of a long drive, a good dinner, and two bottles of wine meant we were all ready for an early night. I excused myself first and went to fetch Dickens and Christie for a stroll on the beach.

Dickens bounced up when I opened the door, but Christie was asleep—curled in a tight ball in the middle of the bed. When I nuzzled her with my nose, she yawned and stretched.

"Hey there, sleepyhead. Do you want to go for a walk?"

Rolling on her back, she stretched out full length and purred. When I placed the backpack on the bed, she crawled in and turned around with her face peeking out. "I'm ready."

I pulled a grey fleece turtleneck over my head and added a red headband—the one my sister had given me last Christmas embroidered with my initials. When we walked outside to the pool and encountered the ocean breeze, I was glad I'd bundled up.

With only a few folks on the beach, I took a chance and let Dickens off his leash. He scampered ahead, barking intermittently at the receding tide. "You silly boy, you can't call it back. It comes when it wants to." Christie was quiet, and I could feel her burrowing deeper into the backpack until she was tucked at the bottom where the wind couldn't reach her.

Near the pier, a lone figure jogged towards us and waved. *Who can that be?* I was almost on top of the person clad in sweatpants and a hoodie before I realized it was Daisy, the Events Coordinator. "Oh my goodness, in that outfit, you're almost unrecognizable."

She laughed. "I'm taking one last opportunity for a long run on the beach before the festival kicks into high gear. After this, it will be nothing but pantsuits until next Sunday." She knelt to pet Dickens. "May I give him a treat?"

When he sat back and barked, "Yes, yes, yes," she had her answer, though it took a chuckle from me to confirm it.

Christie got a head rub when she stuck her nose out of the backpack and meowed, "One for me, please." When no treat was offered, she grumbled and returned to the bottom of the pack.

Daisy continued on her way toward The Grand, and I trudged on into the headwind. Though Dickens would have been happy to stay outside for hours, it wasn't long before I was ready to go in. Like the full-size members of his breed, my boy loved frolicking in the wind and cold. Great Pyrenees were built to thrive in chilly weather and stay out with their herds of goats or sheep in the bitter cold. This weather was right up his alley.

As we approached the pool area, I heard voices. I suspected the people speaking didn't realize how their words carried on the wind, and I sensed some frustration in the male voice. "Yes, Emily, trust me, I've got it all under control."

"I know you say that, Rhys, and no offense, but you can't possibly be as well-versed in the Christie lore as a member of her family would be. I only wish we could have gotten one of the Prichards as a speaker. Given your medical background, I'm confident you'll be fine on the topic of poisons, but the Christie versus Conan Doyle session and the Greenway tour? I'm worried about those."

The man, who had to be Rhys, replied with a laugh. "No worries. Gilbert helped me to prepare, and he'll fill in if I miss any critical points. You know how he loves to talk. As for the special presentation at Greenway, I've given the tour any number of times as a volunteer, and I've read countless interviews with Matthew Prichard about his grandmother's letters—not to mention, I've read and reread the book. Everything will be fine."

By now, I could see them as well as hear them. The elegant silver-haired woman gave her tall, slender companion a peck on the cheek. "You know how I worry. I won't breathe easy until we've gotten through the Sayers versus Christie session, though I'm not nearly as worried about it. You and I have debated that topic enough throughout the years that we could probably do it in our sleep."

"Right, it would only be a problem if you had to shift from Sayers to Christie. There's never been any convincing you that Christie is the better writer."

With that, the gentleman took her arm, and they ambled to the door. "Now, shall we have a nightcap? You did bring my cognac, right?"

I refastened Dickens's leash and murmured. "Did you hear that, boy? Their conversation reminds me of some of the conference worries I dealt with at the bank. And Rhys is probably right. In my experience, things usually work out." *Little did I know.*

# Chapter Two

WENDY AND I MET for an early breakfast while Belle and Ellie slept in. Ellie was worn out from driving the Bentley, a car she didn't often use, and Belle rarely rose before 9 a.m. I told my friend about the conversation I'd overheard the night before.

She chewed a bite of croissant and followed it with a sip of tea. "That's fascinating. I bet there are always hiccups at these things."

"True, though the man seemed to be taking it in stride. It was the woman who was more worried. I think she may be the one in charge of this whole thing, and I feel for her. It makes me glad those days are behind me."

Wendy chuckled. "I wonder if Rhys Ford knows Gilbert is bringing a cat to the King and Queen presentation. Surely, he told him."

Glancing at my watch, I realized I needed to get a move on. "I've got to hurry if I want to be on time to meet Dave and

Gilbert at the train station. Do you want to walk with us to the 'discrete little railway station,' as it's described in the hotel brochure?"

"Of course I do. And I assume 'us' means Dickens and Christie. I'll meet you back here in a jiffy."

Since I'd already fed Dickens and my fussy feline, all I had to do was grab the leash and the backpack. I told Wendy I'd be down in ten minutes. That would give us time to admire the Victorian architecture of the Torquay railway station as we waited for the London train.

I may have lived in the UK for nearly two years, but I never failed to be charmed by the architecture and history, and the small station was picture perfect. I sat Christie in her backpack on the pavement, handed Dickens's leash to Wendy, and pulled out my phone. "Wendy, I want to take pictures of everything this week. This experience will make for a great series of newspaper columns, and my editors love photos."

Though I was an ocean away, I continued to write columns for small papers in Georgia and North Carolina, and my readers were as enchanted as I was with my life in the Cotswolds and trips further afield. This time last year, I regaled them with a description of the Astonbury Fall Fête. Tales from a murder mystery festival would be a first for me and them.

Dickens barked, and Wendy pointed. "Look, there they are." She hesitated and looked at me. "Did they pick up a fashion model on the way?"

I looked up in time to see Gilbert and Dave emerge from the station with a gorgeous redhead between them. The tall, slim creature wearing spiked heels and tight jeans sported a mane of wavy, red hair that flowed past her shoulders, and both men appeared engrossed in whatever she was saying. I watched as she placed her hand on Dave's arm and laughed. Before I knew it, she'd twined her arm in his and leaned in to whisper in his ear. *What the heck?*

Wendy was as taken aback as I was and said what I was thinking. "Who on earth is that? She acts as though she's Dave's long-lost friend."

Gilbert was the first one to look up and must have said something to Dave because he broke into a grin, pulled his arm away, and dropped his bags in one smooth motion.

"Leta," he called, jogging my way. He lifted me off my feet in a hug and murmured, "Lord, how I've missed you."

Setting me down, he grabbed my arm and pulled me toward his two companions. "You know Gilbert, but let me introduce you to Scarlett. She's a Southern girl like you."

Gilbert greeted me with a kiss on my cheek before I shook hands with Scarlett. "Leta Parker from Atlanta."

"Scarlett Callahan. How lovely to hear another Southern accent. I got my graduate degree at Emory, so I know your city well. And this must be Dickens! Dave told me all about him." She patted her knees and Dickens took the hint and placed his front paws on her legs.

Scarlett made appropriate cooing noises. "You're precious."

Christie made her presence known by screeching, "What about me?"

By now, Wendy had joined the conversation, and Dickens had shifted his attention to Dave. When Wendy explained she'd taught high school English in Charlotte, Scarlett gasped and grinned. "Goodness, you ladies are making me homesick. I'm a South Carolina girl, and I got my English degree at Clemson."

Our entourage made quite an impression as we approached the entrance to The Grand. Scarlett alone would have turned heads, but Gilbert in his typical Golden Age attire also got his share of inquisitive looks. No doubt, the lively Southern-accented chatter emanating from the group caught people's attention too. They had to be puzzled by the references to Bulldogs, Yellow Jackets, and Tigers and likely gagging at the mention of boiled peanuts—all typical topics for Southerners in the fall.

Wendy and Scarlett were discussing NASCAR, of all things, as she and Gilbert checked in. I realized Scarlett had shifted gears when I heard her mention the Poison Pens Literary Festival and ask the front desk clerk to ring Emily Paget-Ford's room. I wondered how many members of the Golden Age Literary Association would be here.

I couldn't wait to show Dave our sea-view room, and his reaction was what I'd anticipated. "Wow! Love it, and it even has a balcony." He tossed his bag on the bed and stepped outside, pulling me with him. "Can't you just see us sipping champagne as we gaze at the stars over the ocean, me in my tux and you in your velvet gown?"

*Goodness, I'm glad he's here.* "How very posh. I wonder if we can find Dickens a rubber dog toy shaped like a champagne bottle so he doesn't feel left out." Dickens nudged my leg in what I took as encouragement, and Christie chose that moment to rub against Dave's shin.

Dave tilted my chin up and planted a kiss on my lips. "I can't explain it, but I missed you more these two weeks than I do when I'm away from you for months in New York. That quick overnight with you on my way to London didn't do it. Do you think you're growing on me?"

"That is *so* strange. I felt the same way. Is it because usually when you're here, we spend very little time apart? Whatever it is, I'm glad you missed me." I stepped back and looked at him. "You didn't feel a need to replace me with a tall redhead, did you?"

His mouth formed an O. "Do I detect a hint of jealousy? I haven't seen this side of you before, Miz Parker. Rest assured, I only have eyes for you. Now, Gilbert, on the other hand . . . "

*Maybe I am jealous, or more like territorial—one of the words he used to describe Peter's behavior towards me.*

"Yes, Gilbert did seem quite attentive, but then he's always that way with the ladies—young and old alike. I recall Ellie commenting that he made her feel like a queen." We continued in this vein as Dave explained that Gilbert had bumped into Scarlett when he went in search of a snack on the train and, hearing her Southern accent, brought her back to meet Dave. She sat with them for almost the entire trip. That's when they heard she was on her way to help with the festival.

"Gilbert was quite intrigued by some story about Dorothy Sayers having an illegitimate son, but I didn't catch all of it. You're a Sayers fan. Is it true?"

"I'm a fan, yes, but not so much that I've studied the woman's life. I guess that would have been quite a scandal back in the day. If it's true, I wonder whether it happened before or after she became famous."

Dave rolled his eyes. "Oh well. We can ponder that mystery another time. Knowing Gilbert, he'll chase down the details while we're here. Now, are you ready for a visit to the bookshop? We should be able to fit that in and be back in time for the 3 p.m.

session, right?" On this trip to England, he was killing two birds with one stone—speaking at several literary festivals and, at the same time, gathering data for an article on small, independent bookshops.

He glanced at Christie, who was meowing at his feet. "Do you think that means she wants to go too?"

My sassy cat looked from me to Dave. "Such a silly question. Of course I want to go!"

The sunny morning had turned cloudy, but the weather was still mild. Dickens was in heaven with the wind ruffling his fur, and Christie was snug in the backpack Dave carried.

I smiled when I spotted The Quill Bookshop tucked on a side street, its wooden sign sporting an inkwell with a feathered quill sticking out of the top. As the sign creaked back and forth in the breeze, I imagined myself on a street in a Charles Dickens novel. The image was complete when a bell tinkled as we entered.

A large poster for the Poison Pens Festival was prominently displayed between two tables holding books by Dorothy Sayers and Agatha Christie. Given that Christie wrote over sixty detective novels, I was fairly sure more of her books were tucked away on shelves, but Sayers's eleven Wimsey novels were all there, along with several used copies of a title I didn't recognize—*Hangman's Holiday*. I studied the small placard next to the stack.

"Dave, look at this. I knew Sayers wrote Lord Peter Wimsey short stories, but I've never heard of Montague Egg. Have you?"

"That's a new one on me. Let's get a copy. And look here. Someone's written a whodunit titled *Dorothy and Agatha*. What a find this shop is."

We took two books to the counter and continued exploring. Near what must have been the stockroom door, I spied an open box overflowing with colorful postcards—a few were on the floor. "These look like marketing material about a book or an event."

Picking up a card, I was surprised when I saw the name Scarlett Callahan in large letters. My mouth dropped open. "Dave, is Scarlett an author?"

"Huh? Not that I know of. What does it say?"

I handed him the card, and he pointed to the image as he read aloud. "'Coming Soon, *The Sayers Secret.*' Wow. Get a load of this cover and the tagline—'Sexy and Scandalous or Stodgy and Sensible?' I'd think it was nonfiction if not for the silhouette of a shapely woman on the cover. In all the photos I've seen of Dorothy Sayers, she was short and plump."

Picking up another card, I flipped it over. "And here it says, 'See what critics are saying' and it captures what must be early reviews. 'Clever concept. The image of a brainy, sexy Sayers is compelling.' Dave, I think it must be fiction."

"I think you're right, and since it lists the publisher as Callahan Limited, that tells me she's probably self-publishing it. I wonder whether she tried getting it accepted by a traditional publishing house—no easy feat these days."

We carried the two cards to the front desk. "Excuse me," I said to the young woman behind the counter. "I found these on the floor in the back. What can you tell me about the author of this book?"

She smiled. "I don't know much about her except that she's an American and speaks with the most delightful Southern accent just as you do. And I believe she's helping with the festival. The cards arrived yesterday." Laughing, she pointed to the cover image. "Funny you should ask. Until now, I've never known anyone to use the word sexy to describe Dorothy Sayers."

As we paid for our purchases, I admired the inkwells on display. "With my awful handwriting, these would be wasted on me, but they're lovely."

My hand lingered over the one with a red quill pen perched in it, and Christie meowed. "Looks like a cat toy to me."

Before I knew it, Dave asked the clerk to wrap it and add it to our bag. He reached behind him to pet my cat. "What do you think, Christie? Will it stand a chance on Leta's desk, or will she have to display it high on a bookshelf out of your reach?" The only response was a contented purr.

Lining our purchases up on the bar in our room, Dave turned to me. "Now, what's next on the agenda, Leta? I know you have a plan."

"Of course I do. I want to wander the festival booths downstairs before the kick-off session. And, since you know me so well, what do you think I have to do before then?"

"Oh, that's an easy one. A new activity requires a different outfit. Off with the heavy sweater and jeans and into something else. What's the expression you use? You'll *fluff and dust* and then change clothes, right?"

I left him relaxing on the couch, with Christie reclining on his chest and Dickens lying on the floor beside him. Pulling on a long, red silk shirt and black leggings, I added a belt and black suede booties. The finishing touch was the new necklace I'd found on my Labor Day trip to New York City, a long silk cord that ended with clusters of crystal and black beads surrounding a large oval pearl. When Dave saw me, he gave a low whistle and hummed a few bars of "Lady in Red."

I stepped back and twirled. "Does that mean you approve?"

"You know I do. Red is your color, and that belt shows off your waist." His words made me smile. It was nice that he had no idea how much smaller it had once been. I was by no means overweight and was fanatical about staying fit, but I missed the twenty-three-inch waist I'd been so proud of in my younger days. *Still*, I thought, *not bad for a woman in her fifties.*

When Dave attached Dickens's leash to the new collar I'd gotten him—black with white skulls decorating it—we were ready to go.

Downstairs, we wandered the booths. Because I purchased most of my books at the Book Nook in Astonbury, I was more interested in the booths featuring reading-related items—clever bookends, notecards, magnets, and more.

"Dave, look at this!" I held up a five-inch tall statue of a cat standing with a book in its paws. Tiny glasses sat on its nose. "I have to get this for my sister Anna, and gee, I may have to get one for myself." He pointed out the perfect gift for my sister Sophia, a set of notecards labeled "The Reading Woman." Anything I could easily tuck into my luggage when I traveled home was a plus.

The next booth sported a banner proclaiming "Everything you need to write a mystery." It was filled with books, with topics ranging from how to master suspense and plot to how to develop a convincing character, complete with physical and personality traits.

Dave thumbed through a few. "As if you could learn to write a mystery by reading a few books."

I heard a chuckle and turned to see Daisy Owens. "We've hosted several literary festivals here, and you'd be astonished to know how many would-be writers walk out with a stack of these how-to books."

Holding up *Master Lists for Writers*, Dave asked a question. "Do you ever get to hear whether they find them helpful?"

She shrugged. "From what I've gathered, a creative writing class or a writing coach lays a better foundation, but I suppose books are easier to come by. By the way, did you know your host is a writing coach? Several of her students have gone on to publish books—not all, but a few."

Dave blushed when I told Daisy he would soon have a nonfiction book coming out. She congratulated him and jotted the title on her clipboard before moving on.

When Dave picked up *Deadly Doses, A Writer's Guide to Poisons*, I thought of my friend Bev. "Dave, you know my friend in Atlanta, the one who taught anatomy and biology? As often as I turn to her for medical input, she'd get a kick out of this. I wonder if it has jimson weed in it?" That was something I'd asked Bev to check out recently, and sure enough, there was a paragraph on it in a chapter on poisonous plants. "Okay, I'm getting this to take home to Atlanta too."

Dickens was a hit with the crowd, as usual, and Dave and I took turns explaining he was a dwarf Pyr, a miniature of his larger brethren. One woman knelt to give him a belly rub and read aloud the inscription on his tag, "Dickens the Hero Dog." She gave me a questioning look.

"Oh, he helped me out of a scrape, and a friend gave him that." *He saved her life, but there's no need to go into that.*

Scarlett was manning the table in front of the conference room and greeted us with a smile. "Well, don't you two look smashing." Handing us nametags, she pointed to a nearby alcove. "Your friends are just over there, and I got to meet Belle and Ellie. What a pair they are!"

When we joined the group that included Belle, Wendy, Ellie, and Sue, I made the introductions. "Dave, let me introduce Sue, one of our fellow yogis from the Tintagel trip—yet another English teacher, if you can believe it."

As Dave shook her hand, Sue exclaimed, "I'm so happy to meet you. I had to look up your J.M. Barrie article after Leta mentioned it. You did such a lovely job describing the discovery of the book he wrote for Belle. She just beamed when I asked her to tell me more about it."

Dave shook his head. "It helped that she gave me an exclusive and that I had unlimited access to Wendy and Leta, who found the book in the toybox at Sunshine Cottage. Belle adored the book as a child but never considered that it might be a collector's item. Imagine having the only copy of a book not only written by the author of *Peter Pan,* but written especially for you."

I never tired of hearing the story of how Belle's mother knew J.M. Barrie and how he visited Belle when she was a child and came to be known as her Uncle Jim. Dave had spent the last year researching Barrie and his author friends who had summered in the Cotswolds near Astonbury, and he would soon publish a book about the group, titled *Barrie & Friends.*

Looking up, I saw Gilbert approaching us with an attractive silver-haired woman by his side. *Talk about posh.* She wore her hair in a sleek chignon and was wearing a black skirt and a crisp white shirt with a tuxedo collar accessorized with a large cameo pin.

Gilbert was beaming. "Ladies, you must meet Dr. Paget-Ford, the chairperson of this marvelous event." Introductions were made all around, and after asking us to call her Emily, Dr. Paget-Ford explained she was very happy with the turnout for the event. *So, she's the woman I saw last night.*

She leaned and tickled Dickens beneath his chin. "And who is this darling fellow?"

"My boy Dickens, and tomorrow, you'll get to meet his feline sister, Christie."

"I adore his literary moniker. He'll have to meet Wimsey, my Corgi."

Just then, Scarlett strode up to our group. "Please excuse me, but we'll soon be shifting to the conference room for the presentation. Emily, may I borrow you for a moment?" They stepped to the side and conferred briefly, the tall redhead towering over the silver-haired doctor.

As Dave introduced Gilbert to Sue, Wendy pulled me aside. "I haven't had a chance to speak with you since the train station. What do you think about Scarlett? I mean, forget that she's stunning. There's just something about her that doesn't sit right with me."

"Thank goodness I'm not the only one. I thought I was overreacting because of the way she was hanging all over Dave. I've never considered myself the jealous type, but I've accompanied him to plenty of literary festivals where women approach him, and not a one has ever been quite that, what's the word? Familiar? Forward? Maybe it's just that I've grown accustomed to the

British being a tad more formal, but she got under my skin, for sure."

"No, I don't think it has anything to do with British behavior versus American. Familiar *and* forward are both good words. And, she *was* flirting, no doubt about it."

"True. Okay, now that I've had my say on that topic, I'm ready to enjoy myself. Gilbert has been a hoot already, and I can see he's charming Sue too."

Five minutes later, I heard a bell and saw the doors to the conference open. It was time for the first festival presentation. I caught Dave's eye and nodded toward Sue. He got the signal and offered her his arm.

Sue's face lit up. "Why, you're every bit as charming as Belle said you were." Wendy and I fell in behind them, and we all found seats in the third row.

As the lights dimmed, another woman leaned over the open seat next to Dave and asked if she could join us. A redhead, but very different from Scarlett. This one was about five foot six with a cap of red curls and a smattering of freckles across her nose and cheeks.

All eyes turned to the front of the room, where Emily stood behind a table topped with a short lectern. "Welcome to the kick-off session of the Poison Pens Literary Festival. I'm Emily Paget-Ford, and I'm pleased to be your host for the next few days."

She turned to the woman seated to the left of the podium. "Let me introduce your speaker for 'Archaeology & Agatha'—Kate Ellis, award-winning author of both the Joe Plantaganet and Wesley Peterson series.

"It's the archaeological elements in her Wesley Peterson mysteries that make her uniquely qualified to lead us on a journey through this selection of Agatha Christie books. Sit back and enjoy an hour of armchair travel as we explore the Poirot mysteries *Appointment with Death, Murder in Mesopotamia,* and *Death on the Nile,* along with lesser-known tales that don't include the popular Belgian detective."

It was a treat to hear an author I admired and to discover she was both entertaining and knowledgeable. She opened her presentation with a question about Christie's three archaeology-inspired books that *didn't* feature Poirot, and I realized that the audience was evenly split between avid Christie fans who'd read everything the woman had ever written and those, like me, who had read only a handful. Very few of us raised our hands when she asked "Have you heard of *Death Comes as the End, Destination Unknown,* or *They Came to Baghdad*?"

By the end of the discussion, I had mentally added the three titles to my TBR list. The first person to raise his hand when Kate invited questions was an elderly, white-haired gentleman across the aisle from us. "Thank you for an informative presentation. I've always felt that Christie's depiction of digs was quite accurate. Of the six books inspired by archaeology, the one that doesn't sit well with me is *Appointment with Death.* The notion that the victim is killed with an injection of digitoxin when it would have been more effectively administered in pill form ruins it. These oversights concerning poisons happen all too often in her novels." *That's not a question, and it has nothing to do with archaeology.*

Our speaker handled it well as she looked first at him and then around the room. "I'm sure you'll be relieved to hear that my strong suit is archaeology, not poison, so you're all pretty safe with me." That got the expected laugh. "That said, I can't debate how best to administer the drug. For me, the enjoyment lies in discovering the perpetrator. Next question?"

The man muttered something I couldn't make out before turning and walking from the room. His face was pale and his expression cross, and he wore a dark suit that appeared large on him. *How rude to leave like that.*

The subsequent questions focused on Christie's knowledge of archaeology and her travels to digs in the Middle East with her second husband. Mixed in with those were a few about our speaker's research for the Wesley Peterson series.

As we stood to make our way to the door, the woman sitting beside Dave introduced herself. "Good afternoon, I'm Felicity Jenkins. Thanks for letting me join you."

Sue shook her hand and kicked off our group introductions. "Hello. I'm Sue Fairchild from Dartmouth. And where do you hail from?"

"Oh," said Felicity, "quite nearby. I live in Torquay, but I've only recently moved here from Exeter." Seeing our questioning looks, she added, "I'm a Detective Sergeant at the Torquay police station."

As we went through the rest of the introductions, Felicity feigned dismay at falling in with a group that included a writer and three English teachers. "I think I'll just nod at whatever you say and leave it at that, lest I utter something ridiculous. I adore crime fiction and Golden Age mysteries, but goodness knows, I'm no scholar."

Dave nudged Gilbert as we waited for the crowd to thin. "I didn't get to ask earlier. Do you know the man who exited so abruptly? That was darned rude."

"Ah yes. That's Oliver Fletcher. I can't say I know him well, only in passing, as we're both members of the Sherlock Society, but I *can* say he hasn't always been that way. It's only since his grandson died that he's grown morose and argumentative."

Felicity frowned. "I'm sorry for his loss, but that's no reason to be impolite. I thought the session was fascinating, and who cares whether or not Agatha Christie got every little thing right?"

Gathering in the hall, our group chatted about the events and sights on the program for the upcoming week. Most of us planned to take advantage of all the sessions and tours on offer.

Felicity rolled her eyes. "I'm jealous, but I'm thankful I was able at least to arrange my schedule to work the early shift this week. That way I can make it to the late afternoon and evening presentations, and I've toured Greenway several times and walked the Agatha Mile too, so I'm okay missing those. What are you most looking forward to?"

I caught Dave's eye as I responded. "Dressing up Saturday night! I love that they gave us the option of wearing formal attire or dressing as a character from a mystery. My outfit works either way, as does Dave's."

He bowed. "Tommy of Tommy and Tuppence at your service." He turned to Gilbert. "Who will you be Saturday night—Sherlock? Dr. Watson?"

"Neither. It's a Golden Age author, but someone different. How about you, Felicity? Formal attire or costume?"

"If I said I'd be dressed as a twentieth-century American detective—a Californian—who would you guess?"

I thought for a moment. "That has to be Kinsey Milhone, right? I can't think of anyone else."

"Got it in one. I've always liked her because she's so no-nonsense, and I envy her minimalist lifestyle. All I needed was a simple black dress like the one she carries around."

Explaining that she'd be dressed as Agatha Raisin, Wendy pointed to Belle. "Mum, tell us, are you coming as Miss Marple?"

"Yes, dear, but not the dowdy version with the bag of knitting. I fancy Geraldine McEwan's Miss Marple look, and I think I can pull it off with my blue dress."

Dickens had been patiently standing by my side, but when he barked "Let's go," I knew he wanted a walk. The group took that as a cue to break up after agreeing we'd all meet in the dining room at 6:30.

In the lobby, I spotted Daisy Owens speaking with the elderly gentleman I now knew was Oliver Fletcher. She had her hand on his arm and seemed to be remonstrating with him. I caught the words, "Really, Uncle Ollie, did you have to be rude to Kate Ellis?" *Uncle Ollie? What a small world.*

Seated next to Felicity at dinner, I learned that she had two grown children who had treated her to a stay at the hotel for the week. In turn, I answered her questions about how I came to live in the Cotswolds.

When there was a pause in our conversation, Wendy interjected. "Felicity, we know a detective inspector in Truro who transferred from Exeter. Is there any chance you know DI Jake Nancarrow?" She did, and that led to numerous comments from all the women around the table about how wonderful he was.

Dave laughed. "Gee, I met him a few weeks ago, but I had no idea he had a fan club."

We explained to Felicity that we met Jake—or the dishy DI, as we referred to him—when he investigated a case at our yoga retreat in Tintagel and that we'd reconnected with him when he visited our friend Gemma a few weeks ago in Astonbury. She got a kick out of the 'dishy DI' nickname and promised he'd get a hard time about it the next time she saw him.

The conversation continued on a lively note. Gilbert and Dave regaled us with stories about their recent dinner at the Sherlock Holmes Society of London, which prompted a discussion of Anthony Horowitz's novels. Much like Sophie Hannah had been granted permission to continue Agatha Christie's Poirot series, Horowitz had obtained an official endorsement from the estate of Arthur Conan Doyle to write new Sherlock Holmes novels.

Felicity was a full participant in the discussion of the newer books. "I think Horowitz is brilliant, and I find his books much more readable than the original Conan Doyle stories. The same for *The Monogram Murders,* Sophie Hannah's Poirot book."

Gilbert pressed his hand to his chest in mock horror. "Heavens! You simply cannot think Horowitz's versions are better than the originals." Those of us who knew him saw right away he was joking, but it wasn't until he winked that Sue and Felicity caught on.

Gilbert tried to coax everyone to the bar for after-dinner drinks, but his only takers were Dave, Wendy, and me. As I scanned the wood-paneled room, Wendy nudged me. "Look, it's our resident Amazon. See her in the shadows by the bookcase? Now, I wonder who that is she's speaking with."

"Well, she certainly gets around, and I think that may be the man I saw outside last night." I watched as Scarlett placed her hand on her companion's arm and pulled him into a hug before turning toward the door.

Wendy whispered, "She must know him, right? I mean, she hung on Dave but didn't hug him. And yes, I know Southerners are huggers, but seriously?"

"Yes, but we hug friends and family, not every good-looking male we encounter! And in this case, the person she's hugging looks decidedly uncomfortable."

# Chapter Three

GAZING OUT THE WINDOW, I wondered how chilly it was. "It's a beautiful morning, but I bet I'll still need a warm coat for the tour."

"And gloves and a scarf." Dave grinned. "Correct me if I'm wrong, but you have a perfectly coordinated outfit in mind, right?"

"Of course I do. My black jacket, my red beret, and a plaid scarf, plus my black leather gloves edged in red wool!"

Along with Dickens, we planned to meet our Astonbury friends in the lobby to start the tour. As Dave hooked the leash to Dickens's collar, I read the tour description in the flyer we'd found slipped beneath our door this morning. "The stops are related to the Queen of Crime's life plus a few spots that inspired locations in her novels. I can't wait!"

"Did you notice that Oliver Fletcher is leading the tour?"

"Ugh, that rude man from yesterday? I hope he's more pleasant today. Heaven forbid anyone asks him a question he doesn't care for."

Dave glanced at Christie, who was meowing at his feet. "Do you think that means she wants to go too?"

My sassy cat looked from me to Dave. "He really is slow on the uptake, isn't he?"

As Dave put on his leather jacket, I loaded Christie into the backpack. I pulled her fleece blanket up around her neck, so she could easily duck her head into it if the breeze was too much for her.

Exiting the elevator, we bumped into Daisy Owens, dressed in another dark pantsuit, clipboard in hand. I expected she'd be on duty 24/7 this week. "Good morning, Daisy. We enjoyed day one. How was it from your perspective?"

"It couldn't have been better. Fingers crossed, the rest of the week goes as smoothly." She paused and rolled her eyes. "Well, except for my uncle's behavior in the Kate Ellis session. Honestly, he seems to have lost all his filters."

She laughed when Dave gave her a puzzled look, and I realized he hadn't caught that conversation. "My uncle's down from London for the festival, and he's perfectly charming most of the time. He just has a hang-up about Agatha Christie's expertise on poisons. You're sure to hear more about it today on the Agatha Christie Mile, though he assures me he'll be polite."

Dave chuckled as he told her his grandmother had developed the same issue with filters. She claimed she'd earned the right to speak her mind at her age.

In the lobby, Scarlett was checking names off a list, and she grinned as we approached. "There you two are. Now let me see—are Dickens and Christie registered for this?" She tickled Christie's chin. "If not, I'm sure we can make room for them."

Wendy waved me over to where Belle stood leaning on her cane. "Leta, can you believe Mum is serious about doing this walk? I know she's getting around better, but it's still a mile, and with the stops along the way, she'll be on her feet for at least two hours."

"No, I won't, dear. I have a secret weapon. Ellie found me this fancy new cane with an attachment. Look, it's a seat I can fold down for when I grow weary and need a rest."

I studied the cane. It was wooden with a black derby handle, three legs, and a rubber seat. Leave it to Ellie to find one in stylish polished wood instead of metal. It looked sturdy enough, but I was still skeptical.

When Wendy and I looked at each other, Ellie piped up. "You two. Don't start. When you're our age, you'll realize that you can't afford to let opportunities pass you by. Now that Belle's more mobile, we have big plans."

Sue turned up just then. "Hats off to you, ladies. Not only detectives but also adventurers. You're an inspiration."

Scarlett got the group's attention and introduced our tour guide. "You're in for a treat this morning, ladies and gentlemen. As a frequent visitor to Torquay, Dr. Oliver Fletcher has been giving this tour for years, and you never know what intriguing bits of Christie trivia he'll entertain you with. The Agatha Christie Mile was established in 1990 and includes eleven stops. We'll have refreshments at the Imperial Hotel before offering rides back here."

Today, he was dressed in an overcoat, scarf, and fedora, and the nametag pinned to his pocket had a border of dogs around the four edges with the name Oliver in the middle. He bowed and touched his hat and told us our first stop would be the Torre Abbey Museum where we would explore the Potent Plants Garden. Before turning to exit the hotel, he reached in his pocket and spoke to Dickens. "Hello there, little fellow. Would you care for a treat?"

*Gee, maybe he likes dogs better than he likes people.* It made no difference to Dickens. When Oliver asked him to sit, he obeyed and then eagerly accepted the bite-size biscuits he held in his hand.

I chuckled when he barked, "Thanks, but please don't call me little." He'd been sensitive about his size as long as I'd had him.

Dave waited for Belle and Ellie to get in line and then fell in behind them. "Help me keep an eye on Belle in case she stumbles. I agree with you and Wendy that this walk may be too much for her."

Whispering my agreement, I alternated between watching Belle and glancing at the flyer. "Listen to this, Dave. At the garden, the challenge is to figure out which poisonous plants were used in which of Christie's mysteries. What fun."

A look of exaggerated horror flashed across his face. "What does it say about my girlfriend that she's excited about a poisonous plant tour? Should I be worried?"

Belle glanced over her shoulder. "It's me you should be worried about, Dave. After all, I was a nurse, though I didn't work in the pharmacy as Dame Agatha did."

I watched in amazement as Oliver transformed into the Pied Piper as we walked. Instead of playing a pipe, he offered a seemingly endless supply of treats to the dogs we met. *I wonder whether he has a dog at home.*

Along with background on Agatha Christie, he also offered suggestions on how to spend our free time. On the Princess Pier where Dame Agatha roller-skated as a child, he pointed to Dickens and me. "I imagine you've taken this handsome boy for a stroll on the beach, but have you visited the changing huts?"

*He's charming today.* "Oh yes, I've admired their bright colors and may rent one when it's warmer."

"No need to wait for warm weather. I'm enjoying one this week. Whether you sit in the sun or enjoy a late-night walk followed by a spell of stargazing from a beach chair—the experience is heavenly."

In the garden, Belle opened her cane and sat close to our guide as he began his talk. "Given that over half of Christie's victims were poisoned, I don't think you'll be surprised at the beautiful but sinister plants grown here, including the sources for cyanide, morphine, and ricin—to name only a few. I'll provide some background and then turn you loose to solve the mystery of the story titles."

The group had quite a few questions, and our guide responded with facts and humor. One woman asked whether poisons were more easily disguised in food or drink. Belle interjected that she had used the mortar and pestle to grind up pills for patients who had difficulty swallowing and that applesauce helped camouflage bitter taste.

Oliver clapped. "I could use an assistant for the next tour. Would you like a job? Rest assured, though, I'm not going anywhere near applesauce as long as you're around. Now, one last thing before I turn you loose to solve the mystery of the titles. Dangerous or not, every plant here can be found in an Agatha Christie story. That may be a puzzle to solve another day."

*My, he's almost a different man today.* He was a perfect gentleman the entire way, not to mention a knowledgeable and entertaining speaker, and he refrained from any criticism of Dame Agatha. By the time we climbed the hill to the Imperial Hotel, we were all ready for a spot of tea. Belle admitted she was tuckered out and agreed that riding back to The Grand was a better option than walking.

Wendy and I stopped to admire the artwork in the lobby, while Dave escorted Belle and Ellie to the dining room. As we entered the sunlit room, I scanned the tables in search of the trio and was taken aback to see Scarlett not only sitting beside Dave but leaning into him with her hand on his arm and her lips close to his ear.

Grabbing Wendy's arm, I pulled her back. "Look at that! She's doing it again."

Wendy's reaction echoed mine. "That girl is bold as brass. She has to know you and Dave are together." *My thoughts exactly.*

I did my best to conceal my irritation as we took our seats and was fortunate that Belle and Ellie were having a lively conversation about which actress was the best Miss Marple. Like Belle, I favored Geraldine McEwan, but Ellie preferred Joan Hickson.

It was only when Scarlett excused herself to make the rounds of the other tables that I felt my shoulders relax. Dave nodding in her direction and rolling his eyes as she left helped some. *Is this how it's going to be all week?*

Wendy, Dave, and I decided to walk beyond the hotel and take the path to Beacon Cove, one of Agatha Christie's favorite swimming spots. We ladies excused ourselves to find the loo, as my British friends sometimes called it. It was as we were returning to the dining room that we encountered Scarlett, and she pulled me aside.

She wore an odd expression. "Leta, I have to know. Are you and Dave in an exclusive relationship? Or do you see other people when you're apart?"

*What?* An image of my hands circling her neck popped into my head, but I shook that off and managed to splutter, "And you want to know that why?"

"Why? Because I'm attracted to him, but I wouldn't want to step on your toes. But if you date other people, well . . ."

*Is she serious?* "Scarlett, I have to admit I don't know today's relationship terminology, but let me assure you that we don't see other people. Didn't Dave mention he's moving here to be with me? That's more than exclusive. It's committed."

She shrugged. "He said he was moving, but that could be as much about his book as about you, right? I didn't know for sure."

My hands curled into fists as I clenched my jaw. "Well, now you do."

Wendy knew something was wrong when I caught up with her. "What's going on? You look like you're about to blow a gasket."

"I may kill that girl. She just asked me if Dave was available." I tried to repeat the words she used.

"She what? As if hanging on him at the table wasn't enough? The nerve!"

"Right. And now, what do I do? Do I tell Dave? I mean, I tell him everything, but I don't know how to handle this."

"Uh-huh. Well, given your conversation about Peter's flowers, I think—yes, you tell him. I mean, her behavior is over the top in my book."

*Great. When and how do I do that?*

I wasn't looking forward to seeing Scarlett again and was relieved she wasn't manning the table outside the conference room for the afternoon session. Though Wendy and I hadn't settled on a suitable way to refer to the girl, we'd texted possibilities back and forth for several hours. Female Casanova and temptress were the mildest terms we'd come up with.

As we waited for our friends to join us, I spied the redheaded Amazon dressed in a green cable-knit sweater, tan velveteen leggings, and brown high-heeled booties. There was no question the girl was stunning. She was deep in conversation with Emily and Daisy Owens, and I caught snippets of the conversation. I gathered that something was amiss with the apothecary jars for the upcoming presentation.

Dave looked at me as he'd been doing since we left the Imperial Hotel. I hadn't mentioned my encounter with Scarlett, but he knew me well enough to see something was bothering me. All I'd been able to say so far was that I needed to think something through and would explain later.

I was seated between Dave and Wendy for the presentation, and Belle sat next to Dave. "I know I overdid it today, so I'll be making an early evening of it tonight. I'm not going to miss exploring Greenway tomorrow."

She leaned over Dave and smiled. "Witch. That's the word." It seemed Wendy had told Belle about my Scarlett conversation. Smothering my laugh, I nodded. "I like it. One could almost confuse it with another word."

"Yes, and that would be appropriate too." *Goodness, how I love this woman.*

Thankfully, the lights blinked then, and I was saved from having to explain the cryptic conversation to Dave.

All eyes turned to the front of the room, where once again Emily stood behind the lectern. She cleared her throat. "Welcome to 'A Taste of Murder.'" She beckoned to her left, and a man emerged from the shadows to stand beside her. "This afternoon, I'm delighted to introduce Dr. Rhys Ford. An ardent Agatha Christie fan and the author of multiple articles about his idol, Rhys has read everything she ever wrote, even the novels she penned under the name of Mary Westamacott." *So, he's the man I overheard Sunday night* and *the man I saw with Scarlett.*

"Though his specialty is psychiatry, today he plans to talk about poison. Did you know that to practice psychiatry, one must have a medical degree? That means he knows a thing or two about how to make someone well." She paused for dramatic effect. "But also about how to make someone ill—so ill that the result can be death."

Rhys interjected. "Why, Emily, you make me sound quite sinister."

With a laugh, she responded, "We'll let the audience be the judge of that."

She swept her hand from left to right, pointing to the small row of jars displayed on either side of the lectern. They were a mix of glass and pottery. "We have quite the selection here—some items easily attainable, others not so much. Before the day is over, you'll know a bit about them all."

She had us on the edge of our seats. "Rhys, it's all yours."

He took his cue. "Can anyone tell me the poison Christie used most often in her plots?" A hand shot up in the front row and someone said cyanide.

"Correct. Cyanide is the murderer's poison of choice in four Christie books—*The Mirror Crack'd from Side to Side, And Then There Were None, A Pocketful of Rye,* and, of course, *Sparkling Cyanide.* Now—"

A man stood and pointed a finger at Rhys. "*Dr.* Ford, as a *learned* psychiatrist, you should know that Christie's descriptions of poisons and their effects quite often missed the mark."

*Oh for goodness' sake, it's Oliver again.* He'd transformed into the man we'd heard in Kate Ellis's presentation. His stance struck me as challenging, and judging from Rhys's tight smile, he felt the same way. "Oliver, let's not be so formal. As you well know, you and I disagree on the topic of Christie's accuracy when it comes to poisons, but let us leave that debate for another time. I must point out, however, that *The Affair at Styles* was described by the Pharmaceutical Journal as having 'the rare merit of being correctly written.' I, for one, can't argue with them."

By my side, Gilbert groaned and whispered. "He has a bee in his bonnet about Dame Agatha. Has had ever since his grandson wrote his book, but Rhys put him in his place, didn't he?"

Without missing a beat, Rhys continued. "Now, if you visited the Potent Garden today, you learned that poisons are frequently featured in Christie's novels. Arsenic, strychnine, digitalis, and morphine put in an appearance, as do some lesser-known elements—thallium, taxine, and monkshood. Given how many murder mysteries the author penned, it's no wonder that poisons appear any number of times."

He spent the next thirty minutes pointing to different apothecary jars as he explained the origins and effects of their contents and named the books in which they figured. He ended with something I'd heard before: "And that, my friends, explains why a book on poisons is said to be the most well-worn book in Dame Agatha's library. Now, what questions may I answer for you?"

It was Oliver who was once again the first person to speak up, not with a question, but with an insult. "Quite entertaining, Dr. Ford, but the details you shared are closer to fiction than fact. It's a shame you didn't do your homework."

He muttered something I couldn't make out before turning and walking from the room. He had seemed fine when he led us on the Agatha Mile tour, but now he looked ill. *How odd.*

Rhys shook his head. "Ah well, as you can tell, Oliver and I have a difference of opinion on a few facts, though that doesn't detract one iota from the popularity of Agatha Christie's books. Now, back to questions." His inquisitive audience asked questions that ranged from where to obtain the poisons to how easily they could be detected.

As the hour ended, he uttered one final line. "Now, in case you're concerned about the safety of your meals, please rest assured that these little jars contain either tea leaves or glycerine—nothing stronger." That got the anticipated chuckles mixed with a few theatrical sighs. Based on the thunderous applause that followed, it seemed only one audience member had been disappointed.

"So, Gilbert," I said, "what's Oliver Fletcher's problem? He seems to be spoiling for a fight."

"It's a bit of a story, Leta, best told when we have more time."
Outside the room, Emily and Rhys were chatting with the few remaining guests as Scarlett handed out flyers. "Gilbert, Dave," she cried. "Here's some background for tomorrow's Greenway tour. Oh, and Leta, here's one for you too."

At least I warranted a mention. She ignored poor Sue altogether. I cleared my throat. "Scarlett, I'm sure Sue would like the information too."

Without taking her eyes off Dave, she handed over another flyer. I watched in amazement as she put her hand on Dave's arm. I couldn't help myself. The phrase "brazen hussy" popped into my mind, as did, for some reason, the notice at The Quill bookshop.

*I'll make nice, even though I want to throttle her.* I took a deep breath and dug into my bag for the postcard I tucked in it earlier. I planned to congratulate her on her new book, but when I looked up and saw she had her arm twined in Dave's, that idea flew out the window.

The expression on my face must have said something to Sue because she touched my arm as the group moved away. "Leta, if looks could kill, that girl would be toast. Do all Southern belles act that way?"

*Did I just growl?* "No, we do *not*! What part of Dave and me being a couple does she not get?"

"Well, it's obvious to the rest of us, so I'm not sure what—"

Emily stepped up just then. "Leta, is that one of Scarlett's cards? I understand she rode down on the train with Dave and Gilbert, so I guess she showed them what she was working on. The design is quite eye-catching, don't you think?"

"Yes, it's quite colorful. Dave and I found these at The Quill bookshop yesterday. How marvelous for her that she has a book coming out."

Frowning, Emily snatched the card from my hand. "At the bookshop? The book's not even finished yet." When she saw the back of the card, she gasped. "Sexy and scandalous! What on earth? That can't be right."

As she scanned the information, her face grew red. "She used *my* name! We had this conversation. Either this is a joke or Scarlett . . . No, she wouldn't dare!"

She handed me the card and muttered to herself before turning on her heel and making a beeline for Rhys. *Oh boy. Looks like the fur's about to fly.*

I heard snatches of their conversation and could pick up on Emily's tone but not her words. Rhys, on the other hand, came through loud and clear and seemed equally perturbed. "What do you mean? It says what? Surely the girl has more sense than that."

"Scarlett," Emily barked. "Here. Now."

Scarlett blushed beet-red and disappeared with Emily into the room we'd just left. Rhys rushed over and pulled the door closed, but not before we heard Emily erupt in anger.

Emily's rapid-fire words were clear to the few of us who had not yet dispersed. "This is unforgivable! Do you have any idea what you've done? What this will do to *my* reputation? And yours?"

We missed Scarlett's response when Rhys closed the door. He looked at us and frowned. "I'm sorry you had to witness that. Not quite the professional image we try to present."

Gilbert spoke up. "Don't mention it old boy, but do tell. Whatever is going on?"

Rhys looked around to see, I assumed, who was in earshot. Since it was only Gilbert, Dave, Sue, and me, maybe he'd give us the scoop.

He ran his hand through his hair. "How do I give you the short version? Emily is Scarlett's writing coach, and she's been working with her for nearly a year on this book. The last I heard, it was nowhere near ready for prime time. I have serious doubts it's coming soon, but that's minor compared to the fact that Emily's name is on that card. That's beyond the pale."

I looked at the card and read the line again, "Clever Concept. The image of a brainy, sexy Sayers is compelling." — Emily Paget-Ford. "Oh! The name hadn't clicked with me before. So, Emily didn't authorize the quote?"

"Oh, it's worse than that—it's out of context—like the movie reviews that obscure what a critic says by omitting the full line. Emily described the book that way in its early stages by saying 'Clever concept but poorly executed.' And, bloody hell, she would never have her name associated with anything that used the word sexy to describe Dorothy Sayers. The woman idolizes Sayers."

Gilbert tugged at his collar. "My, my, this is much more than a kerfuffle. This has the makings of a full-blown firestorm."

Frowning, Sue agreed. "You're right. Any Sayers fan would be up in arms, and I can understand why Emily's upset about being misquoted. But what did she mean about Scarlett's reputation? Is the book that bad?"

At that question, Rhys threw up his hands. "I've only heard Emily's commentary as it's been taking shape. She describes it as a mash-up of historical fiction, romance, and mystery with the underpinnings of some dubious research—not to mention it has more than its share of steamy passages. Doomed to fail is how Emily describes it in its current state."

I thought about the Lord Peter Wimsey books I'd enjoyed and the things I'd read about Sayers leaving mystery writing behind. "Oh my goodness. No wonder Emily is furious. Steamy and Sayers don't go together, and when you think that the author turned to religious writing in later years, why—fans and Sayers scholars alike will be appalled."

Rhys stared at the closed door. "Well, if anyone can sort it, it's Emily. If she hasn't already wrung Scarlett's neck, she's for sure reading her the riot act. By now, she's probably whipped out her phone to ring the bookshop manager to tell her to destroy however many cards there are. I just hope she doesn't send Scarlett packing. How we'd manage without her is not something I want to contemplate."

I suggested to Dave that we take Dickens for a brief walk and then grab some blankets and sit by the pool. It was time I told him about the Scarlett conversation.

"Dave, I have a question for you about Scarlett. I know you'll think I'm being silly or overly sensitive or something—but do you think you've given her any indication that . . . "

He looked confused. "What, Leta?"

I felt my face grow hot. "That you're available?"

His mouth dropped open. "Available? As in for another woman? Are you kidding? Of course, I haven't."

As I took him through my conversation with her, his expression went from astonished to horrified. "She had to ask if we were exclusive? She couldn't tell? And the answer to your question is no, I haven't. I'll grant you she's the most forward woman I've encountered in years, but I didn't think it meant anything. Short of pointedly removing her hand from my arm or flat-out telling her not to touch me, what was I supposed to do?"

*Why am I blinking back tears?* "I don't know, Dave. I was so flabbergasted by her question, I was nearly speechless, but I managed to tell her in no uncertain terms that we were exclusive. I even used the word committed. And when I saw her cozy up to you again this afternoon, I didn't know what to think."

In a flash, he threw off his blanket and moved to my chair. "Think this, Leta Parker. I love you. If that girl is misreading our relationship, it's her problem, not ours." He used his thumb to wipe a tear from my cheek. "Got it?"

"Got it." I smiled. "Can we agree to refer to her as that hussy?"

He pulled me into a hug. "Whatever it takes."

We knew our friends would be interested in the scene we'd witnessed between Emily and Scarlett, so we popped by their room. Wendy answered the door and cautioned us to speak softly. "Mum's having a lie-down, and Ellie's reading. Have you come to talk about Oliver Fletcher? What drama."

*She doesn't know the half of it.* "Oh no, we've moved beyond that. You left before the real excitement."

Dave plopped on the couch. "Scarlett and Emily are the news of the hour. Leta, do you still have that card?"

"Scarlett and Emily?" Wendy had the same reaction I did when she read the details about the book. "What? Sexy and scandalous? Dorothy Sayers?" She looked puzzled. "And Emily Paget-Ford calls it a clever concept? Doesn't sound that way to me. It sounds more like an abomination."

"Yup. It's a mess, and it gets better." Dave and I took turns describing the scene we'd just witnessed.

Rolling her eyes, Wendy muttered. "You know, it's this kind of brash behavior that gives Americans a bad name with us Brits. What was the girl playing at?"

Dave frowned. "Well, whatever it was, it backfired. And just so you know, the official title for Scarlett is now hussy. Or is it brazen hussy, Leta?"

Wendy laughed. "I see Leta told you about their encounter. Mum thought witch was a good one, but I adore hussy. It has a nice Southern ring to it. Now, anyone care to take bets on whether we've seen the last of Scarlett?"

By now, we'd made Sue and Felicity official members of our group, and we kicked off dinner with a discussion of the Scarlett and Emily kerfuffle. *What a uniquely British word!* We had mixed opinions as to whether Emily had overreacted and whether we'd see Scarlett again.

When we retired to the bar for after-dinner drinks, Belle and Ellie once again called it a night. This time, though, Sue and Felicity joined us. We ladies snagged a spot in front of the fireplace, while Dave and Gilbert went off to fetch a round of Irish coffees.

As we savored our drinks, I saw Rhys Ford approach the bar. "There's Dr. Ford. I wonder how his evening's gone. Do you think he's been called in as a referee?" My comment prompted Gilbert to wave him over.

"Rhys, join us. We spoke with you earlier during the contretemps, but I didn't get a chance to introduce my friends."

He shook our hands as Gilbert went around the table, and then Rhys turned his gaze to Wendy. Tilting his head, he seemed to study her. "Wendy, Wendy Davies?"

My friend's mouth dropped open. "Rhys, from Oxford? Oh my goodness. No wonder you looked familiar. I can't believe it's you."

Instead of shaking her hand, Rhys put his drink on the low table and pulled her to her feet. He held her at arm's length before pulling her close and kissing her cheek. "I thought you moved to the States. Are you here for a visit?" He looked around. "Is your husband with you?"

Wendy shook her head. "Not a visit and no husband. I'm back for good, have been for two years. We have a lot of catching up to do."

The smile hadn't left Wendy's face since Rhys first said her name. I couldn't help smiling too as I took in how delighted she was to see him. There had to be a story here, and I was eager to hear it. Given the looks passing between the two, I doubted I'd get the scoop until the next day.

I knew I was right when Rhys suggested that he and Wendy move to a small table on their own. "Can you forgive me if I steal her away? We haven't spoken in—how long is it, Wendy?—at least thirty years."

Gilbert clapped him on the back. "Take her away, old man. Just be sure to return her."

Setting my cup down, I caught Dave's eye. "It's time we took Dickens out. What do you say we bundle up and take him to the beach and then turn in?" He smiled and explained to the group that I was known to turn into a pumpkin before ten, sometimes earlier.

Dickens was happy to see us. "Snacks? Did you bring me snacks?"

By now, Dave spoke to Dickens like I did, except he had no idea what Dickens was saying. "You seem to be in high spirits, boy. How 'bout a walk?"

Zipping me into my quilted parka, Dave kissed me on the nose. "I guess you'll have to keep me around since you can never manage the zippers on your own." Early on, he'd picked up on my inability to zip anything. My sister Anna had the same problem. Who knows why?

It was a crisp October evening, and we were the only ones on the beach, so once again, we let Dickens off his leash. I laughed as we strolled past the colorful changing huts. "You know, I've never seen one of these in person, and I'd love to rent one, but not until the summer. Maybe after you move here, we can rent one."

"In warmer weather, yes. You're shivering now even in your parka." A grin appeared on his face. "What do you say we go inside and get you warmed up?"

I was sound asleep when a loud banging on the door woke me. As Dave groaned and reached for the hotel robe, I looked at the clock. It was nearly one a.m. *What on earth?*

Wendy barreled into the room when Dave opened the door. "Oh my gosh, Dave, Leta, come quick. It's Emily. She's dead."

# Chapter Four

By the time I grabbed my robe, Wendy had dragged Dave down the hall to a room near the elevator. Christie never stirred, but Dickens followed me from our room. His soft growl told me that his guard dog instincts had alerted him that something was wrong.

Dave and Wendy entered the room with me close behind. I took in the scene. Dressed in a blue velvet robe, Emily sat in a chair in the living room, her eyes closed and her head lolling to one side. Rhys knelt beside her holding her hand and repeating softly, "Emily, Emily."

Wendy went to him and placed her hands on his shoulders. When she whispered in his ear, he released Emily's hand and moved to the chair on the other side of the small side table. The words "wrung out" popped into my head as Dave pulled me close.

Stunned silence filled the room until Dickens whimpered. "Leta, look at the dog." That's when I noticed the small dog lying on its side beneath Emily's chair, some treats by his head.

I stumbled to the little thing and murmured, "Oh no, not the dog. What happened here?" Dave recovered first. "We need to call a doctor and the police."

Shaking his head, Rhys murmured, "It's too late for a doctor. She's cold to the touch."

I pointed to the phone on the console table. "Let's ring Felicity, since she's already in the hotel. She'll know who to call."

As Dave picked up the receiver, Wendy nodded. "Good idea, Leta." A tear rolled down her cheek. "Is the dog . . .?"

Dickens was licking the little thing's nose and nudging it. "Leta, look, he won't wake up."

When I relayed that news to Wendy, she darted to the bathroom and returned with a fluffy bath towel. "His name is Wimsey. Emily introduced me to him earlier today." She wrapped him in the towel and moved to the sofa with him in her lap. Dickens followed her, whining softly.

Dave hung up the phone. "Felicity's on her way." He moved toward Rhys. "Can I get you a glass of water, anything?"

As though she were a character in a television crime mystery, Wendy cautioned him. "We shouldn't disturb anything else—any more than we already have."

I stood helplessly by Emily's chair as random thoughts flitted through my head. *How did Rhys and Wendy get in the room? Maybe Emily had a heart attack. Except what's wrong with the dog?*

Rhys was oblivious to the look I gave Dave, but I could tell my boyfriend knew what I was about to do. What I wasn't sure of was what his reaction would be—until he nodded and moved back to stand by the phone. That was all the encouragement I needed to study the scene. *Something isn't right here.*

I did an about-face and moved closer to the doorway. Slowly, I turned to the left. Behind the two chairs was a wet bar with several bottles on its top and a small fridge beneath it. *I need to come back to those.* Next, I took in the table between the two chairs. It held two liqueur glasses embossed with what must be the hotel's logo and a pair of blue-rimmed reading glasses. A small crumpled foil wrapper lay by the reading glasses. The glass near Rhys had a brownish film in the bottom, and the one next to Emily held a small puddle of green liquid.

Emily's arm dangled over the arm of her chair, as though she had just set her glass down. *She looks so peaceful.* I didn't want to focus on her lifeless body, but I did. Peeking from the right pocket of her robe was something white. Not a tissue, maybe a card? *Is that why her reading glasses are on the table?*

I forced myself to refrain from tugging at Emily's pocket until I finished scanning the room. On the far wall facing the door was the couch where Wendy sat with Wimsey in her lap and Dickens leaning against her leg. It was centered beneath the window with tables on either side, and I could see lights from the harbor in the distance. Completing my rotation, I turned to where Dave stood by the console table with the wall-mounted TV above it, I didn't see anything out of place. The only things on the top were the phone, the remote control, and a manila folder.

Shuddering, I hugged myself. *Dare I look in Emily's pocket?* When I heard the ding of the elevator, I made a hasty decision. I pulled the sleeve of my robe over my fingertips and tugged what turned out to be a small white card from Emily's robe. It was one of Oliver Fletcher's business cards with the same whimsical border of dogs I'd seen on his nametag. Written on the back were the words *Best Wishes.*

Quickly, I tucked the card back in the pocket and turned just as Felicity entered the room. Her mouth dropped open, and she stopped midstride. *I bet she had no idea there'd be a crowd here.* She wore jeans and a sweatshirt, and her red curls stuck out every which way. I detected a smidgen of something white on her forehead as though she'd hastily wiped night cream from her face. When I touched my hand to my forehead, she rolled her eyes and wiped her face before she spoke.

"Leta, Dave called me—"

A burly man in a suit filled the doorway behind her, speaking into his phone. "Right. The door is open. Got the detective sergeant here. I'll call you back."

Felicity motioned me away from the body and stepped in to check for a pulse. Though Dave had told her that Emily was dead, I knew she had to confirm it. "Ewan, please go to the lobby to wait for my constable, and before you send her up here, tell her to call the coroner. Now, I want one person to tell me what's going on. Who will it be? Dave?"

Dave nodded but moved to my side and put his arm around my shoulders before he spoke. "We were asleep when Wendy banged on our door."

"It was one a.m.," I interjected.

Dave squeezed my shoulder. "Shh, Leta, I'm sure you'll get your chance." He repeated Wendy's words, that Emily was dead, and described what he'd seen when we got to the room—Rhys kneeling beside Emily, seeing the lifeless dog only after Rhys moved to the second chair.

Felicity turned to Wendy, and I noticed for the first time that my friend had her overcoat on. *Where was she at one in the morning?* Her attire prompted me to look at Rhys. He too was dressed for the outdoors.

Taking a deep breath, Wendy told her story. "Rhys was walking me to my room when he noticed that Emily's door was ajar. That worried him, so we pushed it open and saw . . . saw Emily." She gulped and Rhys started to speak, but Felicity held up her hand to silence him. "Rhys called her name and went to her. I think he touched her neck to take her pulse. And, when he knelt beside her and moaned her name again, I knew. I knew something was terribly wrong."

Turning to Rhys, Felicity gave him an inquiring look, and he responded. "Wendy's right. I think I knew before I searched for a pulse that she was gone, but I had to check." He shuddered and repeated what he'd said to us earlier. "She was cold to the touch. I'm . . . I'm not sure what I did at that moment."

Wendy spoke up. "You knelt beside her and held her hand. I knew you were in shock, so I did the first thing that came to mind. I fetched Leta and Dave."

Felicity frowned as she turned to look at the two of us. "So, that's how you two got here. Someone can explain that chain of events to me later."

When Wimsey whimpered, I broke down. Tears streaming down my face, I sobbed. "Something's wrong with the dog. We need to help the dog."

Without missing a beat, Felicity pulled out her phone and shot off a text. "Done. The constable will find a vet. Was the dog on the couch when you lot got here?"

Wendy shook her head. "I guess I shouldn't have moved Wimsey from beneath the chair, but I had to."

"I understand that. How is he? If it's named Wimsey, I guess it's a he." As if in answer, Wimsey stirred.

"Rhys, do you have anything to add to what Wendy's told us?" When he shook his head, Felicity turned and spoke to all of us. "Beyond moving the dog, did any of you touch anything else?"

*Nope, I'm not mentioning the card.* I glanced at Emily's pocket and back up at Dave to see if he was going to give me away. He looked me in the eyes and gave a slight shake of his head. *Phew. We're on the same wavelength.*

As we all replied no, Felicity appeared relieved. "Okay then, I know you're in shock, and I have no further questions at this time, but I will shortly—particularly for Rhys and Wendy."

A young blonde woman in uniform entered the room. "DS Jenkins, I'm here."

"And just in time. Please ring the front desk and tell them we need two adjacent rooms—conference rooms would work. Then, escort these two there, one to a room." She pointed to Wendy and Rhys. "Given there's something wrong with the dog too, I'm treating this as a suspicious death and calling in the Scene of Crime Officers. Goodness knows how long it will be before they get here."

Wendy paled. "You . . . you don't consider us suspects, do you?"

The direct question seemed to take Felicity by surprise, and for a moment, she didn't respond. I watched as she straightened her shoulders and set her mouth in a hard line. "Wendy, I'm not *thinking* anything at the moment. I'm asking questions."

*And to think, only a few short hours ago, Felicity was joking with us over drinks.* "Felicity, do you want Dave and me to stay here?"

"No. You can go to your room, but please don't go anywhere until you hear from me. I may have more questions for you two as well. And, Dave, here's my card in case you two think of anything else." She paused and looked at Wendy.

"Actually, Wendy before you leave, I have a follow-up question for you—what prompted you to fetch Dave and Leta rather than ring the front desk or me or even 999?"

*How will my partner-in-crime answer that question? Will she mention the Little Old Ladies' Detective Agency?*

"Um, they were just down the hall?" There was a question mark at the end of what should have been a statement. *Not good.*

Sure enough, Felicity picked up on the inflection in what should have been a statement. "Are you asking me or telling me, Wendy?"

Now, Wendy flushed. "They're my friends. Isn't that enough?"

She was digging the hole deeper. I cleared my throat. "Felicity, perhaps that's a question I can answer for you when you speak with me and Dave."

When she rolled her eyes, an image of Gemma popped into my head. She irked me no end when she rolled her eyes at me, and I was feeling the same way now. What I wouldn't give for Gemma's boyfriend Jake to be here.

Dave must have picked up on where the conversation was going because he tugged on my arm. "Leta, let's go to our room. If Felicity wants us, she'll know where to find us."

Suddenly, I was exhausted. We'd come to Torquay for a murder mystery festival, not a real-life murder. And now, Wendy had landed in the thick of one.

# Chapter Five

LEGS CURLED BENEATH ME, I sat on the couch in our suite, where Dave joined me with a blanket. He sat on the other end, pulled my feet into his lap, and tucked the blanket around them. "Comfy?"

I smiled. "Yes, though I don't feel like I should be comfortable when my best friend is being interrogated by the police. I feel like I should be doing something. Something to help Wendy or maybe even Felicity. Is it me, or does she seem out of her depth?"

"First of all, I'm not sure I'd label it an interrogation. Don't they usually separate witnesses so that their memories aren't colored by what the other one says? And second, what makes you think Felicity is out of her depth?"

"Not sure. Maybe the fact she just transferred to Torquay and is a detective sergeant. It reminded me that when Jake transferred to Truro, it was for a promotion to detective inspector. So, maybe she was a constable until recently, kind of like Jonas is in

Astonbury. But also, she seemed unsure of herself a few times. Oh, I can't explain it."

He raised an eyebrow. "Perhaps it's her first murder investigation. If we assume that's what it is."

"I *do* assume that's what it is! Felicity used the words 'suspicious death.' That plus the dog, it has to be murder."

"Uh-huh, and if you think she needs help, that would be an excuse for you to get involved, right? Tell the truth, you're itching to play detective, aren't you?"

*Admit it, he's right.* "Sometimes, you know me better than I know myself. Yes, I'm dying to figure this out—poor choice of words, I know. What does that say about me?"

"It wasn't that long ago that you explained that to me. Something about feeling fulfilled because you're such a good observer and listener—that you ferret out things the police can't. Wasn't that it?"

My eyes widened. *So, where does he stand on the topic now?* "Do you think I—we—should get involved?"

A smile tugged at his lips. "Let's say I'm learning there's no point in trying to discourage you. And since I'm here with you, perhaps I can rein you in as needed."

I bristled. "Rein me in? What does that mean?"

"I merely meant maybe I could keep you from putting yourself in danger."

"Perhaps, though you have to admit that I've been pretty good about not taking risks lately. Things just happen. Like I'm in the wrong place at the wrong time."

When he rolled his eyes, I gave him a playful slug. "You know I'm right."

"Sure you are, Leta. Granted, you don't say to yourself, 'Oh, let me go out and confront someone who may be a killer.' But you *do* ask enough questions to provoke someone into coming after you. All I'm saying is that if I'm here, maybe you'll be slightly safer—not that I'm Superman or anything."

I stuck out my tongue. "No. You're just Tommy to my Tuppence, and I think we've just taken on a case. So, what do we do now?"

He suggested a few hours of sleep, and I knew he was right. Much as I wanted to mull over what we'd seen, I knew my brain wouldn't cooperate until I got some rest. When my head hit the pillow, I was out.

It was still dark outside when I smelled coffee. Though it was only six a.m. and I didn't feel particularly rested, there was little chance I'd be able to go back to sleep. When Dave came through the door with a cup of coffee, I stretched and sat up.

He handed me a mug and went to take a shower. I'd barely had two sips before he was back. *How do men do that?*

"I might as well take my shower too, since there's no telling what this day will hold. Sooner or later we need to roust Belle and Ellie. If Wendy doesn't make it back before they wake up, they'll be worried."

My shower took much longer than two sips of coffee. I let the hot water beat on my shoulders as I reflected on what I'd seen in Emily's room. I needed to write it all down before I forgot it. Except I also needed to blow-dry my hair and be ready for action. Hair and makeup won out. *It's like donning a suit of armor.*

When I emerged from the steam-filled bathroom, the door between the bedroom and living room was closed, and I heard voices. Still in my robe, I cracked the door and saw Gilbert holding a cup of tea. *What's he doing here so early in the morning?*

I'd never seen Gilbert look so woebegone. "Good morning, Tuppence. Dave just broke the news to me. I can't believe Emily's dead. Known her a lifetime. Just can't take it in."

"I'll be right with you two."

I threw on jeans, a wool turtleneck, and a scarf and felt ready to face the day—or at least Dave and Gilbert. They looked up expectantly when I joined them. Christie looked up too, but with a demanding meow. "Would you please feed me? These two don't seem to get the message."

As I put a dab in her dish, Dave apologized. "Sorry, Leta, I was so caught up talking with Gilbert, I tuned her out. Good thing I took Dickens for a walk before that."

"Well, if Gilbert's presentation is still on, he'll want a happy cat." I stopped myself. "Oh! I haven't even considered what Emily's death means for the festival. Will it continue or be called off? What will happen?"

Gilbert cleared his throat. "That's what Dave and I have been discussing. I need Dave's help."

"Dave's help? With what?"

"With the presentation. I was awakened by a panicked call from Rhys asking if I could do it without him, but to be effective, the session requires two people. Naturally, I thought of Dave."

Our friend shook his head. "He didn't offer much of an explanation as to why he couldn't be there, only that there had been an emergency and he couldn't make it. Now, I know what the emergency was or is, and I can't believe it. But he made no mention of the festival being canceled."

I stared out the window. The sun wasn't up yet, and the lights still twinkled around the pool. "How much has Dave told you?"

Dave answered for Gilbert. "Only the bare bones, Leta. I thought I'd wait for you. Sharing the details with Gilbert may help focus our minds, and I can take notes while we talk."

I refilled my coffee mug and curled up on the couch. I thought about the vibrant woman I'd met only yesterday. *Could it be as simple as food poisoning—in something she'd shared with her dog?* "Oh no! How's the dog? Has anyone heard?"

Gilbert spluttered. "The dog? Something happened to Wimsey?"

I told him that Dickens had seen Wimsey beneath his mistress's chair. Thinking about the dog almost stopped me in my tracks, but I made myself continue. "I have to believe Felicity will contact us before long and that she'll bring good news about Wimsey. Let me begin with Wendy pounding on our door. And, Dave, did Wendy say anything more as you two went down the hall?"

"If she did, I don't recall. She was pretty much in shock."

I watched as Christie approached Gilbert and looked up at him. She meowed until he put his teacup down. Then she jumped into his lap. She was a sassy thing, but she could tell when people needed comforting.

As Gilbert stroked Christie, I started the narrative with us entering the room. Rhys kneeling and murmuring, Wendy helping him to the other chair, Dickens spying the dog, Wendy sitting with the poor thing on the couch, Dave contacting Felicity.

"It was seeing the dog that triggered the awful thought that this wasn't a natural death. How could Emily *and* the dog have had simultaneous heart attacks or strokes or whatever else?"

"Right," interjected Dave. "And, Gilbert, you know how she is. She shook off her shock and focused on the scene."

That comment earned him a small smile. "I took in every little detail—several bottles on the bar, two glasses on the small side table." I closed my eyes. "I'm picturing the bottles. I think one held crème de menthe because it was green, and the other tall one may have been cognac—Hennessey cognac."

Dave's mouth dropped open. "You're a connoisseur of cognac? How do you know it was Hennessey?"

I used my hands to outline a shape in the air. "Um, it's a distinctive bottle. I don't drink the stuff, but the bottle's pretty. And there was another smaller bottle on the bar too, and I don't know what it was. It looked almost antique and had brown liquid in it."

Gilbert nodded. "The crème de menthe makes sense. That's Emily's drink of choice after dinner. She claimed it helped her digestion and helped her sleep, but we always teased that she simply liked the mint flavor. The glasses on the table—what was in them?"

"The one near Emily held a bit of green liquid. That had to be crème de menthe, and I think the other one was cognac since it was brown. And there was a small foil wrapper too."

Dave was jotting notes. "Gilbert, who do you know that drinks cognac? Who would have had a drink with Emily?"

Tilting my head, I added, "In her robe. A drink with Emily when she was in her robe. That can't be many people."

Gilbert looked from me to Dave. "That's really two questions. I can think of any number of people who drink cognac. As for who would have had a drink with her? Honestly, if you had knocked on Emily's door, she would have let you in no matter whether she was in her robe or not."

He stared at Dave. "She might not have let a strange man in, but if he was a guest at the festival, someone she'd met, like Dave? She wouldn't have been happy, but she would have been hospitable."

I chewed on my lip. "Gosh, in this day and age, I think I'd be more careful. I'd be concerned about letting someone I barely knew into my room—especially at night."

That comment earned an eye roll from Dave. "Admit it, Leta. You might have been hesitant, but you would have let him in. You tend to think you're a good judge of character, so unless there was something overtly threatening or off about the man, you would have politely invited him in."

*He had a point.* "So, it could have been anyone who sat with Emily and drank cognac? That doesn't narrow the field." Something was niggling at me. "Gilbert, how well do you—did you—know Emily? Did she also drink cognac? I mean, why else would she have kept a bottle of cognac on the bar in her room?"

Gilbert's expression went from baffled to horrified. "Emily didn't drink cognac, but Rhys does." He let that hang in the air. "And they're more or less co-hosting this event, though Emily was clearly in charge."

Thinking back to when I saw the two in conversation by the pool, I thought he was right about their roles. And I recalled that Rhys had asked her about cognac. "And it follows that she would have it handy, then?"

He hesitated. "Yes . . ."

He looked as though he wanted to say more. And then he did. "Are you aware that Rhys and Emily were once married?"

My eyes grew wide. "Married? They were married?"

"Yes, but they've been divorced nearly as long as they were together—maybe ten or fifteen years now." He took a breath and then explained. "I mean, they get along famously. They're both members of the Sayers Society and more recently the Golden Age Literary Association, and they attend the same events, literary and otherwise. They often function as each other's plus one." He seemed to run out of steam. "They're great friends."

Another piece of the puzzle surfaced in my brain. "The card. I forgot about the card in the pocket of her robe."

Dave looked up. "Right, I saw you check her pocket, just as Felicity came in the door, but I never asked what you found. I think I figured it was of no consequence, maybe a tissue, or you would have mentioned it."

"It was one of Oliver Fletcher's business cards with *Best Wishes* written on the back." I closed my eyes and thought aloud. "Did Oliver send her a gift? I have too many questions."

Just then, my phone rang. "Maybe that's Wendy." I stumbled to my feet, jogged to the bedroom, and answered it without looking at the screen. Not Wendy and not at all who I expected.

# Chapter Six

"Leta, it's Jake. I just had the most disturbing wake-up call from Wendy. What have you two gotten yourselves into this time?"

*Jake? She called Jake?* "Oh no. That must mean it's bad. Why else would she call you?"

"Leta, you're not making any more sense than Wendy did. She was almost incoherent—something about Exeter and being questioned and wanting me to call Felicity Jenkins."

Now I was stumped. "What? Did she want you to vouch for her or something? I'm confused."

"Well, you're not the only one. Why don't you start at the beginning and tell me what's going on? For starters, where are you two? Are you in Exeter?"

"Hold on. Dave is here too." I strode into the living room and hit the speaker button. "Okay, we're in Torquay, at a literary festival. And, oh, our friend Gilbert, the Sherlock Holmes expert, is in the room with us."

"Tell me this isn't some kind of elaborate joke, Leta. Are the rest of the little old ladies there too?"

Dave took over. "Jake, I know what it must sound like, but this is no joke. What started as a trip to a murder mystery festival has turned into a real murder—at least that seems to be the way the police are leaning."

I listened as Dave succinctly laid out the sequence of events. *This is what comes of starting your career as a newspaper reporter. The facts, ma'am, nothing but the facts.*

Jake let Dave get through the recap, posing only a few questions along the way. I heard him blow out his breath. "Okay, I think I've got it. I bet Wendy connected Felicity's transfer from Exeter with the fact that I used to work there. So, yes, I think she wanted me to vouch for her with Felicity. And that was a good call because I worked closely with Felicity Jenkins before I took the position in Truro."

*Ooh, that's good news.* "So, Jake, can you help Felicity see that Wendy may have found the body, but she can't possibly have anything to do with Emily's death? For goodness' sake, she doesn't need to waste any time thinking Wendy is a suspect when she could be out finding the real murderer."

"Hold on, Leta. We don't know that she considers Wendy a suspect, but even if she does, it's not that simple. This is Felicity's case, and she's on the scene, not me. I can vouch for Wendy, but that's about it. I can't second-guess how Felicity processes the scene and who she questions."

When I looked at Dave and used my finger to point at him and me, he picked up on what I wanted. "Okay Jake, we get that, but there's something else we'd like you to vouch for, and that's the advantage of having Leta and the Little Old Ladies' Detective Agency on the case. You know firsthand how adept they are at ferreting out information. They have an uncanny ability to get people to open up to them, and Leta's talent for connecting the dots at a crime scene is a bonus. Is there some way you can influence Felicity to leverage the LOLs?"

"Bloody hell, Dave, have you gone over to the dark side? I had the impression you looked askance at your girlfriend's escapades."

I spluttered. "Escapades? You call the investigation in Astonbury an escapade? Wendy and I solved that case!"

"Okay, maybe not in that instance, but you have to admit, you two breaking into an office in Tintagel was over the line."

Dave made calming motions with his hands. "I'll ensure no lines are crossed here, Jake, if you can get Felicity to accept assistance from the LOLs."

It took Jake so long to respond, I thought we'd lost him until a loud sigh echoed down the line. "I give up. I'll do it, and, Leta, I'll call you later, but take this as a caution—Felicity and Gemma are two peas in a pod."

Not what I wanted to hear, but it was a good tip. I thanked him profusely, and he promised to text me once he had connected with his former co-worker.

His final words were to Dave. "You're a better man than me."

Gilbert hadn't uttered a word during the whole conversation, and I wondered what he was thinking. "Gilbert, are you okay?"

"Yes, no, I don't know. I guess I'm still processing the fact that Emily's dead. On top of that, it's nearly 8 a.m., and I have a presentation to make at eleven." He looked at Dave. "Can you help me? I've got the notes, and I'm sure you can carry it off. And it never hurts to be self-deprecating. If you lose your way, remind them you're an Agatha Christie fan, not a scholar, and that J.M. Barrie is your field of expertise."

Throwing up his hands, Dave agreed to step in. "I'm all yours Gilbert. Where are the notes?"

The two agreed to shift to Gilbert's room where they could order room service and Dave could study and practice. My job was to locate Wendy and update the rest of the LOLs. Hopefully, I'd hear from Jake soon.

With Dickens at my side, I knocked on the door to our friends' suite. I expected Ellie would be up, though it was pretty early for Belle.

Dickens barked, "I hear Ellie. Maybe she has snacks."

"Uh-uh. Don't you start. You've had your breakfast. I'm the one who could use a snack."

Ellie was tugging on a cardigan when she opened the door. "I heard that. No treats for the boy?"

"Nope. We've got more important things to worry about this morning. Is Belle awake?"

"Not yet, and Wendy's door is still closed. I must have been asleep by the time she came back from her walk last night because I didn't hear her."

Little did Ellie know Wendy hadn't come in at all, and judging from the silence emanating from Wendy's room, she must still be with Felicity. *Not a good sign.* "She went for a walk? Last night?"

"Yes, I was watching the telly when she came in to fetch her coat. She and Rhys were going for a walk on the beach."

*That explained the coats.* "Ellie, I'm afraid we need to wake Belle. Wendy, unfortunately, is being questioned by the police."

When Ellie's mouth dropped open, I added, "She's alright, Ellie, though I'm sure she's in a state."

Ellie shook herself. "I'll wake Belle. Can you make her a cup of tea, please, and perhaps ring room service for a pot?"

I couldn't help smiling. In true dowager countess form, Ellie had taken charge. I rang room service and Wendy, in that order. Tea and toast would soon arrive, but Wendy's phone went to voicemail. *She can't possibly still be with Felicity, can she?*

As if in answer to my unspoken question, Wendy opened the door. Forlorn was the word that came to mind. I sprung up and hugged her. "Oh my goodness, Wendy. You look as though you've been through the wringer. Do you want to lie down? Have a cuppa? Talk? What?"

She was uncharacteristically silent as she kicked off her shoes and threw her coat on a chair. She didn't speak until I placed a mug of coffee in her hands, and then it was only a weak "thank you."

Room service arrived as Belle and Ellie emerged from their bedroom, and Belle went to her daughter. "I don't know what's going on, dear, but we'll sort it."

When Belle hugged her, Wendy collapsed into her mother's arms, and tears coursed down her face. "Oh, Mum, it was dreadful, and I don't think it's over."

My heart was breaking for my friend, and I didn't know what to think. "Wendy, let's get some food in you, while I tell your mum and Ellie what happened after you knocked on my door last night—or this morning, I guess it was."

"Please do, Leta. The less I have to explain, the better."

I laid out what had happened from the time Wendy woke me until she and Rhys left the room with the constable. I had to remind myself this was shocking news to Belle and Ellie, though after seeing the crime scene and rehashing it for Gilbert and Jake, it was becoming less so for me.

Belle rubbed Wendy's shoulders. "You look a bit better, dear. Do you want to tell us where you've been since then? Surely you've not been questioned all this time."

"No, Mum, not all of it. They left me on my own quite a bit. Felicity didn't get to me until after the Scene of Crime Officers arrived, and she came and went a few times after that. I think she may have been going back and forth between me and Rhys."

She looked at me. "Leta, it was just like on the telly. Her constable was the good cop, comforting me, saying she knew this had to be distressing. But Felicity was brutal. She peppered me with questions—accusatory questions. 'Why were you in Emily's room? Why did you go to Leta and Dave and not to me? Where exactly were you and Rhys? How long have you been planning to meet up with him here?'"

*Seriously?* "That woman was in the bar with us. And she treated you like that? Couldn't she tell that you two hadn't seen each other since you were at university?"

"That's why you called Jake, right? In the hope he'd get her to back off?"

"It was more than that, Leta. I was afraid she was going to arrest me!" She blinked. "How do you know I called Jake?"

I was dying to know what happened before Wendy knocked on my door, but I had to share the conversation I'd had with Jake, first. "I was hoping to hear from him sooner than this. Maybe he's having a hard time connecting with Felicity."

A weak smile appeared on Wendy's face. "I hope she listens to the dishy DI."

Wisely, Ellie prompted Wendy. "Why don't you tell us about your walk with Rhys. You two must have been enjoying yourselves if you were out until one." *What a good approach.*

Wendy noticeably brightened. "Oh my gosh, it was magical. The years fell away, and it was as though we were back at school. Except, of course, that we had years of catching up to do. He'd kept up with our chums better than I had and shared what everyone was up to. And who would have believed he's as big a reader as I am? When I told him Mum's nickname was Miss Marple, he cracked up."

Belle looked thoughtful. "Did you date him at university? I thought I met all the boys you were serious about."

"No, Mum. I had a bit of a crush on him, though. He was witty and charming and always surrounded by girls—or so it seemed to me. He was quite the ladies' man at Oxford, and believe it or not, I knew better than to get involved with him. When I married right after graduation and moved to Charlotte, he was still unattached. He didn't marry until he was nearly thirty, but like my marriage, his barely lasted a decade."

*Is now the time to tell her who he married?* "Um, Wendy, did he tell you who his ex-wife was?"

"No. Just that the marriage didn't last, but the breakup was amicable. We had that in common. I didn't see much of my ex, but when I did, we got along fine."

"Wendy, I don't know how to tell you this, but it was Emily—he was married to Emily."

Her face gave new meaning to the phrase "white as a sheet," and I had to strain to hear her whispered response. "That's not possible."

"I'm sorry, Wendy, but she is—was—his ex. I guess that explains why he was devastated."

Moaning, she buried her face in Belle's shoulder. "Why didn't he tell me? What does it mean that he didn't tell me?"

"Perhaps he was trying to figure out how to do that without scaring you off." We could always count on Ellie to be the voice of reason. She made soothing sounds as Belle wiped Wendy's fresh tears with a tissue.

I was trying not to think less of Rhys, but I couldn't dismiss his omission as easily as Ellie had. *Something's not right.*

Belle studied her daughter's face. "Do you feel up to taking us through the rest of your evening? And then I think we need to get you to bed."

"We walked and talked. We sat by the pool bundled in blankets and talked some more. It was the wind picking up that drove us inside." Her eyes lit up. "He kissed the tip of my frozen nose and apologized for keeping me out so late, and we cajoled the bartender into brewing us some decaf even though the bar was closing. I was on cloud nine—until we passed Emily's room and saw the door slightly ajar. And you know the rest."

*Indeed I do. But what does DS Jenkins know that I don't? What made her lean so hard on my friend? If Rhys and Wendy were together all evening, shouldn't she be pursuing other leads?*

# Chapter Seven

Leaving Wendy to the ministrations of Belle and Ellie, I dropped Dickens in my room and went in search of breakfast. Toast was all well and good, but something heartier would be better. I was approaching the dining room when Jake texted me. "Vouched for all of you, but DS Jenkins isn't happy." *Now, what does that mean?*

Next came a call from Dave. "Where are you? Have you had breakfast?"

In no time, Dave joined me, with a file folder tucked beneath his arm. "I need to sit down with these notes and make them my own. Gilbert had only a broad outline of Rhys's part, but as soon as he let Rhys know I was filling in, he graciously dropped by with his notecards and reference material."

"You saw Rhys? What did he have to say?"

"His appearance said it all. He's wiped out, and I wasn't about to ask him questions about anything beyond his take on Agatha

Christie. Believe it or not, he still plans to lead the Greenway tour later today. I'm not sure I could do that if I were in his shoes."

I was disappointed but decided I likely would have done the same as he had. I made short work of breakfast, and we headed to our room so Dave could prepare. After thirty minutes of study, he asked me to play Gilbert to his Rhys so he could run through his part.

Gilbert's notes were clear enough for me to follow, and Dave did an excellent job with Rhys's part. "How is it you're not nervous? You hardly hesitated."

"I did a series of articles on Agatha Christie a few years ago. When I read Rhys's notes, it was like a file drawer in my brain popped open."

"You never cease to amaze me. Way too many of the file drawers in my brain are stuck." As if to make my point, I reached for a vague memory of an old *New Yorker* cartoon about that—to no avail, of course.

By 10:30, Dave was ready to go. He and Christie left to meet Gilbert, while I took Dickens for a quick walk. I wondered how Rhys's absence would be addressed this morning and who would deliver the news about Emily. No doubt the SOCOs, an ambulance, and a stretcher carrying a body would have been noticed by at least a few early risers, and by now, rumors were surely flying.

Walking through the lobby, I saw Daisy in conversation with Oliver Fletcher. She looked harried as she showed him something on her ever-present clipboard, but managed a small smile when he gave her a peck on the cheek. No amount of training could have prepared her to deal with a death at a conference.

I was surprised to see Scarlett handing out flyers at the door to the conference room and assumed Rhys had asked her to stay. He would need all the help he could get to see the festival through to its conclusion, and Scarlett, with her behind-the-scenes knowledge, would be indispensable. Her pallor was visible despite her expertly applied makeup.

Whispering, I put my hand on her shoulder. "I'm so sorry for your loss, Scarlett. I hope you're holding up okay."

"No thanks to you!" she snapped.

*Whoa. What have I stepped in?* "I'm sorry? What does that mean?"

She gripped my arm and pulled me aside. "You're the one who flashed my card at Emily. I don't know where you got it or why you did it, but it's your fault that Emily was furious with me." *My fault?* "And now she's dead, and all I can hear are her angry words. It was a stupid misunderstanding, and we would have worked it out, but now we never will."

As more guests arrived, she shoved a flyer at me and left me standing in shock. I got my wits about me and entered the room, where I found Felicity Jenkins standing alone at the back. Dressed in a dark pantsuit, she looked like a different person from the woman I'd met Monday. "Good morning, Felicity. How are you doing?"

She looked around before leaning toward me. "Not very good, at all, Leta. Never in my wildest dreams did I think I'd be investigating a murder at a festival featuring murder mysteries. Talk about life imitating art."

"Does that mean you've definitely concluded it was murder?"

"You mean Jake Nancarrow hasn't brought you up to speed?" Her expression gave nothing away.

"Only that he told you how adept we LOLs are at unearthing information."

Her hand flew up in the halt position. "Don't start with me. I'll get to you and your lot later."

Jake was right. Felicity's reaction was much like that of Gemma in the early days—before she mellowed and occasionally admitted that our input was valuable. *Time for me to exit stage left.*

As Dickens and I moved down the center aisle, Sue stood and waved us over. "I saved a few seats, but I see from the flyer that Dave doesn't need one. Are the others on their way?"

"The flyer? What?" I hadn't looked at the piece of paper I had in my hand. On it was a headshot of Dave and a brief bio. "Wow. That was quick work."

"I saw Scarlett leaving the business center this morning, and she told me she'd run off new ones because Rhys had an emergency. Hope he's okay."

Dickens yipped as Ellie slid into the seat next to me. Turning around, I searched for Belle and Wendy, but Ellie was alone.

"I'm it for the morning, Leta, but Belle says she's not going to miss the Greenway tour. Am I right in thinking it's still going on?" That question got a quizzical look from Sue, but the lights dimmed, preempting any questions.

It was Scarlett who introduced Gilbert and Dave. She stood between the two men, directly behind Christie, who was perched between them. "Welcome to day two of the Poison Pens Literary Festival. Today, we bring you 'The King of Detectives vs. the Queen of Crime—Conan Doyle vs. Christie.' Though there's no evidence the two authors ever met, much has been written about them both, and this morning, we have the pleasure of hearing a perspective on how their writing compares."

She turned to her right and motioned. "Let me introduce Gilbert Ward, a member of the Sherlock Society who calls himself a *dabbler* in all things Sherlock, but I'm sure you'll soon agree that he's much more than that. He's often called upon to speak of the great detective and his creator, and we're honored to have him with us today. I know you'll find his talk highly entertaining."

Turning to Dave on her left, she continued. "Now, I know you were expecting to hear from Dr. Ford this morning, but due to an emergency, we imposed on Dave Prentiss to take his place. He's a long-time contributor to literary magazines and has written extensively about nineteenth- and twentieth-century authors. It was his article about a previously unknown J.M. Barrie book that catapulted him into the limelight last year, and his book *Barrie & Friends* will be released early next year.

"And last but not least, this beautiful creature is Christie—named of course, for Dame Agatha, though no one's told me whether she has a speaking part." When she reached around Christie and scratched her chin, my cat hissed and promptly bit her finger. I'd never known Christie to do that—a love bite on occasion, but not an out and out bite. *Good judge of character, I'd say.*

Scarlett recovered well with a comment about Christie perhaps not liking redheads, to which my sassy feline responded, "It has nothing to do with your hair. I plain don't like you." *Whoa.*

Dave looked from me to Christie, probably wondering whether I'd somehow put my feisty friend up to attacking Scarlett. I might have if I'd thought of it, and I couldn't help grinning as Scarlett turned the stage over to the trio at the table and moved to the rear of the room. The smile on Gilbert's face told me that we were in for a talk that would be humorous as well as informative.

I could hear whispers around the room asking about the cat and wondered what Gilbert had up his sleeve. I doubted she was here only because of her name. Dave answered my unspoken question when he tickled Christie beneath her chin. As if on cue, she meowed sweetly.

Ever the showman, Gilbert stood and motioned toward Christie. "Before we go any further, let me tell you more about our little friend. Yes, Christie is named for Dame Agatha, but she's here to represent Edgar Allan Poe, the author who paved the way for Conan Doyle and Christie. Let us begin with Poe's influence on the characters of Sherlock Holmes and Hercule Poirot.

"Now, ladies and gentlemen, if I were to ask, 'Who was the better writer, Arthur or Agatha?' what would you reply?" He paused. "Perhaps you would react as I did when I read that question in a blog post not long ago. Because I'm here representing Arthur Conan Doyle, if you will, you might think I would immediately utter his name as my response. And, make no mistake, I love all things Sherlock Holmes, but I also happen to think that Agatha Christie's books represent the best mysteries to come out of the Golden Age. My response is that you cannot compare the two."

He turned to Dave. "Dave, what say you?"

Dave chuckled. "Certainly, I agree with your opinion of Agatha Christie's mysteries. I'd go a step further and say that when Conan Doyle died in 1930, Christie's best works were yet to come. And I know you and I agree that their works are very different. In Christie's early writing, Doyle's influence is evident, but she went on to expand into different subgenres as time went by. Doyle's structure never much varied."

What ensued was a lively discussion of Holmes and Poirot who were as shrewd and observant as C. August Dupin, the detective who appeared in three Poe short stories. "Did you know," asked Gilbert, "that Poe's detective is mentioned by name in *A Study in Scarlet*? And that Conan Doyle credited Poe with inventing the detective tale?"

"And," added Dave, "he gets a mention in *Third Girl* when Agatha Christie explains that between cases, Poirot was writing a biography of Edgar Allan Poe."

As they continued, we were treated to fascinating bits of trivia. Gilbert surprised his audience with a question about Christie's 1926 disappearance. "Who among you knows that Arthur Conan Doyle tried to help the authorities find Agatha Christie when she disappeared in 1926?"

When not a single person responded yes, he chuckled. "By that time, Doyle was well into spiritual phenomena, and he attempted to find the missing author by taking one of her gloves to a medium. As you might suspect, nothing useful came of that effort."

Finally, he returned to the subject of the cat in the room—the one who had long since assumed a sphinx pose in front of him. "As for this splendid creature, though she's graced us with her presence, she has declined to share her thoughts on Edgar, Arthur, and Agatha."

He scratched Christie between her ears and chuckled when she meowed. "She does, however, represent another thing Conan Doyle and Christie had in common with Poe. Can anyone tell us what that is?"

Sue raised her hand. "Is it something to do with Edgar Allan Poe's tale about a black cat?"

"Well done. All three authors wrote tales with a cat in the title, and Poe, of course, was first with his horror story 'The Black Cat.' Conan Doyle came next with his short story 'The Brazilian Cat,' and finally, in 1959, we see Hercule Poirot in Christie's *Cat Among the Pigeons.*"

Dave wrapped up with one final item of literary trivia. "We hope you've found our talk intriguing. Here's one more little-known fact—though Arthur Conan Doyle was invited to be the first president of the Detection Club, which was founded in 1930, his poor health precluded him from accepting the role. Years down the road, Agatha Christie reluctantly became president when Dorothy Sayers died. And so it goes, ladies and gentlemen, so it goes."

Standing with a mic in hand at the back of the room, Scarlett thanked the two men. "We've got a few minutes for questions before we break for lunch."

A question came from the middle of the room. "I wanted to ask this question of *Dr.* Ford, our resident psychiatrist, but I'll make do with his fill-in. Mr. Prentiss, would you care to elaborate on Edgar Allan Poe's state of mind when he wrote his lurid tales? Was he driven by alcohol or drugs or perhaps just demons?"

When I heard his voice, I realized it was Oliver Fletcher, or as I thought of him, "that rude man." Once again, his tone struck me as challenging and his question as off-topic. Judging from Dave's facial expression, I knew he felt the same way.

He cleared his throat. "I've done quite a bit of research into Poe for the dozen or so articles I've written on him over the years. He was not a drug user but was indeed an alcoholic. Poe scholars, however, assert that he could not have written his carefully constructed stories while under the influence."

Thankfully, his inquisitor didn't offer a rebuttal. The remaining questions were about Agatha Christie and Arthur Conan Doyle—and my cat, who by now was washing her face.

Scarlett strode to the front of the room, followed by Felicity. "Ladies and gentlemen, first a round of applause for our presenters. Again, thank you for an informative hour." The applause was heartfelt, and I was sure Dave was relieved.

"Second, before we break for lunch, let me remind you that the bus departs for Greenway at two p.m. sharp. If you haven't already signed up for the tour, please do so at the front desk. And yes, Dr. Ford will conduct the tour, and you won't want to miss it. Now, I must introduce Detective Sergeant Jenkins, who has some unfortunate news to share with us." *Well, that's an understatement.*

"Thank you, Scarlett." Felicity clasped her hands in front of her and cleared her throat. "I am sorry to have to tell you that Emily Paget-Ford passed away last night. As you would expect in a situation like this, the police have been called in, but please be assured we will try to be as unobtrusive as possible."

Looking around the room as if for questions, she continued, "I realize this is disturbing news, and a great loss not only for those who were close to her but also for the literary and mystery communities she was such a large part of. We know she would want the festival to continue, and that is the plan."

Without another word, she walked briskly to the door. The audience looked around as though seeking permission to depart. Her announcement was distressing to me, and I already knew Emily was dead.

It helped that Christie chose that moment to dart up the aisle to my lap, meowing loudly. "Leta, are we going to help? Me and Dickens?"

Though my boy had slept through most of the presentation, he had awakened when Scarlett mentioned lunch and was now fully alert. "Detective Dickens is ready when you are!"

Scarlett took advantage of the barks and meows as a segue. "I didn't quite catch what our four-legged friends had to say, but I want to reiterate DS Jenkins's message that the festival will go on. I know Emily would encourage us to keep calm and carry on, and we will. Thank you for your understanding."

Sue sat stunned beside me. "Leta, you don't look shocked. And neither does Ellie. Did you two already know about Emily before Felicity took the stage?"

I gave her an abbreviated version of the early morning happenings and was surprised to see her eyes fill with tears. *Oh my goodness, Sue's probably met Emily before.* When I asked, she confirmed that she had heard Emily speak through the years at Sayers Society events, though she could hardly claim she knew her.

As we broke for lunch, participants stopped by to meet Dickens and Christie and to comment on how well-behaved they were. Dickens rolled over for belly rubs, and I rolled my eyes. "Christie may be well-behaved, but she's the poster child for sassy and finicky." *And she did bite Scarlett, though that's okay by me.*

As if to prove me wrong, she meowed demurely and stood to nuzzle my neck. "Leta, these are smart people. They love me."

Though Gilbert and Dave graciously thanked Sue and Ellie for their congratulations on a job well done, I could tell they were distracted. As they ushered us from our seats and into the aisle, Dave pulled me back. "Leta, hold up."

"Hearing that last bit from Felicity reminded me of something, Tuppence." Gilbert's use of my sleuthing nickname told me something was up. "I left the bar shortly after you and Tommy, err, Dave, and I saw our ginger friend go into the business center with a laptop. She was in tears."

It took me a moment to figure out he was speaking of Scarlett. *Funny how Brits use the word ginger in place of redhead.* "Did you only see her, or did you approach her?"

"I felt compelled to speak to her. Though she was clearly in the wrong, she struck me as a damsel in distress. Naturally, I offered her my handkerchief."

"And?" *Is he stretching this out on purpose?*

"Well, she was blubbering, and between that and her Southern accent, I'm afraid I didn't understand everything she said, but I got the gist of it. After all but boxing her about the ears, Emily gave her an opportunity to atone for her sins—if you will. Something about striking through every single steamy scene in the book. The rewrites could come later, but Emily wanted proof that she was clear about which passages were offensive and had to go."

"So she wasn't demanding that Scarlett leave?"

"Not yet, but she was proceeding as though her departure was a foregone conclusion. She scheduled a meeting with Daisy Owens to brainstorm ways the hotel staff could fill in, and she would decide about Scarlett only after seeing the marked-up manuscript." With his hand to his throat, Gilbert turned dramatic. "Her fate hung in the balance. Would she be banished from the kingdom or granted a reprieve?"

Dave grimaced. "And Scarlett told him the markups were due to Emily no later than six this morning. Seems like a Herculean feat to me."

I thought back to Scarlett's words. "It was all a misunderstanding." *What she told me doesn't jibe with what she told Gilbert.*

Gilbert nodded. "Right. If anything, Emily's challenge seemed even more over the top than her earlier reaction. But, my big question is, should we tell Felicity—or DS Jenkins? So difficult for me to think of her in her professional capacity."

"She claimed, or threatened, that she planned to question me and Leta," Dave said, "and I'm surprised she hasn't done it by now. We can tell her when she gets to us."

Clapping Dave on the back, Gilbert thanked him and headed to the restaurant while we took the elevator to deposit Dickens and Christie in the room.

Christie was peering from the backpack, and as we stepped off the elevator, she leaped out. "Look, something shiny, Leta." Darting to the end of the hall, she stood on her hind legs and dipped her nose and front paws into a large plant.

Dickens was right behind her. "I want to see. Is it a toy?"

Along with clumps of potting soil, Christie dropped a glass object on the carpet. She didn't want to give it up, but Dave pushed her aside and retrieved a glass vial.

None too pleased, Christie stood with her paws on Dave's legs and meowed her complaints. "Hey, I found it. It's mine."

"Leta, it's a vial like the nurses use when they draw blood. See, it has a small rubber stopper in it, and a tiny drop of liquid."

"Oh my gosh. What's that doing in a plant? Could it be? Is it from Emily's room?"

Maybe I was jumping to conclusions, but we agreed we should contact Felicity. *Goodness knows what she'll think.*

As I flopped on the couch, Dave laid the vial on the console and pulled out his phone to call Felicity. "Give yourself a few minutes, Dave. You've barely had a chance to savor your performance this morning. I hope you know that you came across as every bit the expert. If not for how the day started, a bottle of champagne would be in order this evening."

"Guess that will have to wait until DS Jenkins or the LOLs solve the crime. Do you think she'll be impressed that we've already stumbled across not one, but two clues?"

"Not if Jake's text is any indication. I can picture her now rolling her eyes and labeling us as stumbling, bumbling busybodies. Except for you, of course. I bet she has no clue you're an honorary member of the LOLs."

Dave's face lit up. "I have an idea. Let's *encourage* her to see us as a band of bumbling old biddies plus a clueless old codger—that would be me. Think about it. That way we can snoop under the radar."

I burst into laughter. "Seriously? An old codger? You crack me up. Felicity might fall for that act, but I know of another redhead who doesn't see you that way at all."

"Does that comment mean you can laugh about her now, and you know not to worry?"

When I nodded, he hugged me. "You know, these hints of jealousy are quite flattering. Now you know how I felt when Peter sent you flowers. Not that I was seriously worried."

*But enough that you weren't taking any chances, and I love it.* "Perhaps a little jealousy now and then adds to the romance." I kissed him on the cheek and stood back.

"Now, on to the Felicity plan. If you're serious about crime-solving under the radar, we need to turn this vial over to her. Then what's our next step? Shall we go on the Greenway tour or stay here to snoop?"

"Leta, I *am* serious. As long as we stick together, and I can keep an eye on you."

Though I successfully bit my tongue, the expression on my face must have given me away. "Oh come on, Leta. It's more about my presence at least making a villain think twice. You have to admit I'm a better deterrent than Wendy."

"You're right. She's not much help in that regard." I pictured a would-be attacker grinning at the idea of two petite women fending him off.

Pulling me into his arms, Dave grinned. "Yet another reason for you to keep me around, right? In addition to my witty repartee and expertise with zippers?"

"Hmmm. Not to mention how dashing you look in a tux."

We were interrupted by a knock on the door. It was Felicity, and I was surprised to see her on her own given how things usually went in Astonbury. I looked beyond her as I invited her in. "Are the big guns hiding down the hall?"

She blew out her breath. "As in my DI? He would be if he hadn't been involved in a horrific automobile accident last night." Her eyes glistened with tears, but she blinked them back. "They're not sure he's going to make it."

"Oh, I'm so sorry. How on earth do you work on a case with that in the back of your mind?"

Straightening her shoulders, she answered. "You just do. And now we're short-handed to boot." She moved to a chair and shifted gears. "I just had the most interesting conversation with Gilbert Ward."

She had waylaid him with questions about Rhys and Emily's relationship, and one thing led to another. That told me Rhys was more open with Felicity than he'd been with Wendy. Much as Gilbert had shared with us, he painted the marriage, divorce, and subsequent friendship between the two as amicable and admirable.

"Funny, I could tell he was squirming as we spoke, but it turned out *not* to be about Emily and Rhys. It was his encounter with Scarlett last night that he was uncomfortable about. According to him, the poor girl was in a state."

That sounded like Gilbert. For starters, he was counting on Dave and me to share the Scarlett story, but also he'd be loath to paint her in a bad light.

"I want you two to recount what happened last night after Wendy woke you up, but I also want to hear more about Scarlett and this whole book thing. So let's start with Wendy knocking on your door."

Dickens barked. "What about Wimsey? How is he?"

*How did I forget about the dog?* "Sure, but first can you tell us how Wimsey is, please?"

Her face brightened. "Yes, the little thing is doing well. Rhys told us Emily regularly gave him Benadryl for his skin allergies, so we think whatever else he may have gotten hold of knocked him out. We're still not clear on what it was."

I looked off into the distance. "Do you think it will be the same thing Emily was dosed with?"

She pursed her lips. "Jake warned me about you. I don't know that she was dosed with anything, Leta, and I'm not likely to tell you when I do. Your turn. Take me through last night."

*Dosed. The vial!* "Oh, wait. Christie found something just now in the hall, more precisely, in the plant." I stood and picked up the vial with a tissue as I explained how Christie excavated it from the plant. "A vial near Emily's room is awfully suspicious, don't you think?"

Looking as though she wanted to wring my neck, Felicity pulled a plastic evidence bag from her pocket and motioned me to drop the vial in it. "Just now? And you didn't ring me immediately? What were you going to do, dust it for fingerprints?"

I fudged and glanced at Dave. "We came straight to our room, and Dave was about to call you. Surely, you didn't expect us to stand in the hall with it for anyone to see."

Dave correctly interpreted my look to mean he should go along with my story, and he did even better than that. He returned to the command Felicity had given us before I handed her the vial. "I hope those few minutes aren't a problem, Felicity. Now, shall I take you through last night?"

When she blew out her breath and nodded, he described every detail, right down to me turning in a circle to scan the room. He left out the part about the card in Emily's pocket, though.

Felicity turned to me. "I doubt you observed anything the SOCOs didn't, but can you walk me through what you saw?"

Hopping up, Dave told her to wait as he retrieved the notepad from the console. "We wrote it all down. Would you like me to take you through it?" *So much for his clueless old codger act.*

A bemused expression appeared on Felicity's face as she nodded at him to go ahead. He read my recollections aloud. "Three bottles on the bar—crème de menthe, Hennessey cognac, and an antique-looking bottle of something or other."

"Excuse me, how on earth did you know it was Hennessey? You didn't pick it up, did you?"

I repeated what I told Dave. "No, it was the shape."

Dave continued with the list. "Two glasses on the small table, one with green liquid, one with brown. We think it's logical that it was crème de menthe and cognac. And, oh, blue reading glasses." *Is he going to mention the card?*

I headed him off at the pass. "That's pretty much it, Felicity. As you said, probably the same thing the SOCOs saw. Am I right?"

"Mostly, and thank you for not touching anything. I can't tell you how many people rush in, pick things up, move them around, and generally wreak havoc with the crime scene—or disturb it, as they say on the telly.

"But you did miss one or two things—the manila folder on the console, not that I consider it of any consequence. The dresser in the bedroom was stacked high with folders. I guess Emily was on duty 'round the clock."

"And the other thing?"

"I was wondering whether you'd gone as far as checking Emily's pockets. Guess not. It was one of Oliver Fletcher's cards with a note that read *Best Wishes*. He's a strange man, isn't he?"

"I'd have to agree with that. So I guess that means he saw Emily last night or maybe before that, if the note was in her robe. I wonder, was it only a note or did it accompany a gift?"

"So very curious, Miss Marple!"

Stifling a laugh, I didn't tell her that it was Belle who thought she was Miss Marple. "Guilty as charged. I'm also curious about the little bottle on the bar. Is it an antique?"

"I suppose there's no harm in telling you that." She pulled out her notepad. "It's a handblown Bardinet crème de menthe bottle, and yes, it's an antique. The SOCOs tell me that's why its contents are brown, and it was a gift."

I waited to see what else she would volunteer. When nothing was forthcoming, I primed the pump. "So, was it from Oliver Fletcher?"

Rolling her eyes, she replied, "Yes. We've spoken with him. He saw Emily last night when he delivered the antique bottle *and* the card. He told us this event was her pride and joy and he wanted to wish her good luck." *Interesting, he was cordial to Emily but not to her ex-husband.*

She flipped a page in her notebook. "Now, tell me about the book. Gilbert indicated it caused a furor when you told Emily about it."

"I did not *tell* Emily anything! She was looking over my shoulder when I pulled out the postcard about the book. The way you describe it, I sound like a tattletale. And, if you don't believe me, ask Sue. She was standing right there."

"My, my, did I hit some kind of nerve? Calm down and just tell me the story." *Calm down! That is so condescending.*

Thankfully, Dave took over before I could get any more indignant. He described how we'd visited The Quill and seen the cards advertising Scarlett's book, and how we were intrigued. "I didn't see Leta pull the card from her purse, but I witnessed Emily's reaction. She was fit to be tied. We didn't know the background then. We only knew she seemed horrified with what she saw on the card."

"And," I added, "Emily erupted—that's the only way I can describe it. Even I shuddered when she snapped, 'Here. Now,' to

Scarlett. I mean she had every right to be angry, but she treated her like a child—gosh, almost like a disobedient dog."

Dickens barked, "You don't talk to me like that, Leta. I'm a good boy, right?" I tickled his ears in response.

Felicity was scribbling feverishly. "So, according to what Scarlett shared with Gilbert, Emily told her to pack her bags, but then gave her a reprieve." She murmured almost to herself. "Glad I didn't work for the woman."

My clueless old codger picked up the thread. "Guess it's a good thing Emily backed down, if only temporarily. Otherwise, who would have taken over this morning?"

Felicity scribbled in her notebook. "Yes, and I'm glad Gilbert mentioned the business center encounter. The last time I saw Emily was immediately after Rhys Ford's presentation, and I haven't spoken to anyone who saw her much beyond that time. Gilbert offered that she might have spoken with Daisy Owens about backfilling for Scarlett, but I haven't gotten to her yet. "

I followed her train of thought. "Could Scarlett have been the last person to see Emily alive? Did she have a drink with her, maybe in Emily's room, and then go to the business center? That might tell us Emily was alive before ten."

Dave squinted. "As angry as Emily was, I can't see her sitting down to have a drink with Scarlett, can you?"

A hint of a smile appeared on Felicity's face. "This is what Jake was talking about, isn't it? Except he didn't tell me you'd be involved, Dave."

"Oh, we're like all the other folks at this festival. We just read too many mystery novels and can't help ourselves."

Thankfully, Felicity let it drop. Since we were attempting to come off as bumbling and clueless, I didn't share any of the questions percolating in my brain—any of the several items that needed following up. Dave and I could discuss those later.

As she stood to leave, she glanced at the bar, where I had dropped my purchases from the festival booths. "*Deadly Doses: A Writer's Guide to Poisons?* Interesting reading material, you two."

"That's a gift for my anatomy teacher friend in the States. She's forever reading up on medicine and ailments, and I thought she'd get a kick out of it." My mouth dropped open. "Oh goodness, if this were a mystery novel, that book would be a clue, wouldn't it? Next, you'll want to survey all the festival-goers to see who else bought one."

"If only it were as easy as it is in books or on the telly." A stern expression appeared on her face as she opened the door. "A word of warning. If you or your animals 'dig up' anything else, bring it to me immediately. Do you understand?" She followed that directive with the standard parting instructions to call her if we thought of anything else as we looked back on accompanying Wendy to Emily's room.

Little did she know that we planned to look back on every single thing since we'd arrived at The Grand Hotel. *We're way ahead of you.*

# Chapter Eight

DAVE AND I DECIDED that touring Greenway would allow us to observe interactions among the festival participants and possibly pick up on some telltale sign of a guilty party. Felicity would be focused on The Grand Hotel and tracking down things like the divorce settlement between Rhys and Emily, Emily's will, and the usual leads the police had to follow.

Dave laughed as I set my red beret on my head and grabbed my black wool cape. "Is it a requirement, Tuppence, that you be well-dressed to play detective?"

"Why, of course, Tommy, and it's time we found you a fedora."

We made it to the dining room in time to grab a quick bite and connect with our friends. Thankfully, Wendy looked less distressed, though she was by no means her usual chipper self. I wondered whether she'd spoken with Rhys yet.

With Gilbert and Sue added to the mix, our group now numbered six. Since none of us were looking forward to a bus ride to Greenway, we decided to take Ellie's Bentley and my London taxi.

When Sue heard Ellie was driving a Bentley, she clapped her hands together. "For real? A Bentley?"

Gilbert made as though he was tipping his hat at Ellie. "Dear Lady Stow, I humbly beseech you to allow me to ride in your chariot today."

Sue gasped, "Oh, I beseech you too! Is there room for me?"

Ellie did her best Lady Grantham imitation. "The back seat is available to commoners."

"I claim Wendy and Dave, and I think I'll grab Dickens too." I knew from our last visit that he wasn't allowed in the house, but the National Trust provided a tether wall and water bowls for dogs in the courtyard. Dickens would be in heaven.

Accompanied by my delighted dog, we waited for the valet to bring the car around. Scarlett and Rhys stood by the bus. Dressed in an above-the-knee, figure-hugging denim dress, she was all business with a festival tote bag slung over one shoulder and a clipboard in her hands. It was like a receiving line. Rhys greeted the passengers and shook their hands, Scarlett checked names off the clipboard, and the bus driver helped them into the bus.

Dave took the keys from the valet, a gesture I appreciated, as I wanted to focus on Wendy. "Your ride awaits, ladies."

Dickens barked as he scrambled into the back seat. "Me too, right?"

From my position in the front passenger seat, I observed Wendy in the mirror. "Are you okay if I ask you a few questions?"

"I guess so. You haven't said so, but I know you're trying to work out how Emily died. And I'd be right there with you if .

. . if I hadn't found her. Now I know how you felt when you found Alice. I barely knew Emily, so it's not grief exactly, except over someone so vibrant being cut down in the prime of life. I mean we're her age, and I think we've got a lot of living left to do. Opening the door and seeing her sitting there—it was such a shock. As though she'd nodded off, except . . ." Wendy put her knuckles to her mouth.

"It's okay, Wendy, we don't have to talk about that. Why don't you tell me more about Rhys? We know he's a psychiatrist and an Agatha Christie fan."

She gazed out the window. "He has a flourishing private practice and writes regularly for several medical journals. I thought of Dave when he told me he's recently begun writing articles about Agatha Christie and Dorothy Sayers, with a focus on the psychological makeup of the murderers. And he wrote one or two about Agatha Christie and her use of poisons. I meant to ask him if that was why that nasty man accosted him during 'A Taste of Murder.' That was so rude."

When she paused, Dave glanced in the mirror. "Wow. It would be nice to get to know him better. Maybe I can when this is all over."

"Yes, I think you two would get along famously. He so enjoys the writing and the several opportunities he's had to speak on both the psychiatric and literary topics, that he's stopped accepting new patients. He still has a few long-time patients in London, but that's about it. These days, he's consumed by what he calls his newfound passion—writing." She smiled at Dave. "I kept thinking you and he would have a lot in common."

What bad timing. A chance encounter, a charming companion, a growing attraction—all marred by a dead body. That the dead body was that of his ex-wife complicated things, to say the least.

She seemed to be bearing up well, so I continued with my questions. "And now, Wendy? What are you thinking?"

Her lower lip trembled. "I don't know what to think. That I'm an awful judge of character? That I have unbelievably bad taste in men? I haven't seen him in thirty years. What do I really know about him? Other than that there was an immediate spark between us. And I wouldn't be thinking any of this if only he'd told me who Emily was."

Dave reached over and squeezed my knee and then looked at Wendy in the mirror. "Would you care to hear a male perspective on this?"

When Wendy nodded, he continued. "Had I been in his position, I would have been wracking my brain for a way to bring it up without putting a damper on the evening. I bet every time he thought about mentioning it, he pictured you pulling back and making some excuse to say goodnight. You two talked until nearly one a.m. What would have happened if he told you about Emily after the first hour? A sudden attack of yawning?"

In rapid sequence, three things happened. Wendy's face flushed, she looked at her clasped hands, and a tear trickled down her cheek. "I'd like to believe you're right, not that he was deliberately hiding it from me."

I had to admit his take sounded reasonable. Still, I wanted to know more about the man before I came to any conclusions. I would have been concerned for my friend even in more benign circumstances. After she moved home to England, Wendy didn't date until she fell for Detective Chief Inspector Burton—the silver fox, as we called him when he first appeared on the scene.

Burton rubbed me the wrong way from the get-go and had made Gemma's life a living hell. To Wendy, however, he'd been caring and charming—or so it seemed until his true colors surfaced. The words *condescending* and *overbearing* didn't quite capture it. He treated her like a fragile china doll instead of the bright, capable woman she was. Thankfully, my friend came to her senses and broke up with him.

And now, there was another handsome, charming man in the picture, someone from her past. I worried she would soon shift from questioning his motives to a severe case of ostrichism. That wouldn't bode well for her objectivity—or, for that matter, our friendship.

At Greenway, we met up with our friends outside of the small restaurant and joined the line to enter Agatha Christie's summer home. As we entered, we were ushered to the living room where Rhys would give his introductory talk. From there, we'd be given headsets with his pre-recorded details about each room so that we could wander at our leisure. This was more than the usual tour, as it had been augmented with personal information from Dame Agatha's great-grandson.

Rhys entertained us with additional bits of Christie trivia and challenged us with a treasure hunt—to locate the copy of *Martindale: The Extra Pharmacopoeia*, the book often described as the most well-thumbed in her collection. "You might expect to find it in the library. Perhaps it's there. Perhaps not."

Until then, I hadn't noticed that Oliver was on the tour, but there was no mistaking his voice. "Once again, Dr. Ford, you mislead your audience." *What is it with this man? He's like Jekyll and Hyde.*

Rhys did not react as calmly as he did the day before. This time, he pointed at the elderly gentleman. "Oliver, you may criticize my stance on Christie's description of poisons, but her use of this reference book has been documented countless times." He took a shaky breath. "If you find my talk distasteful, I suggest you enjoy a tour of the gardens rather than a tour of the house."

Among the murmurs in the audience, I heard Gilbert's voice. "Hear, hear. Get thee to the gardens and allow the rest of us to enjoy ourselves." *Leave it Gilbert to say what we're all thinking.*

It was good to see Belle able to climb the stairs in the house. She and Ellie whispered to each other as they walked from room to room, and I could tell they were enjoying themselves. We all laughed at the loveseat-size wooden commode on display upstairs. It was allegedly the one item Dame Agatha had to take with her on the trips to Iraq with her second husband, archaeologist Max Mallowan.

I found the most intriguing part of Rhys's presentation to be the story of the letters Agatha Christie wrote to her mother in 1922 while on a ten-month round-the-world trip with her first husband Archie. She left her two-year-old daughter Rosalind behind for that trip, and it was only when Rosalind passed away in 2004 that her son Matthew pursued turning the letters into a book.

Dave whispered to me. "Can you imagine how interesting those letters are? Just think, they lay undisturbed in boxes here at Greenway for years until her grandson decided to do something with them."

"Uh-huh. I'll have to get the book. I can't believe she visited South Africa, Australia, New Zealand, Hawaii, and Canada—and she took up surfing and excelled at it! I need to tell my sister Sophia about this, or maybe I'll get her the book for Christmas."

Dave nodded. "What was it Rhys said? When you read the letters, you can see her sharpening her skill at building memorable characters. Fascinating." He pulled out his phone and spoke into it. "Note—think about an article on *The Grand Tour* by Agatha Christie. There, maybe that's something I can pitch to the *Strand* or the *New York Review of Books.*"

When he jogged ahead to hold the door open for Belle and Ellie, I waited at the foot of the stairs for Wendy. I knew Dave would tend to Dickens, so I wasn't in any rush.

Wendy grabbed my arm. "Will you look at that?" Her face flushed, and she looked as though her head would explode when she tilted it in the direction of the upper landing. "She's all over him."

"Whoa. She is!" It was Scarlett more or less hanging onto Rhys. Well, maybe that was a slight exaggeration, but as she'd done with Dave, she had her arm twined in his and was whispering in his ear. "The girl's name is perfectly fitting. Puts me in mind of Scarlett O'Hara hanging all over poor Ashley at Tara. Did Rhys have anything to say about her last night?"

Wendy spoke through gritted teeth. "Very little, but what he told me fits with what we've seen. When I teased him about always being surrounded by women at university, I mentioned seeing him with the red-haired Amazon in the bar. He groaned and said she'd provoked the ire of several senior ladies at the Sayers society for her brazen behavior with their husbands, who, like him, were all old enough to be her father—and, in at least one case, her grandfather. I told him she'd behaved the same way with Dave and wondered whether she had a thing for older men. Rhys used the word maneater."

"Okay, so as a personal assistant, I can see why she'd be here helping out, but Emily had to be aware of her protégé's inappropriate behavior, don't you think? How could she not? Surely, she coached her to act—how should I put it? In a more restrained manner."

"You're right, Leta. If I had a student-teacher behave this way, I would have sat her down and told her in no uncertain terms that her behavior was out of line. Emily sure didn't hesitate to set Scarlett straight over her book, so why wouldn't she do the same about her flirtatious ways? Flirtatious! It's so much more than that. Anyway, Emily didn't strike me as a woman who would put up with that."

"Maybe she did tell her to shape up, and then that postcard episode was the last straw. That might explain how extreme Emily's reaction was."

We puzzled over that as we looked for our friends outside. Dave was walking Dickens, Gilbert was on his way to the coffee shop, and the others were seated at an iron table.

Shaking off our serious discussion, we pulled over additional chairs, and Wendy kissed Belle on the cheek. "What did you think, Mum? Was it worth the trek up and down the stairs?"

Belle gave her daughter an enthusiastic response. "Yes. The presentations at the hotel are interesting, but seeing the furnishings here and the books? This is amazing."

I was only half-listening to Belle. My mind kept straying to Scarlett, to Rhys, to Emily's mysterious death—and sitting next to Sue gave me an idea. At our yoga retreat in August, she and her sister got a real kick out of the LOLs and our sleuthing activities, and I thought she'd be tickled if I invited her input now. Not to mention, I found her to be a good judge of character.

"Sue, do you remember how helpful you and Penny were in Tintagel when we were trying to figure out what happened to Caryn? Would you be surprised to hear we're doing a bit of snooping now?"

Her forehead wrinkled as she looked at me. "What?" And then I saw her make the connection. "You're looking into Emily's death? You mean she didn't die of natural causes?"

I explained we didn't know for sure, but that Felicity questioned Wendy, Dave, and me and certainly seemed to be treating it as a suspicious death. I turned to Wendy. "Can you tell Sue what's been going on?"

I hadn't shared my idea with my friend, but she went with it. In a halting voice, she gave Sue the highlights of what she'd witnessed in Emily's room and how she and Rhys had been separated and questioned. "I think I'm still in shock, Sue, and if the way Felicity questioned me is any indication, I'm a suspect. And I think Rhys could be too."

"You? A suspect? That's ridiculous. You only just met Emily."

Belle elaborated. "It's standard procedure for the police to suspect the person or persons who find the body, but there's more to it. Did you know that Rhys Ford is Emily's ex-husband?"

"Everyone—well, everyone in the Sayers Society and the Golden Age Literary Association—knows that. They were a power couple in literary circles, hosting fundraisers for libraries and small gatherings for less well-known authors."

Dave had returned with Dickens and was listening attentively. "And now, Sue? Since they divorced, what's the scoop on the two of them?"

She shook her head. "They get along much the same as they always have. Sure, they don't host soirées together, since they no longer share a home, but they support each other. No one suspected they were getting a divorce until it was a done deal. Then there were the usual rumors. Was it another woman? Another man? As far as I know, it was nothing of the sort, but you know how people are. They adore scandal and gossip, but they were disappointed in this case."

That description meshed with what Gilbert had to say about the relationship, but there was still the financial aspect to consider—or Lucre, as P.D. James famously wrote in *The Murder Room*. "All the motives for murder are covered by four Ls: Love, Lust, Lucre, and Loathing."

Sue looked at Wendy. "That still doesn't explain why you would be a suspect."

Now it was Ellie's turn. "Think about it. In the best murder mysteries, Wendy could be the femme fatale. As the plot thickened, we'd discover that she and Rhys had been meeting secretly for quite some time and planned to meet up at Poison Pens and do in his ex."

By now, Gilbert had returned with a tray of coffees. "As absurd as that is, it would make a great book. Perhaps that's the next move for the Little Old Ladies' Detective Agency—writing a cozy mystery."

Dave grinned. "That sounds like a grand way to keep you ladies from getting into trouble. You can write about dangerous encounters instead of living them. I volunteer to be your editor."

Understandably, Wendy didn't see the humor in the conversation. "Very funny, you two, but at the moment, my number one priority is to get Felicity to take me off her list of suspects."

I didn't realize Rhys was in earshot until I heard his voice. "I couldn't agree more, except I'd add that removing me from the list too would free her up to find the real killer."

When Wendy whipped around, he came closer and touched her arm. "May I speak with you privately for a moment?"

She looked uncertain but followed him as he walked toward the gardens. I couldn't help thinking that in an Agatha Christie mystery, this would be when Wendy disappeared, never to be seen again. I didn't want to think Rhys had somehow murdered his ex-wife, but what if he had? What if he had spent the evening with Wendy to give himself an alibi for the time of death?

# Chapter Nine

Wendy returned much subdued, and the drive back to The Grand Hotel was a quiet one. Though I was dying to know what Rhys had said to her, I respected her wishes when she said she wasn't ready to discuss the conversation.

She unfastened Dickens from his seatbelt as the valet opened the rear door. "Leta, may I take Dickens for a walk? Maybe it will help me clear my head."

Dickens was happy to oblige, leaving Dave and me to face his feisty feline sister on our own. Christie was tucked between our pillows on the bed and didn't move until I stroked her head. Then she rolled and stretched. "Where have you been? I haven't had a treat in forever."

Dave might not be able to understand her meows, but he knew her habits. "Bet she wants a treat, right? I wonder what she misses most—curling up in your file drawer or the handouts she gets when you're at your desk."

I pointed toward the plastic container of treats on the dresser. "I'd say food wins every time, hands down." While he fed the princess, I pulled off my boots and flopped back on the bed. *What a day.*

Dave joined me on the bed, and Christie climbed on his chest and licked his chin. "I think she's beginning to like me. Or at least she does when I feed her."

Little did he know she'd been rooting for me to date Peter ever since we'd moved to Astonbury, but he was right. She'd finally come around to accepting Dave, possibly even liking him. *And that's a good thing.*

"I can't believe your eyes are still open, Leta. Or mine, for that matter. Since there aren't any more tours or speakers today, do you want to do room service or maybe have a late dinner in the bar?"

"Um," I murmured, as I drifted off.

When I woke, the room was dark, and there was a blanket over me. Once again, the door between the bedroom and living room was closed, but I could hear voices. One of them was Wendy's. *Oh my gosh, it's 6:30.* In the bathroom, I studied my reflection and ran a brush through my hair. Room service was sounding better all the time.

Dave looked up when I entered the living room. "Leta, you're among the living." He must have realized how that sounded because he clapped his hand to his mouth. "Sorry, poor choice of words."

It caught me off guard to see not only Wendy but Rhys ensconced on the couch. A bottle of red wine sat on the bar with one glass, and Dave, Wendy, and Rhys had full glasses in front of them.

I poured myself a glass and sat on the floor in front of Dave's chair with my back against his legs. "Is this a meeting?"

Glancing at Rhys, Wendy cleared her throat. "Of sorts. Rhys and I have been going over last night, and we have some details to add. Maybe they're inconsequential. Maybe not."

Rhys reddened. "Before we go much further, I feel I have to explain why I didn't tell Wendy that Emily was my ex-wife." He more or less explained the omission the same way Dave had. That he didn't want the evening to end, and couldn't come up with a way to broach the subject.

Wendy nodded at me. "Can you believe it, Leta? That's almost verbatim the scenario Dave described."

I studied him. "That certainly makes the explanation more believable." *But I'm not sure I'm buying it.*

Either she didn't pick up on it or Wendy chose to ignore my tone. "And he told Felicity right up front, so you know what that means. By now, she's seeing Rhys as her number one suspect, with me a close second. And it doesn't help that I forgot all about Rhys leaving me in the bar last night for a few moments."

Dropping his hand onto my shoulder, Dave asked, "When was this, Wendy?"

Rhys grasped Wendy's hand. "Let me, Wendy. Here's the timeline. After you left to walk Dickens, it wasn't long before the others made themselves scarce too. Wendy and I talked and talked and decided to take a walk on the beach. We went to our separate rooms to get our coats, spent time on the beach, and then wrapped ourselves in blankets by the pool. When it grew too cold even with blankets, we gave up and returned to the bar. The bartender was cleaning and straightening but was kind enough to make us a pot of coffee. That's when my phone rang with a call from my assistant."

"And that's when he left me on my own cradling a mug of coffee in my hands."

"Right, I walked toward the lobby, thinking it would take only a few minutes, that she wouldn't be calling that late unless she was desperate. Sure enough, she needed a copy of an article she was editing for me. I thought I put my latest updates on our shared drive, but she was struggling to find it."

Rhys rolled his eyes. "It wasn't the first time this had happened with us. I'm a bit inept with technology, so it's usually me who can't find something. Anyway, I knew if she couldn't find it, I'd probably messed up. I had no choice but to go to my room and check my laptop, and I was right. I forgot to put my last update on the shared drive, and I had to send it to her." He explained that she often worked late after her children were in bed.

Dave leaned forward. "So you were apart for what, twenty minutes?"

"If that, but there's more to those twenty minutes than talking to my assistant and getting her what she needed. And I think this part could be more significant. As I was closing my door, I heard the elevator, and I looked up to see Scarlett getting on it. And when you consider that Emily's room is very near the elevator, it's not a stretch to think that's where she'd been, is it? Not to mention she was . . . I don't know, distressed?"

*That's pretty much how Gilbert described her.* "That fits with what Gilbert told us. He encountered Scarlett in the business center in tears. This would have been around ten or so, right?"

Rhys shook his head. "No, this was midnight or slightly before. I know because the bartender mentioned closing time was fast approaching, but that Wendy and I were welcome to stay while he continued clearing up."

I looked over my shoulder at Dave and then back to Rhys and Wendy. "Let me think. So, Gilbert saw her before ten, and she told him she had until this morning to get a revised document to Emily. But you saw her before midnight on our floor. That means she saw Emily again after ten, and again she appeared upset."

Wendy sat forward. "What's that about Gilbert? And a document for Emily?"

Squeezing my shoulder, Dave shared what we'd learned from our friend. "Of course, Gilbert's version was much more dramatic, but the upshot was that Emily decided to give Scarlett a chance to redeem herself."

I covered his hand with mine. "Do you think she finished updating her manuscript and went to see if Emily was still awake? Instead of waiting until morning?"

Christie chose this moment to knock her jar of treats to the floor and let out a loud meow. "Talk about waiting. I want my treats now."

Despite the serious discussion, Rhys smiled. "Did she just answer your question?"

"Unfortunately, no. I think we'll have to figure it out ourselves. Rhys, did you notice whether Scarlett was carrying anything? Like a folder? No, that doesn't make sense. If she finished editing the manuscript, she would have left it . . . unless maybe she wanted some input before going any further."

Another loud meow told me Christie was growing impatient—no surprise there. I levered myself up from the floor and gave her a handful of treats as I tossed possibilities around in my brain. "You know, Wendy, you're the only one who went in Emily's bedroom last night. When you grabbed a towel for Wimsey, did you notice the folders in there?"

"Are you kidding? I was in no condition to see anything."

Rhys closed his eyes. "Oh, knowing Emily, I know there were folders, and I imagine there was a box of chocolates on the nightstand. I sent it to Emily wishing her luck with the festival. This was a huge undertaking for her, and I played only a small role." He smiled. "Crème de menthe and chocolate were her two weaknesses."

*And what about the cognac?* "Rhys, that reminds me. Did Emily also drink cognac? There was a bottle of Hennessey on the bar along with the bottle of crème de menthe."

"No, cognac is my drink. She kept it for me. I know it's hard to believe, but we truly were best friends. Better friends than we were a married couple."

Wendy gave me a knowing look. "Leta, there are so many unanswered questions. What are we going to do? Is Felicity open to the Little Old Ladies' Detective Agency pitching in to help with the case?"

Rhys frowned at her. "Little old ladies? What are you talking about?"

It was no wonder that Wendy seemed at a loss for words. There wasn't exactly a short answer to the question. "Um, that will take a bit of explaining. Maybe we should continue this discussion over dinner."

*She's right.* "I agree, Wendy. I have a gazillion questions for Rhys about Emily and Scarlett, and we owe Rhys an explanation about the LOLs." I looked at him. "Until you understand why we're getting involved, you'll think we're just a bunch of prying old biddies."

Standing, Dave added, "Rhys, you may think that even after you hear their story, but Wendy and Leta are pretty darned amazing—as are their partners in crime, Belle and Ellie."

*Belle and Ellie! It's time to put them to work, too.*

An hour later, the four of us were seated by the window at the Ephesus restaurant in Torquay. On a hill above the main drag, it overlooked the English Riviera Wheel and the Torquay Harbour Bridge with its blue lights. When he learned that I was Greek, Rhys suggested it not only for the Greek and Turkish menu but for the stunning view.

"You were right, Rhys, they have a nice variety, but I'm going with one of my favorites, lamb moussaka." Dave opted for beef stifado, and Wendy and Rhys both chose seafood dishes. We shared falafel and calamari as starters.

In unspoken agreement, we didn't broach the main topic until after we'd ordered dessert and coffee. It was Rhys who opened the discussion.

"Wendy brought me up to speed on the LOLs, and I must say, I'm torn between astonishment and shock. Astounded that you really *do* solve crimes à la Miss Marple and Agatha Raisin and shocked at the danger you ladies—well, at least you two—put yourselves in."

Dave gave me an "I told you so" glance. "You know, I keep trying to tell Leta that she takes too many risks, but she doesn't want to hear it. Not to mention, the only serious arguments we have are about her penchant for snooping."

"Or, as my sister Sophia says, my 'unfortunate sleuthing activities.' She refuses to see them as anything more than an entertaining hobby." I wasn't about to mention that my youngest sister Anna agreed with Dave.

Wendy tilted her head. "Perhaps we should get my brother to explain it to her. Peter's a believer in the power of the LOLs, so much so that he hired us in September. He didn't pay us, mind you, but he hired us."

"Well, he paid at least one of you, didn't he?" Dave said.

I knew he was referring to the flowers and elbowed him as he continued. "Rhys, like it or not, they're already on the case. Leta called Ellie before we left for dinner with an assignment for the two senior members of the team, and believe it or not, she's involved Sue too."

As serious as things were, at least his remark got a chuckle from Wendy. "Oh yes, Mum and the dowager countess were chuffed at the task you set them. What's not to like about taking Gilbert to dinner and picking his brain?"

"And Sue?" asked Rhys, "What's her assignment? Does it involve a magnifying glass?"

I shrugged. "First, I have to admit I find it difficult to be objective about Scarlett, and I think Wendy's right there with me, so I asked Sue to keep an eye on our Southern belle."

Dave draped his arm across my shoulders. "You know, that's the nicest thing I've heard Leta call her. My brown-eyed girl has displayed a hint of jealousy when it comes to Scarlett. She hasn't quite turned into a green-eyed monster, but if Scarlett hugs me one more time . . . well, all bets are off."

Wendy came to my defense. "And the nerve of her asking if you were available! Admit it, Dave, the hussy does more than hug you! She pulls you close, whispers in your ear, and all but wraps herself around you." She looked at Rhys. "And, I saw her do the same to you today. With that behavior, it's no wonder she's ticked off more than a few wives in London."

Rhys turned red. "I can't argue with you there. If you can believe it, she's slightly more restrained than she was before, at least according to Emily. Did I tell you that Scarlett's mother is the reason she's here in England?"

He explained that her mother and Emily were good friends. "They met as students at Cambridge when she did a semester abroad, and the two remained great friends. Marilyn lives in Tennessee and has had great success as a romance writer. They always laughed about how she'd turned her degree in medieval literature into a historical romance empire."

Wendy wondered whether she'd read any of her books, but Rhys said she wrote under a pen name, and he didn't know what it was. "Anyway, it seems Scarlett's been a handful for a while. When she told her mother she wanted to become an author, Marilyn saw it as an opportunity to ship her off to England and have Emily take her on as a client. Only she also asked Emily to try to tone down her behavior."

*This is fascinating.* "There must be a story there if her mother had to ship her across the pond for etiquette lessons."

"Emily told me there'd been some kind of scandal at Emory but didn't elaborate. Regardless, she said Scarlett had potential as a writer if only she would listen. If the fiasco with the Sayers book is any indication, her coaching fell on deaf ears, and I suspect pointers on acceptable behavior may have fared the same way."

An idea was forming in my head. "Rhys, this isn't a fully baked thought, but bear with me. I feel as though we need to take a closer look at Scarlett. We know she was in Emily's room at least twice last night, and we don't know exactly how those conversations went—the one right after dinner and the later one. What if Scarlett was so upset she lashed out at Emily?"

Wendy picked up the thread. "And what if Scarlett's behavior with you is more than innocent flirtation? It's not rational, but all that could combine to produce a disastrous situation."

It seemed to take Dave a moment to digest that idea. "Um, Rhys, did Scarlett . . . what's the word? *Pursue* you in London? I mean, more so than the other men you say she flirted with?"

Rhys ducked his head. "I don't know to what extent she *pursued* other men, as you describe it, but since she lives in Emily's carriage house, I ran into her rather frequently. And, I know this will sound daft, but her attention always made me uncomfortable. Made me squirm is the phrase that comes to mind."

I cut my eyes at Dave. "Is that how you feel?" *Does he know this is dangerous territory?*

"Yeah, it was strange, but honestly, Leta, I put it down to her being young and maybe socially inept, until you told me what she said to you." He looked at me. "Uh-oh, was that the wrong answer?"

"You *do realize* that you're the man who said I was oblivious to admiring glances and comments that came my way. Could it be we're alike in that regard, and it takes a bystander to pick up on it? Though I'd say Scarlett goes far beyond glances and comments."

"I'll echo that," Wendy said. "Maybe it takes a woman to see it."

Dave seemed to have been struck dumb, but Rhys jumped in. "Let's set aside the overly forward behavior and focus on Scarlett's multiple visits to Emily's room. I think that bears looking into, but how do you do that? We tell Felicity, right, and let her take it from there?"

Placing a hand on Rhys's arm, Wendy asked the one question we all seemed to have overlooked. "Rhys, did you tell Felicity that we were apart last night for twenty minutes? I didn't because I blanked on that detail."

"Bloody hell. No, I didn't. I can't recall if she asked if we were apart. Did she ask you that directly, Wendy?"

Wendy shook her head. "No, but she's sure to see this as a lie of omission if we tell her now. Isn't that what they call it on all the murder mystery shows?"

Would that put Rhys squarely in Felicity's sights, or would she focus on Wendy? Or would she think they were in it together? Like Ellie had joked earlier.

Dave nodded. "I can hear Leta now, explaining to me over the phone why you can't 'fess up to Felicity—that the LOLs *have* to investigate, and that you have no choice, especially since Wendy's a suspect. It's much easier to see the logic when you're part of the thought process."

I kissed him on the cheek, pleased that he understood. "Agreeing we need to act is one thing. It's knowing where to start that's daunting. Felicity's asking lots of questions, and it's clear she sees this as a murder case, but I wonder whether she's established what caused Emily's death and what made the dog pass out. Whether she has or not, I don't see her sharing that information with us." I looked at Rhys. "I'm sorry, Rhys. This has to be painful for you."

"Yes it is, Leta," Rhys said. "But if talking it through can help find who did this, then let's keep on. I'm not sure I should point this out, but you know I'm a doctor. And I made a presentation last night on poisons. If I may say so, I believe Emily was dosed with something. It might not have been poison, but a lethal amount of a prescription drug would have the same effect. That would also explain poor Wimsey being comatose. The problem is that my being a physician makes me even more of a suspect if or when the police come to the same conclusion—the average person doesn't have ready access to drugs, but I do."

Dave leaned forward. "What if the tea leaves aren't tea leaves?"

*What on earth is he talking about?*

It clicked with Rhys first. "The apothecary jars! Scarlett was in charge of those. That's where we start."

I couldn't see there being anything to that idea, but it wouldn't hurt to let Dave and Rhys pursue that angle. If nothing else, it might trigger other ideas. Dead ends often had that effect.

# Chapter Ten

DAVE COULD TELL I was having difficulty keeping my eyes open, so he took Dickens for a quick walk while I got ready for bed. The only problem was I couldn't turn my brain off.

He did a double take when he walked into the bedroom and found me propped up in bed with pencil and paper. "I expected you to be out like a light. What's going on?"

"Can't sleep. Are you up for talking through a few things? I have a slew of unanswered questions—in no particular order. What could Emily have ingested that would cause her to peacefully die with no violent reaction?"

Dave took the pad and paper from me and began writing furiously. "You think. I'll write."

Christie was stretched out between us, and I scratched her between her ears as I thought. "I want to email my friend Bev in Atlanta to ask about prescription drugs. Would an overdose of pain pills or sleeping medication kill someone? That's a silly question—of course, it would. That's why all kinds of warnings come with oxycodone and such when you have surgery.

"And whatever it was, it could have been in the crème de menthe or added only to her glass or mixed in with whatever pills she may take routinely. I think I read a mystery about someone injecting a piece of chocolate with morphine. There are so many angles to consider."

Dave looked up. "Right, and it didn't appear that she was forced to take something. She looked as though she had nodded off." He looked thoughtful. "The apothecary jars are a good place to start, if only for ideas. I know I'm the one who said the tea leaves might be something else, but why would someone bother to hide the drug or the poison that way? Unless, of course, the killer was trying to implicate someone—like Scarlett."

"You know, Rhys was pretty quick to hop on your idea. And we only have his word he saw Scarlett last night. What if *he's* trying to point the finger at Scarlett?"

"You're just not sure about him, are you? Funny, given your issue with Scarlett, I thought you'd be eager to cast her as the villain. But what would her motive be?"

*My issue!* I took a deep breath to keep from choking him. "That's a tough one. It could be anger, pure and simple. Except I think an angry person lashes out physically or verbally, not by drugging someone. Dosing Emily with something has to be premeditated, doesn't it?"

"Which takes us back to Rhys. He admits he has the where-withal to obtain drugs, but I'm back to the same question. What's his motive?"

Laying my head against the headboard, I groaned. "Means, motive, and opportunity. You know, Lord Peter in the Sayers mysteries says motives are a distraction, that once you know the how you know who. I bet Felicity knows the how. If only she'd tell us."

"Well, let's leave it for now. What else is rolling around in that head of yours? We've got to get it all out if you're going to get any sleep tonight."

"I want to know what scandal Scarlett was involved in at Emory. I bet it had to do with a man. And don't you dare say it. It's *not* because I have an issue with her."

Dave stifled a laugh. "Yes, Tuppence, anything you say."

"And I keep thinking about that awful Oliver Fletcher. As unpleasant as he is, if he's such an expert on poisons, maybe he can give us some ideas. Perhaps Ellie or Belle can butter him up."

"That's a thought. He seemed to take to Belle yesterday, probably because she was a nurse. And I bet if they act as though they suspect Rhys, he'll be pretty forthcoming. It's easy to tell he dislikes Rhys for whatever reason. Didn't Gilbert say something about that being a story for another time? Seems like now's the time."

Closing my eyes, I scooted down in the bed and laid my head on Dave's chest. "Sounds like tomorrow will be a busy day, and we haven't even thought about the festival events."

He kissed the top of my head. "Night, Tuppence."

"Night, Tommy."

I awoke at six with a to-do list rolling through my head—catch up with Sue, get a report from Ellie and Belle, email Bev. The one thing I could do this early was the email, so I fired that off. I'd have to wait a bit for a response, as it was only one a.m. in Atlanta.

As I brewed coffee, Christie strolled from the bedroom and stretched all four paws. "That smell means milk for me, right?"

I poured a tiny puddle into a dish. Much more than that, and she would turn her nose up at it. *Fussy thing.* "Where's your brother? Still sleeping?"

"Yes, and snoring too."

Sipping coffee, I read my emails and posted Greenway photos to Facebook. *I wonder if Emily's on Facebook.*

I'd heard that younger folks didn't use Facebook that much anymore, but lots of people my age did. It made it easy to keep up with friends near and far. I found Emily right away. Most of her photos were taken at dinners or literary events. Many were labeled Sayers Society or the Golden Age Literary Association, and in some, she was accompanied by Rhys. The one that surprised me was of her smiling with Oliver Fletcher at a black-tie affair. The most recent ones came from the festival. *Such a striking, elegant woman.*

I poured a second cup of coffee and considered texting Sue. *Better check on the boys first.* Peeking in the bedroom, I saw Dickens stretch and open his eyes, and I chuckled when Dave followed suit. "Are you ready for coffee?" He rubbed his eyes and gave me a thumbs-up.

The bed was empty, and Dickens was lying in front of the bathroom door when I delivered Dave's coffee. I rubbed Dickens's head. "Are you ready for a walk, boy? I need to throw on some clothes first."

"I'll take him," Dave called from the bathroom.

Bundled up for the chilly morning air, he emerged from the bedroom with a leash and a ball. Dickens pranced by his side, barking. "Ball! We're going to play ball. Maybe I'll find a stick too."

Dave attached the leash and put his gloves on. "Gee, do you think he's excited? I'm going to take him for a long walk and get my blood flowing. Are you okay with breakfast around 7:30?"

"Works for me, and it looks like it works for Dickens too." That would give me time to shower and maybe connect with Sue. Hopefully, Dave and I could dig up some answers this morning and still have time to attend the eleven a.m. session.

My phone pinged with a text from Sue as Dave was walking out the door. "Can you talk? I have clues."

I laughed at her wording and pictured her with the magnifying glass Rhys had mentioned at dinner. "Coffee in my room, thirty minutes."

I was nearly ready when she knocked on the door. "Pour yourself some coffee while I finish my makeup. Then we can chat."

She followed me into the bedroom and perched on the bed with her cup. "I've got so much to tell you, Leta! I had a drink with Scarlett last night, and I've checked Instagram, Twitter, and Facebook. I hit the jackpot."

"Listen to you, Sherlock. How did you manage to have a drink with her?"

"I was keeping an eye out for her like you asked, and I saw her go into the workroom they're using for the festival but didn't catch her coming out. I decided around nine to check the bar before I turned in for the night, and there she was. She was sitting by herself, looking rather woebegone, so I asked her if she fancied company."

"And?"

"She offered to buy me a drink, and I was glad she questioned me when I said I'd have whatever she was drinking. It was a Jagermeister cocktail, which I never could have stomached. I thought young folks did Jager shots, but it turns out they also combine it with gin. Not my cup of tea at all. I opted for an Irish coffee."

As I added mascara and a touch of lipstick, I suggested we continue the story in the living room. Christie made room for us on the couch, and Sue told me what she'd learned.

"Given the way she was dressed—tight jeans, curve-hugging v-neck sweater, dangling earrings—I deduced she was meeting someone. Don't you love that? I *deduced*." Sue looked proud of herself. "I was right about that but surprised that the *someone* was that rude Oliver Fletcher. Who would've thought?"

Sue needed no encouragement to continue. "By the way, he's a retired veterinarian, and she met him through Emily. It seems he and Scarlett have quite a close relationship, and they routinely take evening walks together in London. They were going to walk on the beach last night."

"Did he show up while you were there?"

"No, he rang her to say he was under the weather and when she rang off, she explained to me that he has chronic back pain, and has good days and bad days. I guess that could be why he's so irascible, poor guy."

Rude or not, I was sorry to hear of the man's condition, and it spoke well of him that he was looking out for Scarlett. She probably didn't have many friends here, much less close friends.

"When I patted her on the shoulder, she broke down, and before I knew it, she was sobbing about boyfriends and Emily. I just listened."

"The story she poured out was that she left Atlanta after a bad breakup—and her mother shipped her off to England to take her mind off her broken heart. She must be an incredibly fast worker because she dated someone here, and that didn't end well either. Mixed in with that tale was how much she admired Emily and how she envied the relationship Rhys and Emily had despite being divorced and wondered whether she'd ever find a man like Rhys."

"Goodness, Sue. Even though she irritates the heck out of me, I can't help but feel sorry for her. We found out last night that she was living in Emily's carriage house and that Emily was her writing coach. She'll be at loose ends now. Did she talk about that?"

Sue blinked. "No, not at all. Emily was her writing coach? I mean, yes, I know Emily has—had—an excellent reputation as a coach and she helped any number of struggling writers. What makes no sense is that Scarlett would write a scandalous book about Dorothy Sayers, the author Emily most admired. Who does something like that?"

"That's a good question, Sue. I was flabbergasted that she went behind Emily's back like that. Suffering from a broken heart doesn't excuse that kind of behavior."

Sue's eyes twinkled. "Well, about that broken heart, I have some pretty salacious details. It's amazing what you can piece together from social media."

"Salacious! I don't think I've ever heard anyone use that word! Now you've got my attention."

I was about to get the scoop when Dave and Dickens returned. Dickens bounded in with a red ball in his mouth and dropped it at my feet. "Look, Leta, a new ball. I found it on the beach."

Dave's cheeks were rosy. "Morning, Sue. Great day on the beach, ladies. A cup of coffee and a shower, and I'll be raring to go."

When I told him Sue was about to share spicy details about Scarlett, he asked us to wait for him. "I'll only be five minutes."

While we waited, Sue whetted my appetite by telling me she was feeling sorry for Scarlett until she discovered the whole story—the parts Scarlett had left out. *Maybe it's the scandal Rhys mentioned.*

Christie deserted us for Dave when he sat in the armchair with his coffee. "Make room for me," she meowed as she burrowed her face into his fleece vest.

He stroked her head. "Have you ever noticed how much more affectionate she is when it's cold?"

"Oh yes, I have no illusions about why she likes me. It's about food and warmth. Dickens, on the other hand, loves me unconditionally."

"Okay, you two. I like Dickens and Christie, but I'm dying to tell you what I found out." Sue brought Dave up to speed with a short version of what she'd already shared with me, and then explained how she'd found a treasure trove of information on social media.

I laughed. "Forgive me, Sue, but I've got an image of Dickens finding a bone buried in the garden. You're too young to be an official Little Old Lady, but we could use a social media arm. I google stuff, and I found Emily on Facebook this morning, but I've never been on Twitter, and I rarely visit Instagram."

"If you still taught school, you'd be up on all that, Leta. I've learned all kinds of things from my students. Let's start with Facebook and leave Twitter for last. And, Dave, why don't you join us on the couch, so you can see too."

She pulled out her phone and brought up Scarlett's Facebook profile. The most recent posts were of the Greenway tour on Wednesday afternoon—around thirty photos. "What strikes you about these shots?"

Dave responded first. "They're mostly selfies, and most of them are with Rhys. Is that what you mean?"

"Yes, there's a few of the audience, plus selfies with Gilbert and Oliver Fletcher, but the rest are of Rhys or Rhys and Wendy. And look at this caption for the Wendy pic—'A girlfriend? Give me a break.' Now, let me take you back to Monday."

Swiping quickly, she found the posts from Monday morning. The train ride and the Torquay station were all about Dave with only one or two photos of Gilbert. Dickens appeared once, as did I when Dave lifted me in his arms outside the station.

I pointed. "What? Look at this caption where Dave hugs me. 'Don't tell me he has a girlfriend?' Good grief, Sue. Does this happen every time Wendy or I appear in a photo?"

Dave found his voice, "But I told her I had a girlfriend, that I was moving to England to be with you."

"Except, Dave, she claims she didn't know why you were moving here. Did she choose to deliberately miss that point?"

Sue scrolled forward. "Now look at these photos of our group at dinner Monday night. You dominate the pictures, Dave, though there are a few of you and Leta. And yes, another strange note about your girlfriend. And remember, Scarlett wasn't with us at dinner, so these seem to me like the ones she took of her professor and his wife in Atlanta. I'll explain that in a minute. You see the same theme for the Agatha Christie Mile on Tuesday morning—it's mostly you and one of you and Leta."

I stopped Sue and had her scroll back to the picture of Dave and me at dinner. "Oh for goodness' sake. Do you see the caption? 'Handsome Dave Prentiss and his grey-haired girlfriend?' My hair's not that grey!"

As Sue scrolled further, I saw lots of photos of Dave taken from all angles, one a close-up of Dave reaching over his shoulder to pet Christie in her backpack. There were a few of Belle and our tour guide in the Potent Plants Garden, and one of me and Dave with another girlfriend caption.

A shot of Scarlett in her striking green outfit came next. "Gee, these almost seem normal—selfies of her dressed for the afternoon presentation."

Then, as in the Greenway posts, Rhys was front and center as he gave his Taste of Murder talk. These pictures and the ones at Greenway seemed to indicate she had shifted her focus to him. *Is it possible she got the message that Dave was off-limits?* I voiced that thought and gave Sue the gist of the Imperial Hotel conversation.

Sue's mouth dropped open. "First of all, I can't believe she asked you that. But second, she either didn't get the message or she was taunting you. Remember what happened after Rhys's presentation, as you pulled that postcard from your purse?"

I could feel my face turning red as I looked at Dave. "How could I forget? She was all over him again, as though she and I had never talked."

It was Dave's turn to blush as Sue continued. "And by the next day, Leta, Dave is very decidedly back in the picture. Look at the

Conan Doyle versus Christie presentation. What do you notice, Dave?"

Dave squirmed. "Um, I seem to be the star. Well, there's a handful of Gilbert and one of me and Leta, but the rest are only of me."

Sue pointed to the photo of Dave and me. "And, wherever Leta appears, the same strange girlfriend caption shows up, just as it does for Wendy at Greenway."

I was struck dumb, a rare occurrence for me, and Dave was suffering the same affliction. It took Sue to state what was becoming obvious. "Can you say *stalker*?"

"Surely not," I babbled in disbelief. "A brazen hussy, yes, and snarky, but a stalker?"

Dave looked at Sue. "I'm afraid I agree with Sue. What else would explain these posts?"

"I might be inclined to look for a different explanation if I hadn't spent hours going deeper into her Facebook history and then searching Twitter. This is not some fascination with handsome men. It's handsome *older* men, and it's an obsession. More than that—in at least one recent case, it appears to have turned deadly."

*Is this the scandal?* "Was this is in Atlanta?"

Sue nodded. "Yes, at Emory."

I could see the wheels turning in Dave's head as his eyes moved from Sue to me. "Deadly? For whom? The man or the girlfriend?"

Holding out her hand for the phone, Sue took it from Dave and switched from Facebook to Twitter. She read aloud, "Emory student arrested for drunk driving in stalking incident turned deadly."

My hand flew to my mouth. "You mean someone died?"

"No, but nearly." She explained she'd located a short article in the Atlanta Journal-Constitution. The rest she gleaned from Twitter, Instagram, and Facebook.

"Here's what I've pieced together. If you begin when she was at Clemson, you can see a history of what may have started as serial infatuations with mostly older men but began to escalate. That's why I labeled it an obsession. Every once in a while, the object of her affection, if you can call it that, was someone her age. Initially, it was pictures of the men. Then photos of their girlfriends and spouses started to appear, all with some caption like we saw here. I have a feeling she may have been reprimanded at Clemson for harassing a professor, but don't hold me to that."

Dave's brow furrowed. "Serial. A single infatuation at a time?"

"Astute question, Dave. Several times, I noted two men appearing in photos for a month or so before one seemed to fall by the wayside, almost as if she was deciding which one to pursue."

He groaned. "I can't believe this. I'm not sure I want to know, but tell me what happened in Atlanta."

Sue laid out what she had surmised. "She had a brief relationship with a fellow grad student. I almost see that as her attempt to straighten up—to date someone her age. While he was still in the picture, one of her English professors started to appear in her Instagram and Facebook posts. And soon, the grad student disappeared altogether."

I took a deep breath. "Did the professor have a girlfriend?"

"Oh, much worse. He had a wife, and she's in the photos at Emory events and several times at restaurants with her husband. That's why I called Scarlett a stalker. I think she was at the restaurants but not with the couple. The shots were more like those she took of our group at dinner."

By now, Dickens had moved to my side. He could always sense when I was agitated, and he laid his head on my knee. "It's okay, Leta. I'm here."

Sue looked at both of us. "The professor's wife dropped him off at a MARTA station—I take it that's the tube in Atlanta—and was nearly home when she was involved in an accident with a drunk driver. It was Scarlett."

Dave blanched. "Good Lord. Was she killed?"

"No. Fortunately, only minor injuries, but the whole story came out after that—the affair, Scarlett stalking the professor and his wife, and him trying to break it off. Of course, very little of that was in the paper. The sordid details were only on Twitter."

"Leta, have you told Sue what Rhys said last night, about Scarlett's mother shipping her off to Emily? This has to be the scandal he mentioned."

Sue had a confused expression on her face. By the time I finished a recap of Rhys's revelations, it had changed to a look of horror. "Oh my God, do you think she killed Emily to get her out of the way?"

I stuttered, "But they were divorced!"

"Except by all accounts," Dave said, "they were good friends. They liked each other."

I couldn't believe what I was thinking. "So, Scarlett eliminated the competition? It wasn't a spontaneous act triggered by their argument? It was premeditated?"

"Remember, Leta, what you said last night? If it was done in anger, it would have been something more physical? Maybe the book ultimatum spurred Scarlett to act when she did, but she had it planned all along."

*Is this the same man who thought I had an issue with Scarlett?* "I guess my *issue* with Scarlett was more than warranted. There was just something not right about her, and Wendy sensed it too. Oh no, what about Wendy?"

Dave knew right away where my mind had gone. "Wendy and Rhys. If Scarlett cleared Emily out of the way, where does that leave Wendy?"

First Sue frowned. Then her mouth fell open. "You mean she could see Wendy as her competition now, and . . . and go after her?"

I pondered that possibility. "The thing that puzzles me is the difference between the Atlanta scenario and this one. Scarlett was having an affair with her professor before she stalked him and his wife. Is she having one with Rhys? Aaargh."

Dave rolled his eye. "If they're involved, he had a chance to tell us that over dinner. I know I made excuses for him not telling Wendy that Emily was his ex-wife, but if Scarlett is or was his lover, then he lied to us."

"And if he lied about that, what else has he lied about?"

Sue held up her hand. "I know you two have more experience in this sleuthing thing than I do, but whether or not Rhys lied about an affair doesn't matter at this point, does it? What I've discovered about Scarlett seems pretty damning, and I think we should tell Felicity. And I think she's dangerous. We didn't look at all the Facebook photos, but Rhys dominates the most recent ones taken in London. It's not until the train ride to Torquay that Dave begins to share the stage with him."

Dave and I looked at each other, and I grumbled. "Based on our last conversation, I'm not sure I can suggest to Wendy that Rhys hasn't been aboveboard about an affair. I'll need to think hard about how exactly to present this, and I may need your help, Sue."

Sue offered to write up her findings, complete with links to the newspaper article and the most telling Twitter comments. When she left us, Dave and I agreed we were at a loss as to how to proceed.

I sighed. "One thing's for sure. There's no way I can get any additional information from Scarlett. But, if we're going to leave no stone unturned, I want to find out whether Belle and Ellie discovered anything relevant over dinner with Gilbert."

Dave nodded. "The one thing I wish we knew is what was used to poison Emily. And, of course, we have no idea whether that's what the police have concluded—that she was poisoned. I mean, heck, she could have taken an accidental overdose of something for all we know."

"And if we think Scarlett set out to eliminate the competition, how would she get her hands on poison? Unless it's some common household item, or maybe Scarlett takes sleeping pills and she hoarded them to use on Emily."

He shook his head. "But how would she get Emily to take them? Oh hell, I don't know what to think!"

The one time he'd been around for a Little Old Ladies case, it had been more of a literary mystery. He and Gilbert had discovered factual errors in a handful of allegedly rare documents, and the two of them had a grand time ferreting out clues at a flea market. Somehow, this time, the stakes felt more dire.

"Dave, that puzzle may be better left to Felicity, but I think there's something you can do. How would you feel about confronting Rhys about his relationship with Scarlett? Maybe there isn't one, but if there is, we've got to look out for Wendy. It's bad enough she found a dead body, but she's in for a world of hurt if Rhys has been lying to her—and us."

He blew out his breath. "And I'm the best person to do this because?"

"Because you're a man! He's much more likely to come clean with you than with me."

"I was afraid you were going to say that. Okay, I'll find him now, though it would be an easier conversation over a beer. Here's hoping a strong cup of tea will do the trick."

All I wanted to do was have a leisurely morning—eat a nice breakfast, wander the booths, maybe take a walk—but there was work to be done. I grabbed Dickens and headed down the hall. *Time to convene a meeting of the LOLs.*

# Chapter Eleven

ELLIE OPENED THE DOOR at my knock, and she looked over my shoulder. "Good morning, Leta. Dave's not with you?"

I fudged. "No, he had things to do, and I was eager to hear how your dinner with Gilbert went. Is this a good time? Have you been to breakfast?"

"We're a bit at loose ends this morning. We were debating whether to order in or visit one of the cafés. And now Wendy's gone to fetch Wimsey from the vet so Rhys wouldn't have to go. The poor man has his hands full. Anyway, we were about to ring for room service."

Wendy's absence could be a blessing in disguise. That way if I sounded at all suspicious of Rhys, she wouldn't be around to pick up on it. "Well, I haven't eaten either. May Dickens and I join you?"

After placing the breakfast order, Belle and Ellie filled me in, and I could tell they were quite pleased with themselves. It never took much to get Gilbert talking, and Saturday night had been no exception.

Belle folded her hands in her lap. "Leta, you tasked us with finding out more about Oliver Fletcher, who we now know is a retired veterinarian." I interjected that I'd only just heard that detail from Sue too. "Well, it has no bearing on Emily's death, but Gilbert also told us the poor man has cancer. Not only that, he lost his only grandson not long ago. I *do* feel sorry for him."

I looked at Ellie, who had lost a husband, a son, and a grandson in the past year. *This has to be a difficult topic for her.*

As if she'd heard my thoughts, Ellie spoke up. "But it's worse than you suppose. His grandson committed suicide. I cannot begin to imagine how awful that is, and yet . . . "

Her voice tapered off and Belle patted her friend on the knee. "I'll tell her the rest, dear. Gilbert said that Oliver Fletcher blames Rhys. It seems the young man wrote a book about all the things Agatha Christie got wrong in her books—particularly about poisons. Why anyone would want to do that, I can't fathom. What is it they say? Her books are outsold by only the Bible and Shakespeare? What point is there in denigrating her now?"

Ellie must have seen the puzzled expression on my face. "You must be wondering what the book and Rhys have to do with the suicide. It seems the grandson couldn't find a publisher, not unusual in this day and age, and he was despondent about it. I gather he hadn't held down a job nor had much success in his life, and that he lived with his grandfather."

"Um, how old was he?"

It was Belle's turn. "Late twenties, I think. I can't imagine Peter living with me at that age, but I gather this young man had some emotional issues. And that's where Rhys Ford comes in. He was his psychiatrist for close to ten years."

I closed my eyes as I tried to grasp the scenario. "So, he'd been seeing Rhys for ages, was despondent or depressed over his book, and he committed suicide. And his grandfather blames Rhys? Why? Because he was his son's psychiatrist?"

Belle shook her head. "Oh, it's more complex than that. Yes, he feels—justified or not—that Rhys let his grandson down, that the antidepressants he prescribed were useless. But, as Gilbert says, the man has a bee in his bonnet about the book. He felt Rhys should have been more supportive and encouraging, and given his connections in the literary world, he should have helped the boy find a publisher."

"Seriously? My understanding is he writes the occasional article about Agatha Christie or Dorothy Sayers. How connected can he be? And that's what all the jibes were about? He has it in for Rhys?"

"Yes," said Ellie. "Which would be a great motive if Rhys had been the victim instead of Emily."

Glancing at Ellie, Belle added, "And let's not forget we learned that Emily was the young man's writing coach. That could explain why he was cordial to her but not to Rhys."

"Wait a minute! Isn't it more likely he would blame *Emily*? Not that it's rational by any means, but wouldn't he think Emily had failed his grandson?"

Ellie shook her head. "We said as much to Gilbert last night. It seems he did initially blame her too, but she helped him to see that it's ultimately the writer's responsibility to take the coach's guidance." She smiled. "It occurred to me that Emily was a strong woman. Can't you hear her saying to him, 'We need to talk?' I imagine her sitting him down and setting him straight."

"Oh yes, much like a teacher has to do with a doting parent who thinks little Johnny can do no wrong." Belle laughed. "Wendy used to tell me those stories."

"Did Wendy tell you that Emily was also Scarlett's writing coach? We learned that from Rhys last night—and speaking of Scarlett, Sue reported in this morning."

The senior LOLs assured me Wendy had filled them in on our dinner conversation, so they knew about the writing coach angle and our suspicions about Scarlett. When I mentioned that Sue not only had drinks with Scarlett but also checked social media, they were all ears. I was about to embark on the stalker tale when Wendy, Wimsey, and Dave arrived.

Dickens leaped up to greet the newcomer, eager as always to make friends. Wimsey, on the other hand, was a bit standoffish. Poor thing. He'd lost his mistress and spent the night at the vet and had to be disoriented. I wondered whether he sensed that Emily wouldn't return.

Looking up at me, Dickens barked. "Leta, he looks like Blanche. Do you think he wants to play?" Blanche was Ellie's Corgi, and the two dogs were great friends.

Distracted by the looks on Dave and Wendy's faces, I didn't answer Dickens. *Are they distressed, confused, angry, what?*

Dave answered my question before I could ask. "I was leaving Rhys's room when Wendy stopped by to let him see that Wimsey was okay. That's the good news. The bad news is that Felicity was on her heels with more questions for Rhys. I heard something about key cards as we were ushered out."

Room service arrived before he could elaborate. As though they had anticipated a group meal, Ellie and Belle had ordered two baskets of drop scones and a heaping plate of bacon. In unspoken agreement, we all helped ourselves before continuing the conversation.

By now, Wimsey was following Dickens around, and they both sat by the food table expectantly. When Dickens barked, "Please," I gave them each a tidbit of scone.

"That's it, you two." They took the hint and wandered to the couch.

I looked around the room, wondering where to begin. "Dave, I was starting to tell Ellie and Belle what Sue told us about Scarlett this morning. Shall I begin there and then let you tell us about your visit with Rhys?"

"Yes. For now, I'll just say it was a satisfactory conversation."

*Now, what does that mean? No entanglement with Scarlett?*

"Okay, let's start with Sue finding Scarlett in the bar." I recapped the intriguing tidbits Sue gathered over drinks—details that led her to google Scarlett Callahan and to search social media. "The newspaper article prompted Sue to turn to Twitter, Instagram, and Facebook, and what a disturbing goldmine that turned out to be."

Reaching for my phone, I pulled up Scarlett's Facebook profile and motioned Wendy to sit by me. The shocked expression on my friend's face as I scrolled through the earlier posts from Scarlett's time at Emory told me she was getting the picture.

"Bloody hell, did she stalk them? And the Twitter posts? Did she purposely run into the professor's wife?"

Dave's early career as a newspaper reporter was helpful here. "Wendy, the paper doesn't say that. Even if the reporter had a suspicion, he or she would have been careful not to say it without any proof. The article mentions drunk driving, nothing more, but when you combine it with the Facebook posts? It looks as though someone drew that conclusion and had no compunction about saying it on Twitter."

Wendy was connecting the dots just as Dave and I had. "So this had to be the scandal Rhys mentioned. The scandal that prompted Scarlett's romance author mother to send her over here. Except, based on what Rhys told us about the girl's behavior in social settings, she hasn't learned any lessons."

"No, she hasn't." As I scrolled forward, I realized we'd been going so fast earlier, that I hadn't focused on the posts of Rhys in London.

Wendy spotted them immediately. "Whoa, wait a minute, Leta. Has she been stalking Rhys? Look at all these photos of him, him and Emily, and quite a few selfies of Scarlett with Rhys. There's even one of Rhys at dinner with another woman. And what's that caption?"

"Oh my goodness! It's the same caption she uses later for me and you, Wendy!" Catching Wendy's horrified expression, I explained she'd understand in a minute, and I scrolled forward to the shots on the train where Dave first began to show up.

She pointed to the picture of Dave hugging me. "Clearly, you *are* Dave's girlfriend. What on earth does she mean?"

As we showed the posts to Belle and Ellie and scrolled back and forth, Ellie answered Wendy's question. "I think it means she's sizing up the competition—trying to determine what her chances are with these men she admires."

"Admires?" I pointed at my phone. "I think it goes way beyond admiration. I have an image of the spider and the fly. This may be overly dramatic, but given what happened in Atlanta, I think she's obsessed with Dave and Rhys. Except she hasn't made up her mind yet."

Moving ahead on Facebook, I showed Wendy how the posts shifted between Dave and Rhys and pointed out the girlfriend caption on Wendy's picture and again on mine.

"Oh my gosh, Leta! We could both be in her crosshairs!"

Ellie looked into the distance. "But I wonder . . . yes, she is apparently a stalker, and *maybe* she purposely caused an accident in Atlanta. But we don't know that for sure. Don't we hear we shouldn't believe everything we read? And what is it they say about Twitter? Anyone can post anything—they don't have to be knowledgeable or have proof. People can say anything, and from what I've heard, it spreads like wildfire.

"This whole social media thing is far worse than village gossip ever was. I can see her as a stalker, but beyond that, I think you girls may be jumping to conclusions that aren't warranted. Scarlett may see Dave or Rhys as boyfriend material, but is she necessarily after either of you?"

Dave cocked his head. "There's another difference between the situation in Atlanta and what's going on here. I haven't been involved with Scarlett, nor have I encouraged her, and based on what I heard from Rhys this morning, he hasn't either."

Wendy frowned. "Of course, he hasn't. He told us that last night." She looked from me to Dave. "Wait a minute. You mean you doubted him?"

Thankfully, Dave responded first. "Wendy, it's what we said last night—the spouse or boyfriend is always the first suspect. And there's that twenty-minute gap. If you weren't involved with him, you'd be the first to say we should dig deeper, wouldn't you?"

If looks could kill, Dave would have dropped dead that instant, and when Wendy turned her glare on me, I felt like my days were numbered.

"He's right, you know." I kept my voice low and calm. "You and I know that people lie. I understood why he didn't initially tell you about Emily being his ex-wife, but then I worried that if he'd had a fling with Scarlett, he might shy away from telling you that for the same reason. I mean, he's an attractive, single man, and—"

"Yes, he is, Leta. He's an attractive, single man, who I happen to like—*really like*. And you're implying he's not trustworthy. Give me some credit!"

Was this the same woman who moaned yesterday that maybe she had awful taste in men? Was it so hard to believe she could have misjudged someone she'd hardly known in college and re-connected with less than 48 hours ago?

Judging by her stance, hands on her hips, chin jutted out, it was. "Wendy, I was worried about you, and I didn't want you to get hurt. I'm sorry if I offended you."

"Right, that's what people say when they apologize but don't think they did anything wrong."

The angry words were too much for Belle. "Enough! You're acting like teenagers instead of grown women who are best friends. Wendy, I understand you can't bear to hear a word against Rhys, and Leta, I can see you had Wendy's best interests at heart. It happened. It's done. Let it go."

Dave came to my side and hugged me. "Would it help if I reminded you that, not long ago, Tuppence misjudged me? You may recall she thought I was a murderer, even though she *really liked me*, as you put it, Wendy. And I've more than managed to forgive her. Please tell me you can do the same."

When Wendy gave an almost imperceptible nod, I couldn't tell if I was in the clear or not. "Truce?" I whispered. Her second nod was slightly more vigorous. *Thank goodness.*

Ellie folded her napkin in her lap. "Now, let's return to the matter at hand. Felicity is questioning Rhys. Can we agree that she may have uncovered facts we're unaware of? And, Wendy, please bear with me. As painful as it is to consider, we have no way of knowing all the ins and outs of his relationship with Emily. If this were an Agatha Christie mystery, we'd soon learn that Rhys is deep in debt and stands to gain from Emily's will, or that Emily was dosed with some exotic poison that only Rhys has access to."

Wendy grimaced. "If we're going to compare this situation to mystery novels, then may I point out that quite often, the most obvious suspect isn't guilty?"

As Belle sipped her tea, she studied her daughter. "Let's say that's the case here. Are we then looking at Scarlett as the likeliest suspect?"

*I am!* "Ellie, I take your point about not having any proof that Scarlett meant to harm her professor's wife, but given her pattern, isn't it possible she's escalated? I know I'm not a psychologist, but still."

Ellie took a moment to reply. "I suppose. We certainly read about children who abuse animals and escalate as adults. Anything is possible."

"I think we're missing some vital information." Dave pointed out. "Correct me if I'm wrong, but in your other cases, the police were busy uncovering or ruling out suspects you couldn't possibly have known about. By now, I expect Felicity has checked Emily's emails and phone messages and more to determine what was going on in Emily's life beyond this festival."

Wendy sat up straight. "Yes! Maybe that's why Felicity is speaking with Rhys. She's set her sights on a person we've never even met. And she's ruled out Rhys the same way Gemma ruled out suspects when that awful magician was murdered in Astonbury. Gosh, was that only a year ago? It seems like a lifetime."

*Sounds like wishful thinking to me.* "So, are we saying we should sit back and let Felicity do her job? That she doesn't need our help?"

There was a moment of dead air before Wendy exploded. "Of course not. Whenever we get involved, we uncover critical clues, don't we?"

I chuckled. "It depends on who you ask. Jake would admit we're a huge help, but getting Gemma to agree would be like pulling teeth."

The corners of Dave's mouth turned up. "Just as I suspected. There's no way the LOLs are stepping aside. So, where do we go from here? Do we tell Felicity what we know or suspect about Scarlett and hope she checks it out? Do we create one of your famous case maps where we list all possible suspects, no matter how far-fetched? What?"

Belle gave Dave an affectionate smile. "If you keep this up, Dave, we may have to change our name."

He didn't miss a beat. "Would Dave's Little Old Ladies' Detective Agency work?"

Gales of laughter greeted his proposal.

# Chapter Twelve

WE WERE DEBATING NEXT steps and how to divvy up assignments when Wendy's phone pinged with a text. "It's Rhys. He says everything's fine and wants to know where Wimsey and I are." She looked up. "I'm telling him to join us. We need to hear what Felicity had to say before we finalize our next steps."

Rhys looked haggard when he entered the room, and I thought it was no wonder. The man was mourning the loss of a woman who was not only his ex-wife but also his friend, and he was attempting to run a literary festival at the same time.

He accepted Ellie's offer of a cuppa and pulled up a chair from the small dining table. "Am I glad that's over! For now, at least. I feel as though DS Jenkins has cleared me, but I guess I can't be sure."

He looked at the ceiling. "Where do I begin? First, she told me Emily was dosed with liquid morphine. It was in the crème de menthe. Of course, she wanted once again to know whether

I had been to Emily's room Saturday night or earlier, whether I'd had a drink with her. I reminded her that yes, I already told her I had a drink with Emily before I went to the bar Tuesday night and did the same Sunday and Monday evenings. It was our custom when we were together. And Tuesday night, in particular, she wanted to talk through the Scarlett debacle before she sat down with Daisy."

*Good plan on Emily's part.* "Oh, that makes sense, Rhys. As the events coordinator, Daisy could pitch in to take on some of Scarlett's tasks. Was she meeting Daisy Tuesday night?"

"Yes, Leta. She thought Daisy was very capable. Now, where was I? Oh, Felicity asked about the chocolates. When did I deliver those? I didn't. I asked the front desk to handle that."

*Logical questions.* "Rhys, Gilbert told us Emily loved her crème de menthe. Was that common knowledge? Did Felicity—I mean DS Jenkins—ask who else would know?"

"Yes, and I told her it was fairly common knowledge. She had lots of questions about the morphine. As I said last night, I'm a doctor and have access to drugs. I prescribe antidepressants, anxiety meds, and sleep aids for my patients—but liquid morphine isn't something I'd have a reason to give anyone, and I told her that."

Belle tilted her head. "Rhys, was Emily in good health? Would she have told you if she wasn't? I ask because liquid morphine is most often prescribed when a patient is in extreme pain. Is there any chance Emily had a prescription for it?"

A horrified expression appeared on his face. "She was fit as a fiddle, and if she weren't, I would have been the first to know. It may be difficult to believe, but she was my best friend." He glanced at Wimsey. "It's Wimsey, poor thing, who's in poor health, though Emily takes—took— good care of him. He had a few teeth removed last week."

Wendy looked at Ellie and explained that Wimsey took pills for skin allergies and was still on pain meds after his dental surgery. "I know you and Mum will be fine with him staying with us for the rest of the week, and since you're so good with Blanche, may I ask you to give Wimsey all his medications?"

"Of course, dear. I'll take good care of him. Where will he go after this?"

Rhys held up his hands and said, "I'm not sure. He was never far from Emily's side, and I'm not sure I can give him that much attention. I'll figure something out, though."

In typical fashion, Wendy scrunched her mouth to one side. It was her thinking look, and her next words told me her brain had leaped to another topic. "Rhys, as we were leaving your room, Felicity said something about a key card. What was that about?"

"Crikey, she actually rattled the cuffs when she asked about that. I knew I was in trouble when she asked me why I hadn't mentioned being in my room near midnight. She had checked mine and Wendy's key card records. Thank goodness, I could show her the text message that sent me up there. She called my assistant right then and there to confirm my story.

"She seemed amused when I insisted on pulling out my laptop to show her the email I sent. Do the police get some kind of kick out of making people squirm? That's sure how it felt."

Wendy gaped. "She checked my key card too? Do I look like a murderer?"

"Not to me, but being seen with me could be a liability."

"So, Rhys," Dave asked, "did you take the opportunity to tell Felicity you saw Scarlett?"

"Yes, I did, and that's when she let me have it. I'm not exaggerating when I say she was hopping mad. I thought she was about to grab me by the collar when she got in my face. Good thing I'm a psychiatrist and know not to react when people get overexcited."

I'd seen Gemma explode on more than one occasion, though she never quite got in my face, as Rhys put it. No wonder Jake said she and Felicity were two peas in a pod. I wondered if it was a tactic taught at the police academy.

When Ellie spoke up, I knew she was thinking of Gemma's boss. "Ah yes, I've seen our local DCI act the same way with Leta. The difference is he towers over her when he yells. Our girl never backs down, though." She had to be thinking of that day in the kitchen at the manor house. I yelled and told him to stop bullying me, but I *did* manage to stop shy of calling the man a sexist pig.

Ellie continued. "Now, this is important, Rhys—how much did you tell Felicity about Scarlett? Did you share the stalker story?"

"No, only that I'd seen the girl getting in the elevator on our floor—where else could she have been? I was still coming to grips with the idea that Scarlett could be a stalker, and Dave mentioned having your friend Sue tell Felicity the story, since she's the one who dug it up."

*Fatal Attraction!* "Rhys, the only thing I know about stalking is that movie with the dead rabbit and the incidences of celebrity stalking. What makes a person do it?"

He sighed. "That's what I've been running through my mind. First, it's much more common for men to be stalkers. Regardless of whether it's a man or a woman, though, the research shows that certain mental health conditions often appear in stalkers. For women, it's most often borderline personality disorder—not always, but often."

Belle leaned forward. "How does that manifest itself, Rhys?"

"Someone with borderline personality disorder can feel anxious about being abandoned by those they care about. What would we, on the outside, observe? Someone who doesn't want to be alone, who may come across as needy, even demanding. Stalkers are the extreme."

Dave held up his hand. "But who's the *stalkee*? Is that a word? I mean, who gets stalked, the person they care about or the person who seems to be in the way?"

"Either or both. Leta mentioned the movie where Glenn Close kills the rabbit. She stalks Michael Douglas because she wants him to be with her, but she goes after his wife because she sees her as being in the way. Of course, that was a movie. And please remember that people can be needy or demanding and not have any kind of mental disorder."

Wendy blanched. "So, if Scarlett suffers from BPD, she wants affection from you and Dave, and she doesn't hesitate to throw herself at you. Maybe that's a form of being demanding." Wendy looked at me. "Leta, she's overly affectionate with Rhys and Dave, but for me and you, she could be dangerous."

I grimaced. "The question is which one of us, and the answer depends on which man she ultimately settles on."

Squeezing Wendy's hand, Rhys murmured, "And she may have already killed Emily."

*My thoughts are swirling. Lust, love, lucre, loathing.* "I wonder whether we can convince Felicity that lust was the motive for

Emily's death. Or is she still looking at you, Rhys, with the idea of lucre—who benefits?"

When he gave me a questioning look, I explained that the *four Ls* were the motives P.D. James ascribed to murderers. "But you think you're in the clear, Rhys? I don't want to get too personal, but please tell me there's nothing amiss with your finances, nothing that the police would see as a motive."

Wendy gave me a stern glance. "No, Leta. Rhys and I have been all through that. Sure, he and Emily are beneficiaries in each other's wills, but neither of them was in dire straits, desperate for money."

Stifling a chuckle, I exclaimed, "Good to see you still have your detective mojo, Wendy! No stone left unturned."

She stuck out her tongue. "In that vein, this LOL wants to know how Felicity left it." She turned to Rhys. "And to Leta's point, did she say you were in the clear?"

"Not in so many words, but she told me to get on with the festival and to stay out of her way so she could do her job. I took that to mean she was done with me."

Dave looked at Rhys. "I'm not sure how much detective mojo I have, but I started to ask you this question before Wendy and Felicity arrived. Who else at the festival knew Emily as more than a passing acquaintance? When the LOLs say 'leave no stone unturned,' they mean it."

Rhys ticked off names on his hand. "That's a short list. Scarlett, Oliver, and Gilbert. If there's anyone else, it's news to me. And they all liked Emily. Even Scarlett, despite the argument."

Something was stirring in the back of my mind. "Rhys, maybe it's not a London connection. Is there anyone in Torquay she knows? For example, I'm sure she knows the manager of The Quill. Anyone else like that? Someone with a booth, perhaps?"

He must have felt as though he were on the hot seat. "I'm wracking my brain, Leta, but other than Daisy Owens and the catering manager, whose name I can't recall, no one's coming to mind. I mean, of course, she knows—I mean knew—Kate Ellis and the rest of the speakers, but not well at all. As for the booths, the members of the Golden Age Literary Association handled all that." He looked at us. "I'm not helping, am I?"

"Rhys," said Wendy, "everything helps. Now, you're not on the program today, so is Scarlett handling today's events?"

He nodded. "Yes, but it's primarily this afternoon's Wimsey & Campion session, the comparison of the characters Dorothy Sayers and Margery Allingham created. This morning is free time for guests to explore the area on their own, and it's a stroke of good fortune that Scarlett's on tap to be available in the lobby to answer questions. I shouldn't have to see her until late this afternoon. Maybe by the time I do, I'll be able to speak with her as though nothing abnormal is going on."

Ellie took charge. "Ladies and gentlemen, we have a good many moving parts to consider, and I think it's time we informed DS Jenkins of Sue's social media findings. By *we*, I mean me and Sue. I'll ring her, and the two of us will track down DS Jenkins. My imperious dowager countess tone combined with Sue's facts can't fail to convey how very critical the situation is." She chuckled. "Poor Felicity will think she's been visited by Violet Crawley."

The expression on Rhys's face was priceless, and Ellie answered his unspoken question. "Yes, young man, I am the Dowager Countess of Stow, and I plan to use that title to full advantage."

Belle chuckled. "Well done, Ellie. If you look down your nose at Felicity that same way, she'll be quaking in her boots."

Agreeing to keep each other posted, the group broke up. Wendy and Rhys left to walk Wimsey together before going their separate ways. Then Wendy would stick with Belle and Ellie, and Rhys would focus on the behind-the-scenes work for the festival.

I yawned. "What I want is a nap, but I think I'll review the notes Dave made about our visit to Emily's room to see if they trigger any thoughts."

Belle smiled at me. "If you don't need Dave, dear, may I borrow him? I want to explore the booths downstairs and could use your young man to carry my purchases."

I chuckled, and Dave preened. *Young man indeed.*

With Dickens lying by my feet, I settled on the couch with Dave's notes and my tablet. "Dickens, did you have fun with Wimsey?"

"Yes, but not as much as I do with Blanche. He's a sad little thing."

I reminded him that Wimsey had been sick. "And Dickens, he's lost his mistress."

He stood and put his paws on my lap. "Leta, I don't ever want to lose you."

Rubbing his head, I thought of how sad I'd been when his predecessors died and assured him I wasn't going anywhere. "You don't have to worry about that, Dickens."

"But Wimsey loved Emily, and she's gone."

*My sweet boy.* To distract him, I nudged his ball with my foot, and that did the trick. He rolled it around the room and tossed it in the air before returning to lie by my feet. "You know, Emily fed him *people food* and special pumpkin treats too."

"People food. That's nice."

"Wimsey especially liked the boiled chicken and baked dog biscuits she made him. Why don't I get chicken?"

"Because you get enough people food from my friends. They seem to think I don't notice all the scraps they give you. I suppose I could try my sister Anna's biscuit recipe, though. Her dogs seem to love them."

I thought my sister spoiled her animals no end. Not only did she bake them dog biscuits, she also allowed them on the furniture and in her bed—even the Great Dane. I could never figure out how she and Andrew made room for all five cats plus the dog. The furniture was a bridge too far for me, but baking dog treats might be fun.

"Dickens, should we take Wimsey with us to the beach later, with two balls?" That might cheer him up.

Dickens barked his happy bark. "Yes! With the new red ball I found!"

My tablet alerted me that I had an email, and it turned out to be from Bev. I already had the answer about what Emily had been dosed with because Felicity shared that information with Rhys. But I'd also asked Bev a second question—what could have made Wimsey pass out. Her love of dogs and her anatomy teacher background resulted in answers I never would have found on my own.

I scanned her detailed write-up and visited the links she sent me. The upshot was that anxiety meds and pain meds were available for dogs just as they were for people, and that any number of them could have triggered Wimsey's symptoms. That jibed with Wendy's information that the poor little thing was on pain meds after his surgery. So, perhaps there was nothing sinister about him being comatose.

Dashing off a quick reply, I thanked Bev for the information and told her about the liquid morphine. Then I turned my attention to Dave's handwritten notes and added the information about Wimsey.

I rang Wendy. "Hi, I have a question for you about Wimsey. What medications does he take?"

She rattled off two. "Why?"

"Bingo! My friend Bev says that tramadol can cause extreme drowsiness. That medication combined with the Benadryl for his allergies could have made Wimsey nearly comatose. I suppose Emily could have been so distracted Tuesday night, she gave him too much."

"Except that seems like a strange coincidence, doesn't it? Emily is dosed with morphine and never wakes up, and Wimsey suffers an overdose? I think you could be on to something about it being a combination of the meds the poor guy is on. I'm just not sure. Let's see how Ellie and Sue fared with Felicity and take it from there."

Hanging up, I set aside my doubts and captured my top-of-mind questions. What was in the vial Christie found? Was it Wimsey's regular meds that made him sick or something more sinister? Was it Scarlett? How could Scarlett sneak morphine into Emily's glass of crème de menthe without her noticing? How would Scarlett get her hands on liquid morphine in the first place?

Thoughts of the redheaded Amazon led me back to Facebook. *Maybe we missed something.* I started with the posts from her days at Emory. The young man she dated before the affair with her professor was fit and good-looking. To me, he was more attractive than the professor, but looks aren't everything.

For a month or so after the drunk driving incident, there were no posts at all. They picked up again when she moved in with Emily late last year. Still infrequent, they were typical tourist shots—Westminster, the Tower of London, the British Museum, and such. I found photos of Scarlett and Emily—at lunch, at dinner parties, walking Wimsey—innocent photos of friends.

After a few weeks of that, a young man began to appear in the posts. He must have been a friend of Emily's because many were of the trio in her dining room or the garden. Tall, dark, and fit, he had an engaging smile, and it wasn't long before Emily disappeared from the photos. Now, the posts looked like dates—a picnic in the park, dinners out, and a few days touring Stratford on Avon.

*Is it my imagination? Does he look familiar?* Then it hit me. The Atlanta grad student, Dave, and this young man had similar builds and coloring. *So is she attracted to Dave's dark good looks?*

I was reviewing the captions when Dave opened the door. "Uh-oh, you look like the cat who ate the canary. What have you found, Leta?"

"It's hard to say, but at least it's something new. It appears Scarlett may have had an age-appropriate boyfriend in London. His name is Marko. Take a look."

Joining me on the couch, Dave read the captions aloud. "Marko and me. Roses from Marko. Red & Marko." He frowned. "It sounds almost normal, doesn't it? No snide captions. I wonder what changed."

I scrolled forward until his photos became less frequent. "Hmmm. It's all about Marko for several months as though the romance was heating up. Here's a Valentine's Day shot of them. She's smiling as she pulls a ribbon from a wooden box. Soon after that, the posts with him slow down, and, by the end of February, he hardly appears at all."

Quickly scrolling, I caught the change. "Oh my gosh, Dave, it's Rhys. Now, it's all about Rhys."

Dave reached for my phone. "It's the same pattern that emerged when she was in Atlanta. Except the relationship with Marko seems more serious than that with the Emory grad student. I wonder who broke up with whom."

"I have a funny feeling she may have broken it off. There's just something about the later pictures of the two of them, the way he seems affectionate, but she seems distant. No more shots of her twining her arm in his or kissing his cheek. I wonder who he is."

"Well, it's for sure, you can't ask her, but maybe Tommy can."

"And what exactly would Tommy's excuse be for how he found out about Marko and for why he wants to know?"

"Um, well, that's the tricky part. I'd have to feign interest in her—a romantic interest."

I hit him over the head with a pillow. "Are you crazy?"

He kissed me on the cheek. "Nah, just yanking your chain."

Christie jumped in his lap as I continued to scroll through the Facebook posts. I thought I was done when I reached the Greenway pics, but Scarlett had added one this morning. "Oh for goodness' sake, she's at it again. Look at what she's posted now."

It was a shot of the four of us—Rhys, Wendy, Dave, and me—entering The Grand last night. "And look at this caption—'What do these tall, handsome men see in these old women?' Old?! The nerve of her!"

I was livid, and Dave was concerned. "Sweetheart, I know you're furious, but I'm worried. This seems beyond being rude, almost as though she's trying to provoke you and Wendy. Think about it—she never insulted her professor's wife in the Atlanta posts. Is this a form of escalation?"

"Except she has no idea we're looking at this stuff, right? We only stumbled across her on Facebook because Sue thought to look. But you're right, it seems designed to provoke. Funny, she never posted anything rude like this about Emily."

Closing my eyes, I reflected on Scarlett's behavior over the last few days. "You know what? I don't think there's an ulterior motive here. I see this as who she is—a self-centered, brash young woman with no regard for what others think."

"I feel as though I should lock you in this room until we know that Ellie and Sue have spoken to Felicity and that she's taken this seriously. She already knows that Rhys saw Scarlett that night on Emily's floor, so surely, she'll take the girl in for questioning."

He took my chin in his hand. "But you'd never let me do that, so how 'bout we spend the day ambling along the waterfront. We can visit the English Riviera Wheel, have lunch, maybe do a bit of shopping, and be back in time for the Wimsey & Campion session."

"Shopping? You *do* know the way to a girl's heart."

# Chapter Thirteen

KNOWING A FERRIS WHEEL was no place for dogs and cats, we left Dickens and Christie behind. "Dave, I sometimes get nauseated on rides, so let's do the ride before we shop, while I still have food in my stomach. Besides, we don't want to have packages—"

He stopped me as we rounded the corner into the lobby. "Whoa. That was fast."

Felicity and Scarlett stood by the lobby doors. I doubted that most people would pick up on the fact that Felicity was holding Scarlett's arm, but I did. "Oh my gosh, Dave, she must be taking her to the station."

"As well she should. Sue built a pretty convincing case for Scarlett being dangerous." I must have been inching forward because Dave grabbed the back of my parka. "Hold on, Leta. We don't need to get involved in this."

Too late. Either Scarlett heard him or she had a sixth sense. She looked over her shoulder, and in an instant, she whipped around and started toward us. Thankfully, Felicity held her back, but she couldn't stop her scream.

Her face purple, Scarlett gesticulated wildly with her free arm. "You crazy old bat! I'll get you for this."

Her vitriol was like a physical blow, and I shrank back. Dave must have felt it too, because he pushed me behind him, almost as though her words could harm me.

When Felicity jerked her through the doors and into a waiting car, I realized I'd been holding my breath. "Oh my gosh. What just happened? Is she blaming me?"

Dave steered me toward a chair and lowered me into it. He knelt in front of me. "It's okay, Leta. She can't get to you."

I shuddered. "She can't get to me if . . . if Felicity has enough to hold her. And why me? Is it because of you?"

Clasping my hands, he murmured. "I don't know. Would she have reacted the same way if she'd seen Wendy instead of you?" He rubbed my arms. "Are you going to be okay? Do you still want to go out?"

"Yes. If we stay here, all I'll do is worry. Let's go."

And I did worry, but only intermittently. As we walked, my phone pinged with texts from Wendy and Ellie alerting me that Felicity was questioning Scarlett. I responded that, unfortunately, I knew firsthand what was going on, and I relayed the words that had been flung at me.

I was right about riding the English Riviera Wheel first, as I'd have been sick for sure on an empty stomach. A plain old Ferris wheel was bad enough, but the rotating gondolas on this one almost did me in. It helped that the views were entrancing.

We went for the low-key carousel ride next, with me on a stationary horse and Dave standing beside me with his arm around my waist. I leaned into him. "Remember when we did this in Central Park? This is much more my speed than twirling cups or roller coasters."

Ducking in and out of the shops on the Promenade, I delighted in the end-of-the-season bargains. A straw hat with a large black grosgrain ribbon was a must-have, as was a wide-brimmed, red hat with a UPF 50+ rating. *Heaven forbid I get sun on my face.*

Dave adjusted the brim of the red hat. "You and your hats. How many red ones do you own now?"

I laughed. "I've updated my fashion rules, you know. When I worked, I said a girl could never have too many white tops, black skirts, or red jackets. Now I've added leggings and hats to the mix—with red on the top of the list, of course."

Lunch at Maisie's Tearoom and the stroll past the changing huts almost succeeded in banishing the scene with Scarlett from my mind. Looking forward to the 4 p.m. session, I brushed my windblown hair and changed from jeans into plum-colored leggings and a long black sweater. I was applying lipstick when someone knocked on the door.

Dave hollered he'd get it, and I heard Ellie and Belle. When I walked into the room, the looks on their faces told me something was wrong, and it was Ellie who spoke. "Leta, I want you to prepare yourself. Scarlett's back."

"What . . . what do you mean, back? They let her go?"

"Yes, Felicity brought her back, but not before she called to let me know. She particularly wanted me to get to you before you bumped into Scarlett."

"I—I can't see her. I'm not going to be attacked again—verbally or otherwise."

Ellie studied my face. "Are you sure, dear? I can understand if that's how you feel, but you know she can't hurt you while we're together."

"As in sticks and stones may break my bones . . . ? I don't know. It shook me." *Was it only a year ago that a different woman screamed at me and then assaulted me with a cane?*

Putting his arm around me, Dave guided me to the sofa. "Leta, we'll do whatever you want to do. We can pack up and leave now if that's what you want. But if you want to stay, I promise, I'm not letting her get anywhere near you. If she even looks at you wrong, I'll be in her face."

"I want to go to the Wimsey & Campion session. I don't want to be intimidated into missing it. But there's a little voice telling me not to take any chances. You know, I'm basically a wimp at heart."

*Is it possible for three people to roll their eyes simultaneously?* I listened as Belle, Ellie, and Dave ticked off examples of my being the least wimpy person they knew.

"I think the difference is that in all those examples, I didn't have time to think, so I didn't back down. This seems different."

Belle grimaced. "I don't care for this expression, but Wendy said if you balked, I should tell you to put your big girl pants on."

*Well heck.* My friend who threw caution to the wind at every opportunity had spoken. "Okay, but we're for sure taking my little hero dog. If he'd been in the lobby when Scarlett called me an old bat, he'd have been all over her."

Dickens cocked his head and barked, "Bat? Like the one you keep by the bed?" He was thinking of the cricket bat I kept by my bed to protect myself. In Atlanta, it had been a baseball bat.

I ruffled his fur and stood. "Come on, boy, we'll be late if we don't get a move on."

I braced myself as we exited the elevator, but when we reached the conference room, it was Wendy sitting at the table out front and Rhys greeting guests at the door. Wendy came out from behind the table and hugged me. "I knew you could do it. "

"Where is she?"

"Rhys told her if she wants a chance of finishing out the festival, she needs to stay out of his sight. She has strict instructions to speak to no one—to confine herself to the workroom or her hotel room until further notice. Felicity told her not to leave town. Otherwise, Rhys would have already sent her packing. As it is, we've only got a bit over 48 hours, and this will all be behind us, regardless of whether Felicity solves the case or not."

"Did you see her?"

"Yes, about an hour ago when Rhys was reading her the riot act, and if looks could kill, I'd be a puddle on the floor."

I heard someone clear their throat behind me and whipped around as though I'd been struck by a cattle prod. "Oh my gosh, Felicity, you scared the devil out of me."

Shaking her head, she pointed toward a bench close to the elevator. "Let's talk. After the confrontation in the lobby, I feel like you need to know why Scarlett isn't behind bars."

I couldn't wait. "She's guilty, but you don't have enough evidence to hold her, right?"

"Something like that. I'm going to tell you more than you need to know because Jake says I can trust you and the rest of the

LOLs." A hint of a smile appeared on her face. "He's a good judge of character, but I still don't know how you ladies charmed him so completely."

As Dave followed us down the hall, he mused, "Maybe he has a thing for smart, spunky, women."

Felicity shook her head and shifted gears. "As far as this case, here's what I know. The morphine was in Emily's glass, but not in the bottle of crème de menthe. We found Rhys's prints on the crème de menthe and cognac bottles along with Emily's, and that evidence fits with what he told us—that the two of them had drinks together several evenings. I had hoped to match Scarlett's prints to the other sets of prints on the bottles, but no luck. And the vial Dave found? It contained a trace amount of liquid morphine, but had been wiped clean."

"But you know Scarlett had the opportunity because Rhys saw her, right? And the motive could be twofold—the argument over the book *and* the stalking thing. That's not enough?"

"You're right, Leta, that she had the opportunity. She admits she delivered her manuscript to Emily at precisely the time Rhys saw her catching the elevator down. She claims she planned to slip it under the door because when she texted Emily, Emily said she was going to bed and to wait until morning. Instead, Scarlett got impatient and went to Emily's room anyway.

"She also claims she found the door slightly ajar and that there was a room service tray outside the door, which I can confirm. The SOCOs made note of the tray at the scene later. According to Scarlett, she thought Emily had dozed off in her chair, so she quietly left the folder on the console and pulled the door to, possibly not all the way closed because she was trying to be quiet. She doesn't know."

"Oh come on. That's not believable. Isn't it more likely Emily let her in? Because if the door had been ajar, wouldn't Scarlett have been suspicious? Wouldn't she have thought to check on Emily? I bet she told you she was distraught over their argument, right? And that's the excuse for not thinking straight."

"How did you know?"

I shrugged. "I know that people lie. I can hear her now—'Oh, Emily gets distracted from time to time. Probably put the room service tray in the hall and didn't pull the door quite closed.' What about the rest of it, the snarky Facebook posts, the stalking?"

"Leta, I think there's a case to be made that the girl's a stalker. That combined with Rhys placing her at the scene was enough to bring her in—to see what I could get out of her—but I got nothing. With the fingerprints a bust, I have no evidence that she murdered Emily. There's no way I can charge her.

"Sure, she was angry about the book. Sure, it looks as though she's attracted to Rhys and Dave. And the snarky Facebook posts? Let me tell you, if she were my daughter, I'd lock her in her room and throw away the key—not to mention her computer and her phone. And I'd get her straight to a psychiatrist. She's got anger issues for sure."

*And yet, she's not behind bars.* "So, let me get this straight. She's got anger issues, but I'm powerless to stop her from threatening me, much less insulting me on social media. She had the opportunity and at least one motive, if not two, but you can't find any evidence that points to her as the murderer—no fingerprints, nothing."

"I'm sorry, Leta. Not one iota. She was seen on Emily's floor, but she has a good reason for that. We even have the text messages between her and Emily. I hoped I could provoke her into saying something I could use. Heck, I even told her she couldn't hold a candle to you and Wendy in the looks and brains department, and that Dave and Rhys *obviously* preferred mature women."

I gaped. "That didn't work? She didn't lunge across the table at you?"

"No. She's a cool customer—well except when you're around. I can't explain that. With me, she was quite uppity." Felicity tilted her chin up and put her nose in the air. "She said, and I quote, 'It's clear you know nothing about men—older men fall all over me.' Anyway, that's neither here nor there. I've got nothing and no hope of finding anything."

When I shook my head and straightened my shoulders, Dave pulled me to my feet. "I recognize those signs. We're walking into the Wimsey & Campion session with our chins held high, aren't we?"

Assuring us she wasn't yet ready to shut down the investigation, Felicity set off down the hall while we returned to the conference room. Belle and Ellie had saved us seats on the far right of the room, nowhere near the center aisle where we might have seen Scarlett. But Rhys had banished her, so there would be no chance encounters.

Dave and Wendy flanked me as we walked to our seats and Rhys closed the conference room doors. I fixed my eyes on the front of the room as he introduced Sarah Smith, and soon I was able to lose myself in her words. She compared and contrasted the two characters, and I learned that Albert Campion was initially seen by many as a parody of Lord Peter Wimsey. I'd watched the BBC Campion series on TV but hadn't made that connection. I nudged Wendy. "Yet another series to add to my ever-growing TBR list."

When Wendy asked if Dickens and I would like to join her on a walk with Wimsey, Dickens answered in the affirmative, and we agreed to grab our coats and meet outside. Dave needed to make some calls to New York and was hesitant to let the two of us go off on our own, but Wendy assured him that our redheaded nemesis wouldn't dare approach us, and if she did, we'd handle her. Me? I wasn't so sure about that.

# Chapter Fourteen

As Dickens and I approached the pool area, Wendy texted me that she wanted to postpone our walk for thirty minutes—Rhys needed her help.

I replied, "No worries. Dickens and I will go on ahead. Text me when you're done, and we'll walk back to meet you."

With Dickens and his red ball, I walked to the beach. The day had grown cloudy and blustery, and the beach was deserted, so I let him off his leash. Barking in delight, he scampered ahead. *If I keep breaking the leash laws, sooner or later, I'm going to get a citation.*

My thoughts were a jumble as I pondered Emily's death, Scarlett's hostility, and Felicity's dilemma. Could the LOLs have gotten it so wrong? Granted, we seemed to be wrong as often as we were right when it came to identifying the guilty party, but who else could it be if not Scarlett? *Who am I kidding? The truth is it could be someone we've never met.*

As I threw the ball for the umpteenth time, I replayed what I knew. Yes, it was an LOL pattern to land on someone as the likeliest suspect before striking him or her from the list. Come to think of it, in this case, that someone was Rhys. Which meant that Scarlett was suspect number two. When Shakespeare's quote popped into my head, I chided myself. *Silly girl, it doesn't always "follow, as the night the day," that suspect number two is the murderer.*

Dickens dropped the ball at my feet. "What's wrong with you, Leta? You look sad."

Ruffling his fur, I shared my thoughts. "Dickens, I'm bamboozled, and I don't know what to think. It's not as though Gemma or the detectives on the telly are any better at this than I am or have their eye on the right person from the get-go. As for Scarlett, maybe it's because I want to throttle her, but it's hard to believe she's not involved somehow, someway."

"Then, let's play ball."

"That's the best idea I've heard. Let's head back toward the hotel. Wendy and Wimsey should be here soon."

I threw the ball and Dickens took off. What was I overlooking? Who else at the festival knew Emily well beyond Rhys and Scarlett? Sue only knew her from afar. But what had Rhys said? Both Gilbert and Oliver Fletcher knew her fairly well. And there was Daisy Owens too. Enough! Now, I was clutching at straws. It was time to go back to the drawing board. Time to gather the LOLs and the clueless old codger for a powwow.

When my phone rang, it was Wendy. "I'm at the pool and headed your way, and I need your help."

"What's wrong?"

"Well, first, Rhys is in a tizzy because he can't find Scarlett. Goodness knows what he's going to do if she's abandoned him. I told him she was probably pouting and would surface before long. I mean, the GALA members do lots of the work, but Scarlett has all the details.

"But, more importantly, he pointed out to me that without Scarlett in the picture, it's likely Felicity will, once again, view him as the strongest suspect—as the former spouse. And you know that he's no more guilty now than he was in the beginning."

"Funny, I just told myself we needed to put all our heads together and do a case map the way we've done in the past. Why don't you tell Belle and Ellie we'll meet in my room in, say, an hour, and I'll call Dave about ordering a bottle or two of wine."

I was texting Dave the plan when Dickens skidded to a stop and dropped the red ball at my feet. "Leta, do you hear that?"

"Hear what, Dickens?"

"It's a phone. Don't you hear it?"

Dickens ran ahead and stopped in front of a white changing hut with a bright blue door. I followed him, and then I heard it too. "I bet someone left the phone behind after a day in the sun. If the door's unlocked, maybe we can grab it and see if we can find the owner. I bet the concierge can help."

Throwing the ball for Dickens, I knocked on the door to be sure the hut wasn't occupied. No one answered, but the door was unlocked. *Perhaps they went for a walk and will be back shortly.* I pulled the door open, revealing a small shadowed interior filled with beach paraphernalia. It was difficult to see, but I made out a chair standing in the middle of the small space and another on its side. What looked like a windbreak was rolled up against the back wall. *Now, where's the phone?*

When the phone rang again, it lit up just long enough for me to see that it was in someone's lap. The person was sitting on the floor next to the windbreak. I was apologizing for intruding when some sixth sense told me something was off.

Pulling my phone from my pocket, I turned on the flashlight. One leg curled beneath her and one stretched out, Scarlett leaned against the wall, her head just beneath the shelf that spanned the rear of the hut. *Oh my gosh, her tongue.*

Backing away, I tripped and sat down hard on the wood floor. *Shake it off, Leta. You're in shock.* I reminded myself that when Dickens and I stumbled across a dead body at the cricket pavilion the previous year, I'd managed to get my wits about me, and I needed to do that now. There was no doubt in my mind Scarlett was dead, but I had to check. I'd never forgive myself if she was still breathing and I failed to get help quickly enough.

As I turned to get on my hands and knees, I saw a lantern hanging on a peg to the left of the door. It took several tries to get it lit, but when I did, I carried it to the back of the hut.

*You can do this, Leta.* Putting the lantern on the floor next to Scarlett, I removed my gloves and tried to avert my eyes from her face as I felt for a pulse. The image of her tongue hanging from her mouth was the stuff of nightmares. No pulse and her skin was cold to the touch—but then, of course, she was in an unheated hut. *What is she doing in a changing hut?*

More carefully this time, lest I trip again, I crossed to the door and looked out. *Where is Wendy?* With the sun going down, it was getting darker on the beach, but I glimpsed Wendy off to the right. She was close, and Dickens was running to greet her and Wimsey. I waved frantically. "Wendy, this way. Hurry."

My friend waved back and headed toward the line of changing huts. "What are you doing here, Leta? Have you decided to rent one?"

Running down the stairs, I grasped her arms. "Wendy, it's Scarlett. She's dead."

"No!" She dropped Wimsey's leash and darted past me, stumbling to a halt inside the door. Speechless, she turned to me.

For a moment, even Dickens and Wimsey seemed stunned—until they recovered and ran towards Wendy. "No, you two." I grabbed them and hooked their leashes to the railing before joining Wendy.

"How did you—what made you look in here?"

"Dickens heard her phone."

As she repeated my words, I knew she was in shock too. "Dickens heard her phone . . . and you found her?"

"Yes. I . . . I checked for a pulse, Wendy. She's gone."

"Who? Who could have . . . ?"

We huddled in the doorway. No matter that we considered ourselves detectives, two dead bodies in two days was too much. "Wendy, we better get Felicity down here. Dave has her card. Let me call him."

Stepping outside, I dialed Dave and told him the situation. I answered his questions in short staccato sentences. "Yes, I'm sure. Strangled, I think. It's her tongue. No, I only touched a lantern. Yes, I'm okay. Wendy's here. Please, just find Felicity."

Wendy came to my side. "I heard you say strangled. If this were a movie, that would be it, right? Because her mouth is open as though she's trying to get air." She stuttered. "And her tongue . . . oh my gosh."

When Wendy shook herself, I knew she was trying to collect her thoughts. "Leta, you know how Gemma says you have an amazing eye for detail. Have you looked around?"

"Oh goodness. No, and we need to. Like we did when we checked Alice's flat. We took photos too. Hurry, before Felicity gets here. And for goodness' sake, we need to put our gloves on."

Tuning out the barking dogs, I took in my surroundings. The hut was well-stocked. In addition to the chairs and the windbreak, I saw a stack of blankets, a small cooler, and a table. A large wooden chest with its lid open sat next to the cooler.

On the shelf above Scarlett, I saw a hot plate with a teapot, a cozy, and a set of delicate teacups. They seemed much too fragile to use in a changing hut. The pattern on them was faded—pink flowers surrounding the letter O. The only other item was a tin bottle of some kind. "Wendy, what is that tin thing?"

She studied it and snapped a photo of it and everything else on the shelf. "It says Jagermeister and has the distinctive logo, a deer with antlers. Must be some kind of collectible." She knelt and with her gloved hands picked up a cup on the floor next to Scarlett. She sniffed its contents. "And given the licorice smell, that's what was in this cup." Carefully, she placed the cup back as she'd found it.

When she stood, I glimpsed a shattered teacup in the corner. Picking up the largest piece, I saw that it was still wet with tea. *Did Scarlett's attacker drink tea with her?*

We both jumped when the phone in Scarlett's lap lit up with a text. Without missing a beat, Wendy picked it up. "It's from Rhys. There's a whole string of texts from him—increasingly frantic ones—wanting to know where she is. That makes sense. But look at this." She held the phone out to me. "Oliver Fletcher is looking for her too."

I was too busy taking in the scene to give that much thought. On a mission to absorb every last detail, I moved to the wooden chest. Constructed of dark wood, it measured about 2' x 2' and held brandy, gin, and tonic. It also contained a decorative wooden box with several miniature bottles nestled inside. I lifted the small box and found an inscription on its side.

"Wendy, look at this. These miniature bottles and the box are inscribed, 'Red & Marko, February 14th.' Oh my gosh, it's the London boyfriend!"

"Huh? Boyfriend?"

I told Wendy about the additional information I'd found on Facebook. "This goes back to what I suspected—that after Valentine's Day, Scarlett began to back off. I bet this was a gift from him, and it was too much for her. Maybe she wasn't as serious as he was."

Wendy held one of the bottles in her fingers. "That would fit the Atlanta pattern, wouldn't it? She tries dating someone her age, but it doesn't last. And it was after this that she turned her attention to Rhys, and then Dave caught her eye. What I don't get is why all this stuff is in a changing hut in front of the hotel. Why not in her room?"

My mouth dropped open. "Wendy, could this be the hut Oliver mentioned? And if he and Scarlett walked most nights in London, were they doing the same here?" *And is that why he's looking for her?*

"And then sitting in beach chairs stargazing? Wrapped in blankets sharing a nightcap? Could be. But why Scarlett? This is the first I'm hearing about the whole walking in London thing. Like you said, we need a case map, so we can see all these bits in one place. That's the only way we'll be able to make sense of everything."

She was right. The LOLs had been going in different directions, and the data we'd collected had been shared haphazardly. It was time we got organized, and I had a sudden horrifying thought. "Wendy, if we'd done that earlier, would Scarlett still be alive?"

And that's when the barking resumed in full force, and I heard voices. Wendy quickly returned the miniature bottle to the small box and tucked it inside the chest. When she looked at her hands, I knew we were thinking alike, that it was a good thing we were wearing gloves. "Leta, we haven't touched anything except the phone and the lantern, right? And, if I don't mention the phone, that's no big deal, is it?"

"Uh-huh. That way, Felicity can't get upset with us. We did the right thing. We called the police and stayed at the scene. We didn't disturb anything—much." *Just a small white lie.*

Felicity was first up the stairs, followed by Dave. With a powerful flashlight in one hand, she held out her other arm to bar him from entering the hut. That motion did nothing to deter the two dogs, who were straining at their leashes.

"Bloody hell, am I destined to find you two standing over dead bodies? What are you doing here? Let's have it."

We walked her through the innocent scenario of taking the dogs for a walk. Innocent right up until I opened the door to the changing hut. She listened as I told her I'd checked for a pulse and as Wendy explained about getting there right after that.

"Stop right there. Wendy, you weren't with Leta when she found Scarlett?"

"No, I was on my way to meet her."

Felicity studied me. "Tell me again why you came into a changing hut, and this hut in particular?"

"I already told you, I heard a phone. Well, Dickens heard it first. His hearing's better than mine. He ran this way, I followed him, and then I heard it." *Why am I babbling?*

"What did you do when you first opened the door?"

Closing my eyes, I replayed the scene in my head and tried to be as accurate as possible for Felicity. "It was dark in here. I noticed shapes, and I recall wondering how I was going to find the phone. And then it rang or something, and it lit up. That's when I saw the body—only I didn't know it was a body." I shook my head. "I grabbed my phone and turned on the flashlight, and that's when . . . that's when I knew it was Scarlett. That's when I saw her tongue."

When I shuddered, Dave wrapped his arm around my waist and pulled me to his side. His tone was stern. "Felicity, Leta's white as a sheet. How much more do you want to know?"

"Stay out of this, Dave. I'll decide when I'm done. Leta, continue."

My voice broke as I took her through my falling down, finding the lantern, and taking Scarlett's pulse. "And then I looked for Wendy."

Felicity pounced. "Not me? You didn't think to find me?"

Stunned, I stuttered, "Not then, but once Wendy was here, I called Dave because he has your number."

"Okay, we'll come back to that gap. Now, let's hear what you two did while you were waiting."

Wendy picked up the story, but when she got to the part about the miniature bottles, she turned to me. I knew she wanted me to explain the conclusions we'd drawn.

When I mentioned Jagermeister being Scarlett's drink and this being Oliver Fletcher's hut, Felicity's jaw tightened.

"What makes you think this is his hut? And what does Jagermeister have to do with it? This is what comes of rank amateurs meddling in police work."

*She was so nice to me earlier when she told me about letting Scarlett go. What's going on?* "Felicity, I'm sorry. I know I'm rambling, but it makes sense when you know all the puzzle pieces. Let me see if I can do a better job of laying it out, please."

Crossing her arms, she tapped her foot. That told me I had one chance to get it straight.

"These are the facts. He told our tour group that he rented a beach hut for the week. Sue saw Scarlett drinking Jagermeister at the bar, and that's also when Scarlett told her that she walked most evenings with Oliver Fletcher. The thing that confuses me is the letter O on the mugs instead of F. Unless the monogram is for Oliver. Look at the tin on the shelf. I don't think it's a stretch to think this is his changing hut and that he invited Scarlett to use it."

Staring at the shelf, Felicity nodded but didn't look convinced. "I suppose that's one possibility. You *do* have an amazing eye for detail *or* a knack for spinning yarns—I'm not sure which."

Wendy gaped at her. "Well, if you hear her out, you'll know it's more than a possibility. But if you don't want to listen, maybe we should adjourn now."

I could almost hear Felicity's teeth grinding when she responded. "Wendy, I decide when we adjourn, got it?"

With a grimace, she turned to me. "Now get to the point. I've already been through the stalking scenario with your lot, so let's hear the rest of this one. Once the Scene of Crime officers get here, it will be a crowd scene in this tiny place."

I pointed to the wooden chest. "It's just one thing. That little box inside? Don't kill me, but I picked up one of the miniature bottles."

"You what?"

"I know, I know, but I was wearing gloves. The label reads 'Marko & Red, February 14,' and I know who Marko & Red are. Scarlett is Red, and Marko is a man she dated when she first came to London. I found that on Facebook."

Wendy picked up the story. "Which isn't evidence of anything other than Scarlett spending time here. It tells us she didn't just happen upon an unlocked hut."

"But Leta did, right? She chanced upon an unlocked hut that happened to hold the body of a woman who threatened her and chased her boyfriend?"

*Oh my gosh. What does she mean by that?*

Dave cleared his throat. "May I make an observation?"

Rolling her eyes, Felicity nodded. "Sure, why not? Next, we'll be playing the game of Clue."

"Nothing in this scenario changes the fact that Scarlett was a stalker, but it pretty much puts paid to the idea she killed Emily, doesn't it?"

Felicity chewed her lip. "That would be my first conclusion unless we have two killers running rampant at a literary festival. An idea that beggars the imagination. A young woman, the picture of health, dies in a changing hut, for goodness' sake? There's no way she died of natural causes."

Dave's brow furrowed. "And her death means we got the motive wrong too."

"We? It was your lot that was all hyped up about a stalking scenario."

That was too much for Wendy. "Excuse me, did you have another motive in mind? You sure didn't correct Ellie and Sue when they came to you with the stalking story."

Felicity scrubbed her face with her free hand. "No. No motive and no evidence even remotely pointing to the killer. All we know for sure is that Emily ingested a lethal amount of morphine." She closed her eyes. "The only person closely connected to both victims is Rhys Ford."

Wendy seemed on the brink of launching herself at Felicity. "You can't be seriously looking at Rhys again. What? Scarlett was a major pain so he killed her?"

"Or", Felicity said, "he killed her because he thought she killed Emily."

*Could she be right?* "But, Felicity, he's been tied up with the festival all afternoon. When could he have come down here?"

Dave looked from me to Wendy. "Think about it. Rhys dashing down here to do in Scarlett is about as likely as Wendy and Leta doing it together."

"Except, Dave . . . they weren't together. Wendy found Leta alone here with Scarlett. How do we know Scarlett wasn't alive when your girlfriend arrived?"

I gasped. "What are you saying?"

"That it's not so far-fetched to think you killed her. You and Scarlett had a volatile relationship. You could have walked in here. She said something to set you off, and you lashed out."

Wendy put her hands on her hips. "Now wait just one minute. Never mind that Leta wouldn't hurt a fly, much less strangle someone. You honestly think she got the better of a young fit woman who towers over her? Puh-leeze."

Felicity wouldn't back down. "Not just any woman, a stalker. A girl she was afraid of. That's a motive, and I can quite easily see her strangling Scarlett in a fit of rage."

*Stop talking about me as though I'm not here.* "Look at me! You think I killed her? Me?"

She was beginning to look quite pleased with herself. "Yes, I do. And you just told me how you knew where to find her. You thought there was an Oliver Fletcher connection, so you came looking for her in a changing hut. Maybe you didn't plan to kill her. Maybe you merely wanted to reason with her, but whatever you had in mind, you wound up strangling her."

Silence echoed in the tiny changing hut. If not for Dave's arm around me, I would have sunk to the floor. But Dave *was* holding me, and he took charge. "That's enough, Felicity. Are you arresting Leta?"

Her expression hardened. "Not yet, but I'm done with her for now." She glowered at me. "Can I trust you to return to your room and stay there until further notice?"

Her words reached me as though from a distance, and I managed to nod. Dave turned me around, and we left just as the SOCOs arrived.

Wendy trailed behind us with the dogs, and I heard Dickens. "Leta, let me get to Leta. She needs me." I dropped to my knees in the sand, and he ran to me. Only when he licked my face did I realize I was crying. I pictured myself in handcuffs and shuddered. *Can this really be happening to me?*

# Chapter Fifteen

SOMEHOW, DAVE KNEW I couldn't deal with words. He lifted me to my feet, returned his hand to my waist, and gave me Dickens's leash. Even Wendy was silent. We got as far as the elevator before encountering anyone we knew. When the doors opened, Oliver stepped out with a coat over his arm, took one look, and offered his assistance.

"My goodness, this young lady is near to passing out." Dave took Dickens as Oliver tugged me toward the same bench I'd occupied hours earlier—hours before I'd been accused of murder. After directing Wendy to fetch tea with lots of sugar, he knelt in front of me. "Put your head between your knees." He waited a few seconds. "Feel better? Okay, hold that position a bit longer and then slowly raise your head."

"Thank you, Oliver."

Dave rubbed my back. "You're pale, sweetheart. Maybe the tea will help."

As Oliver put his coat on, he told us that if I felt faint again, I should have my blood pressure checked. Wendy returned with the tea, and he looked on approvingly.

He reached in his pocket and brought out dog treats. "Here you go, Wimsey—and your name is Dickens, right?" *He really is a kind man.*

"Alright then, I'm off. You haven't by chance seen Scarlett, have you? We're supposed to go to dinner, but she's not answering her phone."

He rambled on before any of us could respond. "She was already distraught over being questioned about Emily's death, and now she's had a tiff with Rhys, though she hasn't explained to me yet what that's all about. Such a distressing week."

Dave stood and put his hand on the older man's arm. "Oliver, I'm sorry to tell you Scarlett is dead. That's why Leta is feeling faint. She found her."

*And now I've been accused of murdering her.* I looked at the elderly man. "She was in a changing hut."

He shook his head. "Right. We often meet there. I'll fetch her now."

Struggling to my feet, I grasped his hand. "No, Oliver. She's dead."

Now, it was my turn to sit him on the bench. He looked at me. "You must be mistaken. She can't be dead."

Wendy could tell I was in no condition to comfort him and offered to accompany him to the dining room for tea. She whispered to me, "You and Dave go on. I'll sit with him a bit and see if there's someone I can contact. Maybe Mum or Ellie can help, or could be Felicity can get a Family Liaison Officer to step in. And, here, can you take Wimsey? I'll be up as soon as I can."

In the elevator, I leaned against Dave. "They're not family."

"What was that?"

"They're not family, he and Scarlett, but they're close."

"Don't worry about it, Leta. Wendy will take care of him."

When I collapsed on the couch, Dave brought me a glass of water, and Christie climbed into my lap. "Leta, you look awful. What's wrong with you?"

As I stroked her back, Dickens filled her in. "She found a dead body, that Scarlett girl. And she almost fainted, but the man with dog biscuits helped her." Of course, he didn't know the whole story—that I'd been accused of murder—but Christie got the picture.

She licked my chin. "Scarlett? Is she the one with red hair? I didn't much like her."

Not to be left out, Wimsey chimed in. "She was nice sometimes, but she argued with my Emily."

Dave could barely get near me with the animals crowded all around. "Funny, how they sense things aren't right, isn't it. Now, don't you want to take off that jacket?"

"I didn't realize I was still wearing it, maybe because I'm cold." Leaning my head back, I sighed. "Climbing in bed beneath lots of blankets sounds like a good idea."

Bending over me, Dave felt my forehead. "I'm calling Belle. You say you're cold, but your head is hot. We need a nurse." He tucked a blanket around my legs and went into the bedroom. I heard him on the phone and knew he must be updating Belle.

*How can this be happening?* I knew I needed to think, but I was struggling to form cohesive thoughts. Leaning my head back, I closed my eyes, which did nothing to fire up my brain.

When Christie meowed, "Hey, watch it," I opened my eyes. Dave was unzipping my jacket and tugging it off, and I didn't have the energy to protest. Before I knew it, he'd swung my feet up on the couch, put a pillow beneath my head, and covered me with a blanket. Christie wasted no time before stretching out on my chest with one paw touching my chin.

I was vaguely aware that Dave was on the phone as I lay half asleep. Who knows how long I might have dozed if I hadn't heard knocking at the door? Propping myself up on my elbows, I was thankful to see it was Wendy with her mum—not Felicity or her constable come to take me away.

"Leta, you look like death warmed over."

"Good to see you too. Tell me you have good news."

She looked at Dave. "Now she thinks I have magical powers? No, not exactly good news, but not bad either. Believe it or not, Felicity had a lengthy conversation with Oliver Fletcher, who confirmed that your assumption was correct—he *did* rent the changing hut, and he and Scarlett took nightly walks. Well, except for Tuesday night, when she was working frantically to edit the manuscript to suit Emily."

"You know, Leta, Felicity being in charge of this investigation worries me. I feel like she's checking the instruction manual to figure out what to do next instead of *knowing* what to do. Does that make sense?"

"I told Dave the first night that I thought she was out of her depth. Is that what you mean?"

"Yes. Anyway, I called Mum to sit with the poor man while I went to tell Rhys what was going on. I've been busy."

"Did you tell him that your best friend was now a murder suspect?"

"Of course! I told him the whole story, and he was shocked. He was as convinced as we were that Scarlett had killed Emily, but if someone killed Scarlett, that means a murderer is still running loose. I was almost out the door when he called me back.

"It suddenly hit him that he didn't know where the festival paperwork was—timelines and all the who, what, when, and where. When he was unable to locate Scarlett earlier, he visited the workroom but found only the laptop and random bits of information, like the flyers for the individual sessions. What he needed were the file folders."

I rolled my eyes. "Good grief. That's no way to run an event. It should all be in the workroom, organized and accessible."

Wendy agreed. "Well, you and I know that, and if Emily were still alive, I'm sure she'd have it well in hand. At the moment, it's a complete mess. Since it couldn't have vanished into thin air, I suggested he check Scarlett's room, but of course, he didn't have a key."

"Let me guess," Dave said, "Felicity had already sent someone to plaster yellow tape across the door. How on earth will Rhys function now?"

When a grin appeared on Wendy's face, I knew she had pulled a fast one. "Ah, Dave, I'm nothing if not resourceful. Felicity hadn't made it to Scarlett's room yet, so I beat a path to the front desk and did my distraught maiden act—something to the effect of, 'Oh no. Doctor Ford is beside himself and needs a copy of his speech from Scarlett Callahan's room. Can you let us in, please?' It worked like a charm."

Belle looked at her daughter. "I guess I should be grateful you didn't break in like you did in Tintagel."

"Oh come on, Mum. We had a key that time, so it wasn't quite breaking and entering."

I felt my face getting red. Wendy had a penchant for taking risks I would never consider. Yes, the break-in was productive, but it was also dangerous, and Wendy came close to dying. Not only that, the escapade caused Dave and I to have one of our biggest arguments.

"Whatever you say, dear. Did you find what Rhys needed?"

Wendy did a fist pump. "Oh yes, we gathered up everything we could find—folders, notebooks, and even scraps of paper. Rhys went back to his room, and I headed for the changing hut.

"I can't say that Felicity was pleased to see me, but when I told her what Oliver said about the changing hut—that he met Scarlett there—she followed me to the hotel. I'm telling you, Leta, I had to bite my tongue to keep from chanting 'told you so,' but I knew that wouldn't help matters."

Belle looked at me. "I plied him with tea and tried to get him to talk, but he was like an automaton. When he did speak, he kept saying he needed to find Scarlett, that they were due at the Imperial Hotel for afternoon tea. Poor man."

Patting her mother's hand, Wendy picked up the tale. "He was lucky Nurse Davies was on hand and that Felicity was gentle with him. She acted as though she knew nothing about his relationship with Scarlett. I mean we LOLs knew a little bit because of Sue, but it was you, Leta, who twigged to the fact they were quite close. What I find hard to believe is that Felicity let me and Mum sit there as she questioned him."

"Perhaps, dear, you don't give her enough credit. She could tell that he felt comfortable with us and may have thought that our presence would put him more at ease. We've all witnessed his obstinate side."

"Well, whatever it was, I wish you could have been a fly on the wall to hear Felicity. Butter wouldn't melt in her mouth. 'Dr. Fletcher, I understand you had plans with Scarlett. Oh, you knew her before the festival. Such a lovely girl, wasn't she?' Felicity's tone was entirely different from what it was with you. And it worked. Though he seemed befuddled, he shared key details about their relationship."

Dave held up his hand. "Hold on a sec, let me grab my notepad."

I smiled. "We'll soon need one of those sticky flipchart pads so we can wallpaper the room with our thoughts, and we need Ellie, maybe Sue too."

With Dave back in the room, Wendy continued. "Remember when Mum and Ellie told us that Oliver Fletcher's grandson died not long ago? Well, get this—he was friends with Scarlett. And remember, we heard Emily was the grandson's writing coach. That's how they met."

Belle nodded. "Yes, I imagine the young man committing suicide, possibly in despair over not being able to get his book published, and his death would have hit Scarlett hard too. Of course, do we ever really know what drives someone to such a desperate act? It may well have been a combination of things."

Dave was furiously jotting notes. "We're going to need that flipchart sooner rather than later. Okay, Wendy, what else?"

"Well, the long and short of it is that Scarlett filled the void when his grandson died. Maybe he did the same for her given she had no family here and couldn't have had many friends. Emily and Oliver both lived in Mayfair, not far apart, and he and

Scarlett got in the habit of taking nightly walks and having the occasional dinner out."

"Leta," Belle said, "you may have forgotten, but the grandson lived with him, so it must have been a devastating loss—even more so than losing a grandson one hardly ever sees."

Dave's eyebrows rose. "This sounds like some gigantic jigsaw puzzle—one where we keep finding pieces on the floor."

Christie meowed, "I like puzzles. They make the best toys."

Lifting Christie into her lap, Belle answered Dave. "Remember that Rhys was the grandson's psychiatrist, and unreasonable as it sounds, Oliver blames him for the boy committing suicide."

"Seriously? Why?" I had forgotten Dave wasn't in the room when Belle and Ellie told me that.

Belle sighed. "Two reasons. He thinks the meds Rhys prescribed didn't work, and he thinks Rhys should have used his literary connections to help get the book published. It seems the man was grasping at straws, but grief works on people in different ways. Anyway, none of this came up in the conversation with Felicity. It's what Ellie and I learned from Gilbert the other night."

*The grandson and Scarlett.* "So, we have some new info, though it's not anything that tells us who killed Scarlett—or Emily, for that matter—if it wasn't Scarlett. And I doubt Felicity is looking very hard when she's already got me pegged as Scarlett's killer."

Dave sat forward. "Emily and Scarlett! What were Felicity's words about more than one killer? Before she went off on you? 'It beggars the imagination.' If her working theory is only one killer, how can she possibly be looking at you, Leta? Because that would mean that you killed Emily *and* Scarlett."

*Great. When Felicity takes me away in cuffs, it will be for two murders.*

# Chapter Sixteen

DAVE'S ASSERTION GALVANIZED THE LOLs. Belle called Ellie, and Wendy went in search of a flipchart pad. I suggested we needed food, and Dickens barked his agreement.

Room service menu in hand, Dave called for heavy finger food and several bottles of wine. Usually, it was Wendy and I who took turns documenting our thoughts on the large sheets of paper, but this time Dave took my place. He and Wendy conferred about what to tackle first—the timeline or the players—and I agreed with their logic to tackle the people first because the timing for when the morphine had been administered to Emily was difficult to pin down.

Right or wrong, we felt we should look at the two murders as connected. If we changed our minds, whatever details we documented would still be useful.

When Ellie arrived and announced she had lined up a solicitor for me, I couldn't make up my mind whether I felt appreciative or horrified—appreciative that she was looking out for me or horrified that I could soon be behind bars.

Being the accused was very different than being the detective. More than once, the LOLs had been spurred to investigate a murder because someone we knew was on the suspect list—wrongfully so, we thought. And for those cases, we had uncovered information that cleared a friend and pointed the police in the right direction. Now I had an inkling of how the accused felt. No matter that our crew of amateurs hadn't failed yet, I was scared and not at all confident that the LOLs could help me. *It's not rational, but it is what it is.*

Dave, as he often did, sensed my distress. He handed me a glass of wine and kissed the top of my head. "I know you're scared, Leta, but it will be okay."

As we sipped and munched, Wendy took the lead. "For the benefit of the clueless old codger who's joined our ranks, let me remind you that while Dave and I may wield the pens, all input is welcome and will be captured."

That lightened the somber mood, at least temporarily. "Now, we think we should start with who at the festival knew Emily."

Belle interrupted her daughter. "Can we first capture who visited Emily the night she died? That would help me keep things straight."

"Sure, Mum. Here's what we know." Wendy recited the details as she wrote. "Scarlett two times, Rhys once, Oliver Fletcher with a gift, and Daisy to work on a plan. I'm pretty sure Scarlett was first, followed by Rhys. Felicity may know the timing of the other visits, but we don't, except for what she shared with you, Leta."

I frowned. "Right. If Scarlett was telling the truth, Emily was either asleep in her chair or already dead when she delivered the file. That's the question—was she honest with Felicity or not?" I ticked off more questions. "After Rhys, what was the order of the visits? Could Scarlett have been there a third time? The second time to drug Emily and the third time to be sure she was dead? And no matter what Daisy, Oliver, and Scarlett told Felicity about *when* they were there, any one of them could have lied."

Pointing at the list, Ellie made another observation. "And let's not forget that someone else could have visited her unbeknownst to any of us."

Wendy nodded. "Aargh, you're right." She scrawled *Who Else?* on the page and stood back. "Okay, I suggest we let this simmer and instead work on who's who. If we assume that no one snuck in here and chose a random victim, then that means there had to be a motive for killing Emily. Take it a step further, and that means the killer was someone *here* who knew her—and not just in passing. I mean, Sue had met her before, but she didn't *know* her."

Dave's next sentence made me feel better. "And that takes Leta out of the picture because she only met Emily Monday." *If only Felicity will see it that way.* "So, we want to capture everything we know about the participants who knew Emily prior to the festival. So far, we've come up with four—Rhys, Scarlett, Gilbert, and Oliver." He wrote those names on one page. "Who are we missing, ladies?"

I held up my hand. "There's Daisy Owens. She would have been in constant contact with Emily during the planning stages of the festival, and Emily likely traveled here a few times for meetings."

For the moment, no one had any additional names, so Dave added *Daisy* to the list, and then he scrawled *Gilbert* across the top of another page. I was pretty sure none of us considered our friend a suspect, but Dave thought tackling him first would allow us to ease into the process.

Belle and Ellie tag-teamed as Dave wrote. *Sherlock scholar, knew Emily from Sayers Society and her GALA group, knows Rhys, G & Rhys on schedule to present together, knows Oliver from same groups plus the Sherlock Holmes Society, encountered Scarlett in biz center.*

Standing back, Dave eyed the list. "Not very much, but we can add more if something comes to mind. Let's shift to Daisy Owens, since she seems as unlikely a suspect as Gilbert."

Daisy's page was brief. *Event coordinator, mid-50s, efficient, organized, pleasant, knows Oliver, met with Emily Tuesday night.*

I remembered meeting her on the beach the first night. "I almost forgot. She's a jogger."

Dave added the words *jogger* and *works out* to her page. He explained that when he asked at the front desk about a gym, the clerk told him there was one within walking distance and volunteered that Daisy used it.

*Something was niggling at me.* "Oh, I almost forgot! She more than *knows* Oliver. She's his niece."

Belle looked at me. "His niece?"

"Yes. I heard her call him Uncle Ollie the first day, and she mentioned the relationship the morning of the Agatha Mile excursion."

Ellie cleared her throat. "It seems to me we should do a bit of digging on her." She looked at Dave. "The gym could be a good place to start. Are you up for it?"

I could tell Dave was happy to have an assignment. "Sure, and should we also ask Sue to work her social media magic, or attempt it ourselves?"

When we agreed I'd contact Sue, Dave turned to Wendy. "Do you want to handle the list for Rhys?"

"Not really, but I know we have to do it."

I watched as the list took shape. *Married to Emily 15 years, divorced 10, no children, psychiatrist, member of Sayers Society and Golden Age Literary Association, published Agatha Christie articles, knows Gilbert & Oliver, Oliver's grandson was his patient, OF blames him for grandson's suicide, congenial relationship with Emily.*

Belle added, "We should note that he and Emily had a nightcap in her room on the night she died, and she kept a bottle of cognac for him."

Wendy gave her a stern look. "Yes, Mum, but they did that Sunday and Monday night too."

"Now, now," said Ellie, "let's add that the will doesn't indicate a financial motive. And he sent her a box of chocolates. They did seem to have a lovely relationship for a divorced couple."

When I said, "We should probably document what we know about his relationship with Scarlett, such as it is," Wendy glared daggers at me.

Fortunately for me, Dave knew enough that I didn't have to say anything more. He walked to Wendy's flipchart page and began writing. *NO affair with S, uncomfortable with her advances, knows there was a scandal in Atlanta.* He tilted his head. "Maybe we should start the Scarlett list and come back to this one. Rhys gave us plenty of information about her, and so did Gilbert and Sue."

Ellie frowned. "I know we need to talk about her, but I can't understand how her death is connected to Emily's. It must be, but what one person could have a motive for killing them both?"

No doubt thinking of Miss Marple, Belle responded. "Look at it a different way. Maybe the circumstances of Emily's death created a motive for killing Scarlett."

Dave rubbed his face. "Huh?"

"What if Scarlett knew who the murderer was? It could be a clue she was unaware of—something she saw without realizing its significance. But the murderer knew he'd slipped up—he'd been seen or left behind something that would lead to him—and it was only a matter of time before our Southern belle figured it out. Scarlett being taken in by Felicity would have worried him."

I studied Belle. "And when Scarlett came back, the killer took the first opportunity to silence her—maybe followed her to the changing hut?"

"Or," mused Ellie, "someone killed her for a different reason. Someone was sure she killed Emily and that someone took their revenge."

Wendy exploded. "No. No way! That makes Rhys the best suspect. First, it was 'who benefits' when Felicity looked at him for Emily's death. Next, she flips and says 'oh dear me, Scarlett killed her,' and then points the finger at Rhys for that murder. He would want her arrested and tried. He would never hurt anyone."

"If you all agree it wasn't *me* who killed Scarlett, and Wendy is adamant it wasn't Rhys, that only leaves three people—Gilbert, Oliver, and Daisy. How likely is it that any of them killed her?"

Dave tugged on his collar. "Let's finish what we started before we rule anyone out. Isn't that how you ladies typically approach your detective work?"

*He's right.* "I think me being in the mix is muddying the water. Maybe I should take a bottle of wine and retire to the bedroom."

"Not on your life, Leta. We've each got different details to add, and we can't afford to miss out on yours." Wendy all but stamped her foot to make her point.

She wrote *Scarlett* on the flipchart. "Let's take this sequentially. What do we know about her life before she moved to England? And yes, it's the stuff of soap operas, but we've got to capture it."

The details poured out faster than she could write. *Clemson grad, Emory grad school, student/boyfriend, professor/boyfriend, stalked him, engineered car accident with wife, arrested for drunk driving, (see newspaper and Twitter), similar pattern at Clemson.*

Belle added, "Let's not forget that her mum is a romance author, and she shipped the girl off to Emily. Funny that we haven't heard anything about her father."

Ellie pursed her lips. "An amateur psychologist would attribute her stalking behavior and obsession with older men to daddy issues."

Grabbing a magic marker, Dave wrote *Scarlett in England* on another page. "Enough pop psychology for me. Let's shift to England."

This was where Dave and I had more information than the others. I pulled out my phone and showed each of the LOLs the Facebook posts of Red and Marko followed by the shift to Rhys.

Ellie voiced the same thing I'd said earlier when I showed them to Dave. *Was that just this morning?* "It's the same pattern. A younger man, more her age, a budding romance, and then what must have been a breakup."

As she fumbled for her phone, I knew Wendy was about to show us the bottles in the changing hut. "And look here. We found that sweet gift box of miniature bottles in the changing hut. Maybe the bottles labeled 'Red & Marko, February 14th' were too much for Scarlett, and that triggered her to back off. That's what I see in these pictures."

Dave closed his eyes. "And she fell into her old pattern, chasing an older man. Why would she still have the gift?"

We all had different answers to that question. It was purely practical—why waste the alcohol? It had sentimental value—someone once loved her. She was the one who broke it off and kept it out of some sense of guilt. Much like the suggestion about daddy issues, this was a digression that added little value.

When the responses tapered off, Dave wrote, *Lived in Emily's carriage house, Emily/writing coach, dated Marko, Marko disappears from FB late Feb, March/Rhys posts start.* And then he stopped.

*He doesn't want to add his name.* "You have to do it, Dave. You and Rhys shared the spotlight for a bit."

We ladies helped him with the wording and soon realized the list was as much a timeline as it was a description of Scarlett. *Dave at the station, Rhys in the bar, asks Leta about Dave, argues with Emily, Gilbert & Scarlett in biz center.*

"Stop," Wendy said. "Let's get back to what we know about her, not where she was when. We know she's friends with Oliver and they walked together. We know she spent time in the changing hut *with* him and maybe on her own too. She's nearly finished a novel about Dorothy Sayers. She threatened Leta. She made snarky comments about me and Leta both on Facebook." Dave wrote furiously.

*What else did Sue tell me? Have we captured it all?* "It seems as though there's so much more, but maybe that's because she's been so unpleasant to me. She may like older men, but she certainly doesn't like older women."

Wendy huffed. "Unpleasant? That's an understatement. She called you a crazy old bat!"

"Then maybe my name should be across the top of a page—Leta Parker, Crazy Old Bat."

The dowager countess put her finger to her cheek. "Leta, that's not a bad idea."

Dave went with it. "Right. We know Leta is innocent because we *know* her, but Felicity doesn't. And I don't want to alarm you, sweetheart, but this could help your lawyer—or solicitor, as they say here. If it comes to that."

*Do they seriously think I can sit here while they talk about me?* "You guys have at it. I'm going to the bedroom." I refilled my wine glass and left the room.

Dickens barked, "Wait for me." He followed me, but Christie and Wimsey stayed behind.

My eyes fell on the stack of books I'd purchased at the Quill. Maybe a murder mystery that didn't involve me would be a distraction. *Dorothy & Agatha, A Work of Fiction*—that might do. A review snippet on the cover described it as, "A clever novel starring two masters of mystery." *Why couldn't Scarlett have followed this author's lead instead of penning a novel that promised sex and scandal?*

It worked. All it took was a dead body slumped over Dorothy Sayers's dining room table on page four. *That was quick*. I was hooked and easily tuned out the murmurs from the other room.

I was dreaming I was in a car with Agatha Christie, tracking down a murderer, when Dickens barked and I came abruptly awake.

# Chapter Seventeen

WHEN DAVE ENTERED THE room and closed the door behind him, the look on his face told me something was wrong.

"Leta, Felicity is here." He took the book from my hands, closed it, and laid it on the bed. "She wanted to speak with you in a conference room, but I suggested you could talk in here. The rest of us will wait in the living room."

"And . . . and she agreed to that?"

"Yes, and just so you know, Wendy very quickly covered up the flipchart pages while I spoke with Felicity and her constable in the hall."

The presence of her constable didn't bode well. "Does she have any idea what we've been doing?"

"When she asked if we were having a meeting, we admitted we were. Ellie took the lead with her faux Violet Crawley voice and said we were comparing notes so that we'd be prepared if and when she questioned us. You should have seen Felicity's reaction when Ellie said, 'Felicity dear, you'd do well to take advantage of the LOLs. I understand Detective Inspector Nancarrow has apprised you of our prowess.' Ellie's dowager countess act is priceless."

Grabbing his arm, I swung my feet off the bed and moved to an armchair. "Okay, there's nothing to be gained by keeping them waiting. I'm as ready as I'm going to be."

Christie flew into the room and leaped into my lap when Dave opened the door. Dickens sat by my legs as Felicity entered, followed by her constable. I watched in dread as Dave left and closed the door.

With only two armchairs in the room, the constable was relegated to the vanity stool, where she sat and flipped her notebook to a clean page. A chill went up my spine when Felicity pulled her armchair around so she could face me. *This is serious.*

"Leta, I want you to take me through what happened at the changing hut. Let's start with how you happened to be on the beach."

"May I ask you a question first?"

She ground her teeth so hard, I was positive they'd crack. "One, only one."

"Do you still think Scarlett murdered Emily?"

"That's the one question I can't answer." When I opened my mouth to respond, she held up her hand. "Stop, Leta, you don't want to push me."

My heart pounded in my chest. *Is she seriously looking at me for two murders?*

"Now, back to my question. What were you doing on the beach?"

"Well, first I attended Sarah Smith's presentation. Then Wendy suggested we take the dogs for a walk on the beach—Wimsey and Dickens—and we agreed to meet by the pool. Only she called to say she needed to help Rhys with something and would be about thirty minutes. So Dickens and I set off without her and planned to meet up with her when she made it to the beach."

She looked at her constable, who was taking notes. "It was your idea to go without your friend? Are you sure you didn't plan to take a walk by yourself all along, as soon as you realized Scarlett was back?"

*Where is she going with this?* "No, I mean yes. I'm sure. It's not unusual for me to take Dickens for a walk, but I only thought of the beach when Wendy suggested it. It could have been a short trek to the green area in front of the hotel if not for that."

"Nothing to do with finding out your nemesis was back on the premises?" When I said no, she continued. "How did you know Scarlett was in the changing hut? And how did you know which one she was in? There are at least a hundred out there in front of this hotel."

"I didn't *know* she was in a changing hut. I had no idea where she was. If I'd thought about it, I would have assumed she was in the workroom."

"Why didn't you look for her there if you wanted to talk to her?"

*She's putting words in my mouth.* "I *didn't* want to talk to her, so I didn't look for her anywhere. You, of all people, know I felt threatened by her. Why would I seek her out?"

Her tone changed. Instead of barking questions, she spoke softly. "That's exactly why, Leta—you felt threatened by her."

She paused. "You were scared of her. And you accosted her, didn't you?"

A quote popped into my head. "To be brave, you must first be afraid." *Is that what she's thinking?*

"You may not believe this, Felicity, but I'm not a brave person. All my life, I've been told I need to be more assertive, and I've worked hard at it. But not that hard. If I'd seen Scarlett in the hotel or on the beach, I would have gotten as far away from her as I possibly could."

"You didn't answer my question, Leta. You accosted her, didn't you?"

"No, I did not! I couldn't because she was already *dead!*"

She nodded at her constable. "Okay, let's set that aside for now. Who told you which changing hut she'd be in?"

I gritted my teeth. "No one told me. Dickens heard the phone, and I followed him to the hut." Christie tensed in my lap.

Now, the questions came at me rapid-fire, and I answered just as quickly.

"How did you know she'd been strangled if it wasn't you who did it?"

"Her tongue. It was her tongue."

"How did you overpower her? Did you drug her with morphine first?"

"Morphine?"

"How convenient that you own the book *Deadly Doses*. Is that how you decided what to drug her with?

"What?"

"Did you smash the teacup?"

"No."

"Did she taunt you? Is that what set you off?"

"No. How could she? She was dead when I got there."

"Or did you go there planning to kill her?"

"No, no, no."

By the time the exchange ended, I was panting, and Christie was giving her low cat growl. "You leave Leta alone." I was afraid of what was coming next.

"Leta Parker, I am arresting you for the murder of Scarlett Callahan. You do not have to say anything. But it may harm your defense if you do not mention when questioned something which you later rely on in court. Anything you do say may be given in evidence." *Shouldn't she have said that to me before she started asking questions?*

When I stood, Christie fell from my lap and hissed. Now, it was Dickens who growled. "Leta, I won't let her hurt you." I might not have been in physical danger, but Dickens sensed the hostility.

I sounded like a suspect on TV. "Please don't put me in handcuffs."

"If you accompany me willingly, I can forgo the handcuffs."

As she ushered me from the bedroom, Dave sprang to my side, but it was Ellie who took charge when Felicity told them she was taking me in. "I'm ringing your solicitor now."

Like the police station in Stow where Gemma Taylor worked, the Torquay station was small. The good news was I wasn't placed in a holding cell. Instead, it was a small airless room with a table and two chairs on either side, where I sat by myself for a very long time. When the constable offered me a cup of tea, I hesitated. *Are they trying to get my DNA? Did I leave DNA or fingerprints behind on Scarlett's neck when I felt for a pulse?*

When she asked a second time, I gave in and accepted. I gulped the weak tea and tried laying my head on my arms on the table, but I couldn't get comfortable.

It seemed like eons before the door opened and a man in a pinstriped suit entered. "Mrs. Parker, Ellie Coates sent me, and you know when the Dowager Countess calls, I'm at the ready. I'm Andrew Lytton."

I learned that he represented Ellie's grandson when he'd been charged with manslaughter and aggravated assault. I could only hope that my innocence would mean the outcome of my case—if it got that far—would be very different.

"I don't know what questions were asked and answered in your hotel room at The Grand, but henceforth, you will answer nothing without my go-ahead. Are we clear?"

My Southern upbringing kicked in. "Yes, sir."

We conferred for about ten minutes before he stood and knocked on the door to alert Felicity that we were ready. By now, it was close to midnight. Not late by most people's standards, but certainly by mine. After an hour of questions comprised primarily of different versions of the ones she'd already posed, my solicitor called a halt. "Are you charging my client? No? Well, then we'll be on our way."

When we walked into the lobby, Ellie and Dave jumped up. Ellie spoke with Mr. Lytton before he took his leave. I untangled myself from Dave long enough to thank the man profusely. I was thankful neither Ellie nor Dave asked me any questions. It was enough for them that I had not been charged.

On the short drive to the hotel, I voiced my random thoughts. "You know, Felicity told us she brought Scarlett in knowing she didn't have enough evidence to charge her—hoping she would trip her up with questions and get what she needed. It didn't work then, and thankfully, it didn't work with me. Right or wrong, it makes me think she's not up to this investigation. Goodness, how I wish Jake or Gemma were here."

From the back seat, Dave squeezed my shoulder. "Now you've got me worried. Did I just hear you wish for Gemma?"

At least he made me chuckle. "I'd much prefer Jake."

"Well, as a matter of fact, you're in luck." I turned to look at him. "While you were comatose earlier, I called him and discovered he was in Exeter because he's making a presentation there tomorrow morning—I guess by now it's today."

"What? He's just up the road?"

"Yes. I told him about you finding Scarlett and Felicity's reaction while we were at the scene. I don't know what I expected him to do, but he was so helpful when Wendy called him, I thought he'd at least have some advice. He's a heck of a guy. Right off the bat, he declared he'd drive here tomorrow as soon as his presentation was over—that he could use a weekend at the seaside.

"Of course, I thanked him and offered to get him a room. I found it interesting that he knew all about Scarlett being brought in and released. It turns out that Felicity has been using him as a sounding board since her DI is still in the hospital. Except that when I called the second time to tell him she'd taken you in, he was shocked. She hadn't put him in the picture about that development."

With a relieved sigh, I leaned back in my seat. "I don't know exactly what he can do, but I'm glad he's coming. I'm more than glad—I'm thankful, ecstatic, happy—and I know I'm tired when I can't find the right words."

I walked through the living room without a glance at the pages papering the walls, shed my clothes, and scrubbed the makeup from my face. When I fell into bed, Dickens stretched out beside the bed, and Christie snuggled beneath my chin. I heard Dave puttering around before he joined us in bed and wrapped his arms around me. When Christie meowed and nipped his fingers, he gave a little yelp. "You silly cat. You have to share."

I awoke to the smell of coffee and knew Dave must be up. Stretching, I rolled over and came face to face with Christie. "About time you woke up. Dave's good with the milk, but not as good as you."

"And I love you too, princess." I looked at the clock. "But it's only six a.m." I stuck my head into the living room to see whether it was safe to appear in my robe. Thankfully, Dave was sitting alone at the table with his laptop.

He looked up as I entered the room. "Good morning, sweetheart. How'd you sleep?"

"Surprisingly well for a woman who spent the evening at a police station. Has Dickens already been out?"

"Yes. Would you like me to call room service for breakfast? I thought you might want to keep a low profile today."

"I don't know what I want to do, but breakfast is a start." I left the ordering in his capable hands and took a quick shower. As I finished blow-drying my hair, the smell of bacon wafted into the room. *Perfect timing.*

"Are you ready to tell me about your experience with Felicity at the station? I could tell you weren't up to it last night."

"Not really, but needs must." I tried to capture the words and tone of the questioning I had endured. Dave's expression moved from distressed to shocked and back, so I must have been successful.

"My gosh, after that, how can you be so chipper this morning?"

"I guess I feel as though I dodged a bullet, though I know another could be on its way. What if the police never identify the killer? Until they do, a cloud of suspicion will hang over my head, and that's no way to live. I'd feel much better if you told me you and the LOLs figured out who the murderer is."

"I wish I could. Maybe if you look over our brainstorming, something will leap out at you. We completed pages on all the players—Gilbert, Rhys, Scarlett, you, Daisy, and Oliver. Maybe that will help."

Groaning, I stood. "I'll need more coffee before I can face what you wrote about me. "

"Well, look at Oliver's page, then. We pulled his together after you left, but again, nothing particularly telling."

His page was affixed to the wall by the bedroom door. Holding my coffee mug in both hands, I read aloud, "*Mid 80s, retired vet, knows Gilbert/Emily/Rhys/Scarlett, grandson committed suicide, Emily was grandson's writing coach, dislikes Rhys, close to Scarlett, rented changing hut, walked with Scarlett, knowledgeable about poisons, knows his Agatha Christie, Sherlock Society, bad back, cancer, rude/mostly with Rhys, stately, dapper gentleman.*

"I can't help but feel sorry for the man. He's lost a grandson and a friend, and he's in poor health. I guess I don't have to like him to feel sorry for him. And he likes dogs, so he can't be all bad. And yet, there's something not quite right."

"You may be thinking something along the lines of what the LOLs discussed last night. According to Wendy and Belle, he was disoriented after hearing that Scarlett was dead. He kept repeating they needed to be on their way to tea as though he couldn't absorb the fact she was dead. But you won't believe this—Belle suggested that he might have killed Scarlett, and doing so threw him into some kind of fugue state."

"Miss Marple thinks he killed Scarlett? And that threw him into shock? Goodness, that seems like a stretch. Isn't it more likely that he was in shock because two people he knows are dead?"

"In the end, that's what we concluded, but not before Wendy imagined a scenario where Scarlett revealed her true colors to him, maybe when she ranted and raved about her experience at the police station. She wouldn't have been able to conceal her anger with you, and he could have suddenly seen the truth in the stalker accusation. He's very much an old-fashioned gentleman. Wendy pictured him putting two and two together, reflecting on the past few months as he listened to Scarlett. What if he saw her fascination with Rhys in a new light? What if he realized it was an obsession and the girl he'd taken under his wing was a killer?"

He chuckled. "I know it isn't funny, but I'm telling you, Leta, Wendy has the makings of a mystery writer. She finished the scene with a flourish—Oliver thought Felicity could be right, that Scarlett killed Emily. He questioned her, she gloated and admitted it. He was horrified that she'd killed his friend and, in a moment of madness, killed her." He pointed to the page on Oliver. "But in the end, we went back to what we knew, and we decided it didn't make sense."

Closing my eyes, I rubbed my temples. "It's amazing the things you can dream up when you brainstorm, isn't it? I can believe that he was blind to her obsession. I can believe he'd be shocked if she told him she killed Emily. But strangle her? Nope. Heck, he'd be even less likely than me to be able to overpower her."

*What am I missing?* "What about Marko?"

"What about him?"

"Well, if we're looking for a connection to both Emily and Scarlett, he fits. We may not know him, but he dated Scarlett and he must have known Emily, since his girlfriend lived with her. I wonder whether Rhys knows anything about him."

Dave snapped his fingers. "Social media. Doesn't everyone have a Facebook profile?"

Grabbing my tablet, I pressed the Facebook icon, located Scarlett's page, and scrolled back to where Marko first appeared. "They made an attractive couple."

When I got to the picture of Scarlett looking at the box of miniature bottles, I stopped. "I think this may have been the beginning of the end for their relationship. You can tell from the angle that it's Marko who took this picture, and Scarlett looks disconcerted. Is that the word?"

Looking over my shoulder, Dave agreed. "It's as though he caught her off guard, and she couldn't compose herself. There's no big smile. I can almost hear her saying, 'I don't know about this.' As if she'd been having fun in the relationship, but wasn't prepared for his romantic gesture."

I thought back to my dating life before Henry. "You know all the dating advice warns couples about significant holidays like this and Christmas."

He kissed the top of my head. "But they worked out for us, didn't they?"

"But maybe not for Scarlett and Marko. Her romantic history indicates that she all but ghosts a young man at the first sign of serious interest. Maybe she's not that rude, but the relationship abruptly fades from Facebook after this—photos of Marko go from several a day to one every few days to none. It's a quick transition. And then she sets her sights on someone like her professor in Atlanta or Rhys in London or you, Dave."

Taking the tablet from me, he scrolled slowly forward. "You're right, Leta. Before this Valentine's Day photo, she documents their dates in gushing detail with multiple photos. After February 14th, the poor guy was lucky to get a post a day with no caption. And then bam, he's gone."

"Dave, click on his name where she tags him in her posts. It's funny that it's only a first name, but it's a tag nonetheless. I know one or two folks who use nicknames."

He touched the highlighted name and it led him to a Facebook profile for Marko. His About info was sparse—Lives in London, BA in Journalism & Media from Leeds University. His posts were nowhere near as frequent as Scarlett's. The Valentine's Day photo was there, but there were also others of him carousing with male friends, presumably in pubs as pints of beer were prevalent. From time to time, there were posts of him with his arm around different women.

"Stop!" I pointed to a photo of Marko and an older gentleman at a restaurant. On the table was a slice of pie with a candle in it. "Oh my gosh! It's Oliver, and look at the caption—Grandad's birthday celebration.' This has to be the grandson we've heard about. Oh my gosh! She dated the grandson who committed suicide?"

"And we think she broke up with him."

"Did she break his heart? Was that a contributing factor to the suicide? He may have committed the cardinal Valentine's Day sin with his gift, but that doesn't mean he was any more in love than she was. So, did Red break his heart?"

Dave nodded. "Well, let's go back to the earlier posts and study them more closely."

Before Scarlett entered the picture, his posts mostly featured shots of pubs and drinking along with the occasional paragraph about how his writing was going. In January, the pubs were a bit less frequent. That made sense as we knew he was spending time with Scarlett.

Things shifted again in March. He continued to mention Emily and her critique of his writing. These were simple one or two-liners—*Good session today. Brilliant suggestion from Emily.* Less sanguine posts about writing began appearing in April and indicated increasing dismay with her critiques. *Bloody hell, another rewrite. More research. Why won't the words come?*

I stopped scrolling when Dave commented on one of the writing posts. "I've never had a writing coach, but I can relate to his feelings. It's frustrating when you spend days writing and rewriting the same paragraph—when the words don't flow."

As for Scarlett, we found a few March and April photos of her that we'd seen earlier on her page. Marko's brief comments were telling. *Missing Red today. Happy times.* The most poignant to me was his final post, a picture of the two of them laughing together.

The words that accompanied it were familiar to me. The therapist I saw when Henry died had that Mercedes Lackey quote framed in her office. *If only. Those must be the two saddest words in the world.* I felt as though it had been written especially for me. To tell me that I needed to move forward.

"Dave, is it possible that he was despondent about his writing *and* Scarlett?"

"Maybe. What doesn't add up, though, is that Oliver blames *Rhys* for his grandson's suicide. Of course, I never thought that made sense. Like Belle said, you never know what makes someone take their life."

Shaking myself, I stood. "I need to step away from this. Maybe write a page on Marko to add to our collection. One thing's for sure—I'm not any closer to clearing my name."

"Why don't you ask Wendy to stop by? When you tell her the news about Marko being Oliver's grandson, maybe she'll have a flash of inspiration."

I couldn't help laughing. "Or another flight of fantasy, right?"

# Chapter Eighteen

WENDY WAS ALL EARS when she arrived with Ellie in tow. "Good grief. How did we miss that Marko was Oliver's grandson?"

Ellie smiled at her. "Come, come, we LOLs aren't mind readers. As far as I know, I've never once heard anyone refer to the young man by name. And yes, I want to hear more about him—but first, can we talk about what transpired with Felicity?"

I took a deep breath. "You two have been remarkably patient about last night, so yes, we can do that." I could only hope that they would fill Belle in so I wouldn't have to keep hitting the rewind button. Living it was bad enough.

Wendy reacted to my ordeal much as Dave had but with more vocals. "Oh my gosh, how could she?"

Ellie tsk-tsked and made soothing comments.

With that out of the way, I walked them through the morning's lightbulb moment, as I thought of it—that we didn't know anything about Marko—and how Dave had the idea to search Facebook.

"I saw him as another person who knew both Emily and Scarlett and thought we needed to learn more about him. If he was connected to them both, maybe he had something to do with their deaths, right?"

"Except," Dave pointed out, "he's dead too, and unless we think his suicide was staged, the three deaths aren't related."

Wendy bolted from her chair. "But what if they are? What if one person killed all three of them? Someone we've never even met?"

I bit my lip and Ellie rolled her eyes, but it was Dave who voiced our thoughts. "Wendy, seriously, a serial killer?"

That stopped her in her tracks. "Ugh. You're right. We've established who the mysterious boyfriend was, but that doesn't get us any closer to proving Scarlett killed Emily or figuring out who Scarlett's killer is."

My shoulders slumped. "Unfortunately, you're right."

Wendy wasn't ready to give up. "Didn't you and Mum tell us that Oliver initially blamed Rhys *and* Emily? Maybe deep down he still saw her as responsible. This could be about revenge on everyone who, in his mind, wronged Marko. Scarlett the uncaring lover, Emily the harsh writing coach, and Rhys—the worst offender of all—the man who prescribed ineffective medications and was no help in getting the book published."

Dave blanched. "That could make a kind of awful sense if not for the stumbling block Leta and I discussed this morning. Even if you believe in a revenge scenario, can you honestly see him overpowering Scarlett?"

Ellie chuckled. "Only in the movies. For that matter, can you see him playing a role for months—convincing her that he's her friend? No one's that good an actor."

Wendy groaned. "Well then, I'm fresh out of ideas. The Marko connection is fascinating but useless."

When her phone pinged with a text, she looked almost relieved. "Perfect timing. It's Rhys wanting me to pop by his room, probably because he needs my help. He's trying hard to keep his grief at bay, and I can't believe he's functioned as well as he has so far."

As she opened the door to the hall, I had a sudden thought. "Wendy, can you ask him what he knows about Emily's relationship with Marko, please? Just in case there's something we've missed. She may well have said something in passing."

Given there'd now been two murders, I wondered how well attended today's sessions would be. Were participants beginning to bail? Would there be anyone left by the time we got to Saturday's crowning events—'Sayers vs Christie' and the banquet?

There were two sessions today: Golden Age Amateurs, covering a selection of amateur sleuths such as Father Brown, Miss Marple, and A.A. Milne's Tony Gillingham; and Little Did You Know, featuring lesser-known authors of the era.

Ellie must have read my mind. "Belle particularly wants to attend this morning's presentation, since she considers herself a latter-day Miss Marple, plus she adores Father Brown. You know that the BBC show is filmed in Blockley, don't you? Anyway, let me be sure she's up and moving."

Left on our own, Dave and I moved the large pages on Oliver and Emily side by side and studied them. "What are you thinking, Leta?"

"Oh, the usual. Is there something I'm missing? Did I rule him out too quickly?"

Dave nodded. "I don't think he's involved, but I know what you mean. It was only yesterday that we were positive Scarlett murdered Emily, and now because Scarlett's dead, we don't know whether to look for a second killer or to believe one person is responsible for both. Well, at least that's where we are. I have no clue what the heck Felicity is thinking."

I was worried about Felicity too—and something else. "They were very different murders, weren't they? I hate to sound like one of those profilers on *Criminal Minds*, but Emily's death seemed calm. What do they call it? Organized?" I hesitated. "Except for the fact that the killer dropped a near-empty vial of morphine in a plant. That seems like a reckless move. Aargh."

"Sweetheart, you're either tying yourself up in knots or you're on to something. What if dropping the vial in the plant *wasn't* a mistake? What if it was part of the plan? To point the finger at someone else?"

His eyes widened. "I think that's it. Wipe the vial clean but stash it somewhere where it was bound to be found. That fits with your idea that Emily's murder was carried out by an organized killer."

"Yes. Calm and premeditated. But the scene in the changing hut was different. It looked as though there was a struggle—like whoever killed Scarlett was angry."

"Leta, do you realize that an angry killer and a struggle could easily describe you? Let's keep that idea to ourselves, okay? I still prefer the single killer theory, if only because it takes you off the suspect list."

Second-guessing myself was a bad habit, and who knows how long I would have kept it up if Wendy hadn't knocked on the door?

Two lime green notebooks in her hands, my friend stuck her head in the door. "I wanted to drop these by. I thought they would be about the festival, but instead, they're Scarlett's journals. Maybe there's something useful in them."

Dave teased her. "Like a page where she confesses to killing Emily?"

Wendy nodded. "Well, anything's possible. What would be even better would be something concrete to clear your girlfriend."

It was no laughing matter, but I couldn't help myself. "Oh, I can see it now. The last entry will be who she's meeting at the changing hut. That would do it."

She dropped the notebooks on the table. "Alright, you two, joke all you want, but I only had to flip through a few pages to find this."

Opening one to a page with the corner turned down, she pointed. "She goes into great detail about the mistake she made in Atlanta, that she should have 'removed the competition,' as she put it, long before the car accident. And she didn't plan to make that mistake again."

I scanned the page. "That's . . . that's diabolical. Maybe we were right about Scarlett all along. Which would mean two murderers."

Dave looked at Wendy. "She was already rethinking the idea that one person killed two people. What were your words just now, Leta? The two murders were very different—organized vs. disorganized or whatever the experts call it?"

Wendy rolled her eyes. "I told Rhys you were probably down here second-guessing yourself, and I was right, wasn't I?"

"Wendy, you know her too well. But think about it. If the journals provide proof that Scarlett *did* kill Emily, then we need to look again at how the two murders are related—or not. What if they aren't? Maybe we need to consider all the people, even beyond Torquay, who could want Scarlett dead."

My friend frowned. "You may be right, Dave, but that's a daunting task. All we know for sure is that neither Leta nor Rhys killed Scarlett. What I want to do is read these cover to cover with a highlighter clutched in my hand. Just saying that makes me think you two should make copies before you start. But I can't. Rhys has enlisted Gilbert to help run the festival, but they still need a gofer, and that's me."

Dave glanced at me. "Okay, then, what if I go to the business center and make copies so we can sit here and read through everything? Maybe we'll learn something beyond what we've inferred from Facebook. Either way, then we can give the notebooks to Felicity, no harm done."

"True. If we can pinpoint any passages in these journals that point to someone else that would want to see Scarlett dead—someone besides me—she might just act, and the sooner she locks up this second killer, the better I'll feel."

Wendy nodded. "Unless, worst-case scenario, there's nothing in the notebooks that points to anyone else and Felicity returns to you as the prime suspect for Scarlett's death."

My shoulders slumped. "You're right, you know. I can see Felicity thinking that Scarlett killing Emily doesn't clear me. It's like the BBC mysteries where the police are hell-bent to charge someone, and in this instance, that someone could be me."

"Leta, I can't imagine how worried you are, but let's focus on the journals. There's not much more we can do at this point."

"Right. There's something about being arrested and spending half the night at a police station that's making me doubt myself—well, I always doubt myself, but today it's more than usual."

I wanted to get out of the room, if only briefly, so Dickens and I accompanied Dave downstairs. At the door to the business center, Dickens balked. "Leta, can't we go outside?"

Looking at Dave, I shrugged my shoulders. "How 'bout if I take Dickens out only to the green area and come right back? I'll be careful, I promise."

"Go, but hurry back."

On the way through the lobby, Dickens and I ran into Daisy Owens. "Leta? You're back? I'm so glad."

"I take it that means you know where I was?"

"Yes, the security guard saw DS Jenkins escorting you out last night. I couldn't believe it when I heard you'd been arrested."

"Trust me, neither could I. The good news is they didn't have enough to hold me. The bad news is I haven't heard word one about them looking at anyone else. By the way, how's your uncle?"

"Not well. He's suffered one loss after another recently. First my cousin, then Emily, and now Scarlett."

*Oh my gosh. I missed that—the grandson had to be her cousin.* "Your cousin? I'm sorry, Daisy, you told me Oliver was your uncle, and I knew he'd lost his grandson, but it just didn't click with me—"

"That Marko was my cousin? That's okay. There's no reason you'd make the connection. It was sudden, and he was so young. Uncle Ollie has taken it very hard."

"I'm sorry for your loss. I lost my husband a few years ago, and I know firsthand that it's not something you get over easily." *Nearly three years now.* "It can't have been easy on you either."

"Thank you, Leta. I don't suppose it's ever easy, but it's been much worse on my uncle. And Scarlett filled that void when Marko died, so it's been a double whammy for him."

When her phone rang, I said goodbye and tugged on Dickens's leash. Unencumbered by my dark thoughts, Dickens was his usual happy self. Questions about Daisy bounced around in my head. *How close was she to her cousin? She has to be a good twenty years older than him. Is Oliver her great-uncle?*

Dickens pulled up short when I stopped in my tracks. *Owens! Did the O on the teacups stand for Owens?*

With the notebooks to read, I didn't have time to think about Daisy. And that's when I realized I'd forgotten my assignment to contact Sue. I pulled out my phone and rang her before it could slip my mind again. "Hi. Yes, it's a bit of a story. I'm fine, but I could use your social media expertise again. No, later today is soon enough." *How fitting it is that the topic for this morning is amateur sleuths.*

# Chapter Nineteen

Plopping down on the couch, I looked at Dave. "I've been thinking."

That got an exaggerated eye roll. "Should I act surprised?"

I stuck out my tongue. "It's very creative, and it's a bonus for you. I think it would be easier if only one of us read through the journals, so why don't you take this opportunity to go to the gym? That was your assignment, right? And then, when you get back, we can take a nice long walk, maybe have lunch at Maisie's."

"Now, that's a great idea. And you promise not to leave the room while I'm gone, right?"

Now it was my turn to roll my eyes. "Scout's honor, Dad."

"Don't joke, Leta. I'm serious about keeping you safe. While there's a killer at large, I'm only letting you out of my sight if you promise to behave."

Christie did her best to keep me from reading. She alternated between chewing the corners of the pages and climbing in my lap to block the view. "Leta, move this stuff so I can curl up in your lap."

Ignoring her, I continued reading. The first notebook opened with Scarlett's arrival in London. She was despondent and repetitive and moved back and forth between lamenting her lost love—the professor—and chastising herself for being stupid.

She detailed her mistakes and what she should have done differently. *Fascinating. She's not one bit sorry for what she did.*

When she wasn't fixated on the past, she talked about enjoying her time with Emily, both the sightseeing and the coaching. From the sound of it, Emily taught her a lot about character development and show versus tell.

*Now I'm getting somewhere.* I'd reached the part where Scarlett met Marko, and this was also the point when her focus began to shift more to her writing and enjoyment of Emily's GALA meetings. I highlighted a section where she described sharing a joint coaching session with Marko. She was enthusiastic about the process of reading and critiquing each other's work and then hearing Emily's take.

For the next half hour, the only sounds in the room were Christie's purring and Dickens's gentle snoring as I flipped pages and made notes. Almost overnight, all mention of the Atlanta professor ceased. No regrets. All the *woulda, coulda, shoulda* comments stopped as the Marko and Red love story heated up. It looked as though Christmas may have lit a fire under it.

The January notes about their romance were a bit TMI for me, with their focus on bedroom details. She wrote that she was in love and there were occasional entries about what marriage to Marko would be like. In late January, she met his grandfather.

*Oh my gosh, I was right!* The word besotted came to mind—until right after Valentine's Day, when the tone abruptly shifted. And, then within a week, the relationship was over. The way she described it, the breakup sounded brutal. And to make matters worse, when he begged, she let him *visit,* as she put it, three times over the next few weeks. I was thankful she didn't share those details.

There was no longer anything romantic in the way she described him, and I found myself hoping she hadn't used these words with him. They were like daggers—clingy, insecure, selfish, child-like. I was horrified, and if he sensed any of those feelings, he would have been crushed.

What an emotional roller coaster it must have been for him. The earlier entries read as though she were madly in love and wanted to spend the rest of her life with him. *Maybe she believed what she wrote—until she didn't.* There was even talk of eloping. And then, boom, it was over. *Was she fooling herself as well as him? Did she do this whenever she fell for a man her age?*

For a few weeks after the breakup, the entries were devoted to the progress with her book and complimentary comments about Rhys. She also mentioned occasional walks with Oliver and visits to museums and galleries. Without the benefit of hindsight, it was easy to read her remarks about Rhys as completely innocent. She noted how good-looking and charming he was and admired his air of confidence. And she mentioned she was in awe of the relationship he and Emily shared. *I could have made the same comments.*

When she wrote of Marko's suicide in early April, she seemed genuinely sad. Briefly. And then she shifted to describing him as a weakling, as someone she never should have gotten mixed up with. It was all about her, not about him.

My thoughts drifted as I tried to focus on the words in front of me. I imagined Marko in despair and recalled his final Facebook post, *If only. Those must be the two saddest words in the world.*

It was shortly after the suicide that the walks with Oliver became a regular thing, and she more or less inserted herself full time into his life. She'd kept up with him after the breakup, but not like this. *Why?*

I pondered that question and concluded, amateur psychologist that I was, that Oliver might have been the one uncomplicated relationship in her life. As long as he remained blissfully unaware of how she'd hurt his grandson, she was emotional support for him. Based on her descriptions, their conversations seemed superficial and benign, the stuff of family dinners: How was your day? Did you catch Father Brown on the telly last night?

A week or two passed with little mention of Rhys, but soon a growing obsession was evident. Though there was no indication that Scarlett's attentions were reciprocated, what had begun as comments about his looks and personality were now fantasies of a relationship between them. The words 'What if' and "When we're together' figured prominently.

Once again, this was TMI for me. It was one thing to dream of a romantic entanglement à la the Hallmark channel, but my face grew hot as I read the between-the-sheets imaginings. *Is this the kind of romance her mother writes?*

In addition to steamy fantasies about Rhys, I picked up on increasing discontent with Emily. Scarlett was excited about working on the GALA's Poison Pens Literary Festival but unhappy about Emily's critique of her Sayers book.

Her disenchantment with Emily had progressed to the point where she mixed nightly rants about her coach with fantasies about Rhys. She was more than unhappy with Emily's coaching. Emily was too straitlaced. Why couldn't she see that the Sayers book needed a bit of spice? Reading between the lines, I surmised that Emily thought the writing was top-notch but couldn't abide the book's premise.

By summer's end, Emily began to figure more prominently as a rival for Rhys's affection. No longer did Scarlett admire the convivial relationship the two had maintained. Now, Emily was in the way, and comparisons to the Atlanta romance began to surface. The venomous entries about Emily continued to the last page. As I picked up the second bundle of pages, I didn't hold out much hope things would change, but they did.

The September entries started with several pages of bullet points about people and places. None of these people had appeared previously in her journal, and I wondered who they were. Perhaps she was widening her social circle.

And then it clicked. These were character descriptions—what authors sometimes call a character bible. Was this evidence she was considering writing a different book? Had she suddenly taken Emily's advice about the Sayers book to heart?

As I flipped back and forth, I realized that the names were new but the descriptions seemed vaguely familiar. *I know these people!* The names had been changed, but I recognized Oliver, Emily, Rhys—and Scarlett. I'd heard the adage "write what you know," but never considered that it could mean turning people from your life into characters in a book.

More typical journal entries covered the next several pages—pining for Rhys, antipathy for Emily, and affection for Oliver. And then what looked like a title page with the words "The Salerno Affair" in all caps. *What?*

"Oh my gosh, Christie. It's a story, or at least the start of one." Christie tucking her nose into her paws told me she wasn't the least bit interested in my discovery.

### THE SALERNO AFFAIR

*"This has to stop," Miranda moaned. "I can't go on loving him only in my dreams. I long to run my fingers through his hair, to pull him close, to kiss his lips."*

*The shapely redhead stared out the window, watching Rochester Salerno stroll through the garden with Phyllis. His chiseled good looks were the stuff of fairy tales, and she imagined him as a knight of King Arthur's court, his broad shoulders encased in a suit of armor—his white-blonde hair and striking blue eyes melting hearts wherever he went.*

*Her heart ached as she gripped the windowsill. She whispered to herself in anguish. "I know he doesn't love her. And Phyllis? She must see she's losing him for good this time. How can she ignore the way he looks at me, the way he caresses me with his eyes?"*

"Oh my gosh. Gag me! Is this for real?" My outburst startled my snoozing cat, and she leaped from my lap. "Sorry, Christie."

I returned to the journal, praying "The Salerno Affair" was a short detour from the usual entries. I wasn't sure how much of this I could stomach.

*It was time for Miranda's daily visit to her ailing mentor. He'd long been urging her to act, to let nothing stand in the way of her heart's desire. He had calmed the girl's wild ravings with practical advice. Now, she would rely on his expertise as she prepared to eliminate her middle-aged rival. Rochester would soon be hers.*

*Dr. Miller sat in his wheelchair by the window and waved as the young girl approached the house. When she entered his room, he smiled. "You seem changed today, my dear. Does this mean you've reached a decision?"*

*"Yes, Dr. Miller, I'm ready. Will you help me?" The tall red-head knelt by his side.*

*"Yes, Miranda, if you are truly committed. This is not an undertaking for the faint of heart."*

*She assured him she was prepared to see it through if only he would lay out the plan for her—the plan he'd teased her with over the past few weeks. And so it began.*

*"First, my dear, take this key and unlock the chest in the corner. In it, you will find the poison I've acquired for just such an eventuality. There's more than enough for your purposes. The rest I'll save for my peaceful departure from my life of pain. Remember, your bargain with the devil requires that you stay by my side when my time is near."*

*She brought the vials to him, and he explained that she must slip the liquid into Phyllis's drink and ensure she drank it all. She had to choose carefully. Did Phyllis always consume a full cup of tea? Did she sip sherry before dinner? The taste would be unnoticeable in tea or juice or a sweet liqueur but, he warned, would only have the desired effect if her rival drank the full dose.*

I rolled my eyes as I read more blather about longing and desire and hatred. It was painful to read, but I forced myself to keep turning the pages. Finally, I made it to the closing paragraphs.

*Miranda sat across from Phyllis with a glass of sherry. It was difficult not to laugh as Phyllis sipped from her large goblet of Amaretto. Every evening, like clockwork, she donned her satin pajamas and matching velvet trimmed robe for their ritual tête-à-tête. Little did Phyllis know this would be the last time she would be able to offer a brutal critique of Miranda's work.*

*As Phyllis yawned and greedily turned her glass up for the last drop, Miranda observed that her pupils were slowly shrinking to pinpoints. Soon, her eyelids began to close. The older woman murmured something unintelligible before her head tilted to the side.*

*Only then did the polite smile on Miranda's face broaden to a grin. A maniacal laugh escaped from her mouth as she thought, "You're mine now, Rochester. All mine."*

This was almost an exact description of the scene I'd encountered Tuesday night, but it had been written more than a month earlier. Sure, some details were different, but there was no mistaking it for anything other than a plot for a real-life murder. *But did Scarlett carry it out?*

I flipped through the September and early October pages until I got to the day Scarlett arrived at the festival. I wanted to throw up when I read her description of the train ride with Gilbert and Dave, not to mention her words about me as a potential rival—one she deemed no challenge. *Oh for goodness' sake.*

I read Tuesday's two entries much more closely. Scarlett's humiliation and anger leaped off the page as she described her argument with Emily after Rhys's presentation. The description of Emily's challenge to her was brief and to the point, followed by a diatribe about Emily's refusal to see her again that night.

The spiteful words made me flinch. *Ugly hag. Hateful witch. I could kill her. A dagger to the heart would do. Stupid woman. What does she know about writing?*

The last entry for Tuesday seemed to have shifted from anger to a matter-of-fact recounting of delivering her manuscript to Emily. *Now, I'll have to wait until morning to receive my sentencing. Fingers crossed, Rhys gets me a reprieve. I need a drink!*

On Wednesday night, the tone shifted again. *Ding-dong, the witch is dead, and Rhys needs me in oh-so-many ways.* That was the only mention of Emily's death—nothing beyond the romantic and publishing ramifications for Scarlett. Not one shred of sorrow.

She alternated between waxing poetic about her relationship with Rhys taking off and *The Sayers Secret* being a hit. Dave had taken a back seat to Rhys in the romance arena—there was even a comparison of the two of them, with Rhys coming out on top. I chuckled at that and the one scathing comment about Wendy, "the pint-sized witch who didn't stand a chance."

I wasn't surprised to find that there was nothing on Thursday. Scarlett wrote in her journal nightly, and by Thursday night, she was dead. Goodness knows what she would have said about me if she'd been alive to write in her journal after her trip to the Torquay police station. Based on her earlier catty descriptions of me, a crazy old bat might have been the nicest thing she called me.

The disappointing part was that there was nothing to tell me who she might have been meeting at the changing hut and nothing that would clear me. If Felicity saw this, she might be convinced it wasn't me who murdered Emily, but she could still see me as Scarlett's killer.

# Chapter Twenty

WHEN DAVE WALKED IN the door, he was on the phone. "Yes, we could use your help, but I don't want to put you in a bad position, and I know Leta would agree." He mouthed the word *Jake* to me. "Right. Okay, we're talking about lunch out, so call me when you're close."

"Thank goodness he's coming, Dave. I'm not any closer to identifying Scarlett's killer than I was when you left."

He chugged a bottle of water and came to sit beside me. "You didn't find anything helpful?"

Leaning my head to the back of the couch, I handed him the stapled pages. "Look at Journal #2, at the pages I've turned down and the things I highlighted. It's horrifying."

After a few gasps and muttered exclamations, his reaction to *The Salerno Affair* was much like mine. "I don't know which is more appalling, her writing or the fact that she's mapped out a murder. It's what we saw, Leta."

"I know. First I gagged at the writing. I can't even begin to describe how bad it is. But the story? Oh my gosh!"

Rolling his eyes, he pointed to the description of Rochester. "It's an over-the-top exaggeration, but this is Rhys, right?"

"It has to be. If you're in doubt, just turn to the bulleted list with the lengthy descriptions of each character. And Dr. Miller? Oliver Fletcher may not be in a wheelchair, but who else can it be?"

He flipped a few more pages. "Oh my gosh. I have dark good looks and broad shoulders—not that I mind that bit of flattery, but seriously?"

"Oh, I think her description is right on. You're not quite a knight of the round table, but you'll do. Now, on a more serious note, turn to Tuesday and Wednesday of this week."

Frowning, he moved back and forth between the entries. "It certainly sounds as though she *wanted* to kill Emily, and 'ding-dong, the witch is dead?' She's overjoyed at her death . . . but she doesn't say anywhere that she did it."

"No, she doesn't. So what do you think? Did she kill her or not?"

He shuddered. "I don't know, but thinking about it gives me cold chills. So much hatred. Thank goodness she didn't have an opportunity to come after you."

"I don't want to think about it either. I need a break."

"Then let me tell you how my sleuthing assignment went." *Oops. I'd almost forgotten about that.*

He drank more water and shared the little he'd dug up. "Just about everyone I encountered at the gym knows and likes Daisy. She's lived here for years and mostly worked in the hospitality industry. It says a lot about her qualifications that she was at the Imperial Hotel for several years until she took the job here about a year ago. I'd think you'd have to be a top-notch events coordinator to work at either of these places."

"Anything about her personal life?"

"I may need some pointers from you, Tuppence. With all the talk of Scarlett being a stalker, I was afraid to point-blank ask whether Daisy was married or had a boyfriend in case I got put in that category."

That made me laugh. "A lesson on how to chat up potential sources? I can probably arrange that, Tommy. The professional info is helpful, though, and when Sue checks social media, maybe she'll get the personal angle."

We were both hungry, so Dave hopped in the shower while I changed into jeans with a long-sleeved T-shirt. *It's a good thing I didn't let him read the first journal, or he'd need a cold shower.*

It was hard to tell who was more excited about leaving the room again, me or Dickens. On the patio, a few brave souls sat with their legs dangling in the pool. I'd learned that the Brits were much hardier souls than I was. Sixty degrees wasn't nearly warm enough for me to venture into the water.

"Dave, I bet the tearoom is crowded. What do you think about calling ahead, and you and Dickens walking to the tearoom to pick up lunch while I sit here in the sun? Then we can have a leisurely lunch. I may even feel up to a bit of brainstorming after that, though my brain has about stopped working."

He looked around, and I knew he was conducting his version of a risk assessment. How likely was it that the plump grey-haired woman on a neighboring lounge chair was a danger to me? Or better yet, the balding man trimming the hedges. The two small children with their coloring books? They didn't look too threatening.

"Okay, but promise me you're not going anywhere. No sneaking off with your magnifying glass, right?"

"Don't be silly. You'll probably have to wake me up when you get back."

I was nearly right. If it hadn't been for the brisk breeze, I would have dozed off. As it was, the wind cut right through my jacket, and I kept thinking how much warmer I'd be in my grey fleece pullover. The more I thought about it, the better it sounded. *I'll dash upstairs, grab my pullover, and be back in a flash. Heck, I think I'll get my gloves too.*

Upstairs, I dug my fleece out of the drawer and smiled at Christie curled up on the bed. Walking through the living room, I took a moment to straighten the two notebooks. *Being in the same room with them is enough to give me the willies.*

My phone rang as I was removing it from my jacket pocket. "Do you miss me already, Dave?"

That got a chuckle. "Oh, I always miss you, but listen. Jake's joined me here at Maisie's. How 'bout the two of us eat lunch here and bring yours back when we're done?"

"That's fine. I was chilly outside, so I came upstairs to change, but I think I'll just stay here. Maybe I'll go over the journals one more time." I got the expected admonishment to stay put and then settled in to read.

As focused as I was on the journals, the knock at the door made me jump. It was Oliver, and he looked startled and confused.

"Oliver, are you okay?"

He rubbed his hand across his forehead. "I think . . . I think I need to sit down."

I ushered him into the room and settled him at the table. "Would you like me to call Daisy or maybe help you to your room?" *Or should I fix him the British cure for whatever ails you.* "How about a cup of tea, while we decide what to do?"

He closed his eyes and twisted his head from side to side, much as I did when my neck was stiff. When he blinked, he stared past me to the door, and I followed his gaze, wondering what had caught his attention.

*Oh my gosh, our notes!* Thank goodness the page stuck to the door was about me and was more playful than serious. *Leta Petkas Parker, Avid reader, petite brunette, ex-pat, loves the color red, mid-50s, met Emily this week, animal lover, accosted by Scarlett, loves Dave and hats, good to her friends, retired banker, columnist.* Not much use in my defense if it came to that, but fun to read.

Still, the realization that the room was plastered with our attempts at sleuthing spurred me to action. I made some inane comment about straightening and grabbed my page and the others and stuffed them behind the coffee table.

I was surprised my visitor had no comment about my frantic bustling around. Instead, he responded to my earlier offer. "Yes, dear, a cup of tea would be nice."

I busied myself fixing the tea, and Christie wandered in as I placed two cups of tea on the table. She stretched one paw at a time, first the two front ones and then the two back ones. "Is it time for milk again?"

"Excuse me a moment while I tend to my fussy cat." I knew she'd give me no peace until I poured her a puddle of milk. "I know veterinarians say milk isn't good for cats, but she only gets a small bit."

"So we say, but as long as she eats well, a little dab of milk won't hurt her. Oh my, this tea hits the spot. May I trouble you for a glass of water, please?" He pulled a pill bottle from his pocket and shook out a small white pill. "This keeps the back pain at bay."

Delivering his water, I sat and added milk and sugar to my tea. Christie leaped into another chair at the table. "He's the man with the dog treats. Does he have cat treats too?"

Scratching her head, I took a sip of tea. *Ugh. I added too much sugar.*

Oliver drank his tea. "Thank you. I had a bit of a spell for a moment. That seems to happen more and more these days. I can't think why I came to see you, but I know there must be a reason."

"No worries. Would you like another cup of tea? Perhaps that will help to jog your memory."

When he agreed that might do the trick, I poured us each a second cup. I was about to sit down when he surprised me with a question. "You know, my wife loved hats too and always carried several when we traveled. Are you the same way?"

*So he did read my page.* I couldn't help smiling. "Of course, and I bought two new hats this week, a red one and a straw one."

He looked wistful. "I'd love to see them if it's not too much bother."

*What could I say?* We didn't seem to be getting any closer to why he had appeared at my door, but maybe a bit more conversation and tea would get us there. If not, my next step would be to call Daisy.

When I returned to the living room with my hats, my guest clapped his hands. "Lovely, my dear." I stirred milk and sugar into my cup, as he told me his wife had preferred pastels for her hats, much like Queen Elizabeth. For the next little while, we sipped our tea while he shared memories of the woman who had shared his life for over fifty years. In turn, I told him a bit about Henry.

Setting his empty teacup down, he smiled. "Ah, now I recall why I knocked on your door. I came to fetch Scarlett's journals."

"Scarlett's journals?" *How does he know I have them?*

He must have seen the question on my face. "Yes, Daisy has been trying to locate them for me, and Rhys mentioned you had them. She knows they'd be a comfort to me, a way to keep Scarlett close. She was a treasure, that girl." A tear rolled down his cheek.

*Did he honestly have no idea what kind of person she was?* "Shouldn't her journals go to the police, to help them figure out who hurt her?" He looked so distressed, I couldn't utter the word *murdered*.

"Well, I understand they think you did it, and if they're that bad at their jobs, what hope is there that they'll find the real killer? You wouldn't have hurt her."

"Thank you. If only the police saw it that way. Still, I think they should see the journals, and then her mother is likely to want them, don't you think? Perhaps when she learns how close you and Scarlett were, she'll make you a copy." *And the truth is I want to look at them again.*

He fixed his grey eyes on me. "Leta, did you read Scarlett's journals?"

I blushed as I thought of the steamy passages, and—I couldn't help myself—I glanced at the table where the journals lay. "Well, I flipped through them. I was hoping to get an idea about how she researched her novel." *I'm outright lying. Who wants to admit they read someone's private journals?*

"And did you read her short story?"

*He knows about that?* And then it hit me. His bad back, the little white pill, Dr. Miller, the vials. *Were he and Scarlett in this together?* I took another sip of tea to delay answering. "No, just her notes about Dorothy Sayers."

"Ah, Leta, I can tell you're not being honest with me. I can see you *did* read 'The Salerno Affair.'" I tried not to laugh when Scarlett read it to me. Truly terrible writing, yet quite believable, don't you think? Now, I really must have the journals."

"No, I don't think so." I stood but had to grab the table to steady myself. "I'm afraid I have to ask you to leave." *What is wrong with me?*

Christie rubbed against my leg. "What is it, Leta?"

Oliver moved quickly and snatched the journals from the table. "We're going to leave together, my dear."

I heard Christie meowing, "What's going on? What's wrong with Leta?"

"Tsk. Tsk. Can't have the cat disturbed, can we?" Christie squirmed when he picked her up, tossed her in the bedroom, and closed the door. That didn't stop the meowing, but it was muffled. When he grasped my elbow and guided me into the hallway, it was all I could do to place one foot in front of the other. *Am I going to die? Like Emily? Like Scarlett?*

I must have uttered some of my thoughts because he responded in a soothing tone. "You're not part of this. You'll be fine as long as you behave."

I was vaguely aware of walking and entering another room. This one was also a suite, but the bedroom didn't have a balcony like ours. Sitting me on the bed, he swung my feet up and around until my head was on the pillow. I could only watch as he closed the curtains and retrieved something from the closet. It was a scuffed black bag with the initials OF on its side. *Is that a doctor's bag?*

As he moved around the room, he spoke to me, always in soothing tones. "Now, dear, I had to be sure we could get you to my room. In my younger days, I would have been able to carry you, but not any longer. Can you believe I used to be able to lift Saint Bernards to the examining table? But age does take a toll."

He carried the leather bag to the bed and sat beside me. "I'm not going to hurt you. I just need to be sure you don't interfere with my plans." I blinked as he raised my eyelids and then took my pulse. "I thought so. You need a bit more, and you'll sleep well for several hours."

With a monumental effort, I licked my lips and managed a few words. " . . . going to do with me?"

"Don't you worry. This is about keeping you out of the way until I'm done. It was an oversight on my part not to think of Scarlett's journals earlier. In my defense, though, I haven't been quite myself."

He pulled a stethoscope from his bag and hung it around his neck. "And this turn of events is partly your fault. You're a bit of a nosy parker, aren't you?" *Gemma's words exactly.*

When he finished listening to my chest, he continued. "If only you hadn't read the journals, but you did, and I couldn't take the risk Scarlett had given away the game. You should never play poker, you know. You're not much good at bluffing. As it is, I've had to accelerate my plan."

"But . . . "

"Shhh. I'll be meeting with Rhys, and once that's done, I'm sure someone will be by to see to you. Or, if things don't go as quickly as I'd like, you may have to sleep a bit longer."

When he wrapped a tube around my arm, I panicked. I knew what was coming, but I couldn't move. "Hate needles."

He smiled as he prepared the syringe. "Oh, you're one of those, are you? I bet you've been that way since you were a child. It will be okay, Leta. Just a little prick, and it will be over."

And he was right.

I struggled to open my eyes. *How long have I been asleep?* My limbs felt weighted, and I heard faint voices. Was someone with Dave in the living room? It wasn't until I tried to roll on my side that I realized something was off. *Where am I?*

When the bedroom door cracked open, I heard someone say, "Now, Oliver, I appreciate the kind gesture, but one drink is enough. Daisy will be wondering where I've gotten to. We agreed to meet this afternoon to prepare for Saturday. Oof."

"That's right, Rhys, sit back down. Are you feeling okay?" It was my captor.

"No, it seems that drink went to my head. How odd. Regardless, I need to be on my way, so no more alcohol for me. Thanks again."

"Indulge me one more minute, Rhys."

I closed my eyes and turned my head away when the bedside lamp came on.

"This is why I insist you drink another toast to Emily."

"What? What is Leta doing in your bedroom? Good heavens, what have you done?"

Oliver brushed the hair from my brow. "Oh, she needed something to help her relax, and it's time she had another dose. How strong it is will depend on you, Rhys."

Looking through the door, I saw Rhys sitting in an armchair. He struggled to his feet as Oliver pulled the rubber tube from his bag. "You have a choice. You can walk out of here or you can save Leta."

He secured the band around my arm, and I watched in horror as he pulled a vial and a hypodermic from his bag. "Which will it be, Rhys? Shall we drink another toast to Emily? Or shall we say goodbye to your friend?"

"Oliver, did you . . . was it you who killed Emily? Bloody hell, what are you doing?"

Images of drinking tea in my room flashed through my brain. Being helped down the hall. *Oh my gosh.* I realized Rhys wasn't nearly as wobbly as I'd been. He could walk out of the room any time.

I tried to sit up, but Oliver pushed me against the pillow. "Yes, Rhys, it was, and she went quite peacefully. You know how she loved her crème de menthe. It only took one large dose in her glass, but then, she's smaller than you, not to mention it blended quite well in that sweet drink."

When I moaned, he shushed me. "It's alright, Leta. I don't think he'll let you die, though he managed to do just that with my grandson. Now, Rhys, I can fill this hypodermic for Leta, or I can pour the morphine in your cognac. Which will it be?"

"She has nothing to do with this! You're mad, Oliver. Let her go."

My captor ignored him. "Did you know, Leta, that my Marko died from a morphine overdose? And I'll soon join him, but not until I've seen to you."

It seemed a lifetime before Rhys responded. "Leave her be, Oliver. Let's drink another toast."

*How did I ever think this man killed his ex-wife? He's sacrificing himself for me.*

Soon, I heard the clink of glasses. "Here's to the lovely Emily. Do you miss her, Rhys?"

"Of course I do. What reason did you have to harm her, Oliver? I know you blame me, but Emily? Why Emily?"

"Have another sip, Rhys. Marko was despondent over his writing, and Emily's harsh criticism fed his sense that he was a failure. That's one reason she had to die."

He was so calm, as though his words were utterly rational. "I wonder. Do you feel her loss as keenly as I feel that of my grandson?"

There was no response from Rhys. *Is he going under or simply speechless?*

"Shall I quote Elizabeth Barrett Browning for you, Rhys? 'How do I love thee? Let me count the ways.' It seems fitting."

Raising myself to my elbows, I watched in horror as Rhys took another sip. His tormentor continued to quote lines from the poem as he returned to the bedroom. Setting his glass on the bedside table, he rummaged in his medical bag. *Did he lie? Is he going to kill me too?*

"Please no," I gasped when he pulled several vials and an envelope from his bag.

"I'm not going to hurt you, Leta, but you need to sleep until this is all over." He emptied two vials into his glass and, once again, tied the band around my arm and filled the syringe.

Last, he placed the envelope on my stomach. "Now, I need you to promise me that when you wake up, you'll read this. Do I have your word?"

When I nodded yes, he tossed back his drink and plunged the needle into my vein.

# Chapter Twenty-One

WHEN I CAME TO, the room was dimly lit, and I could hear voices. Turning my head, I was relieved to see Belle sitting in a chair reading.

She looked over her spectacles and smiled. "Ah, Leta, how are you feeling?"

That was a good question. I closed my eyes and thought. *Where am I now? Oh my gosh, Rhys!*

Tears came to my eyes. "Belle, is Rhys . . . is Rhys dead?"

"No, love, he's alright. You both gave us quite a scare, but you're fine. Let me tell Dave you're awake."

When she opened the bedroom door, two furballs burst into the room. One landed on my chest and one put his paws on the bed by my side. They barked and meowed over each other, but I caught bits of what they were saying.

Dickens barked. "The dog treat man kidnapped you, Leta!"

"I told Dave that as soon as he came in the door, but he didn't listen," meowed Christie.

Dickens defended him. "But he figured it out."

I closed my eyes as jumbled memories surfaced. Groaning, I looked at my arm. *Needles, I hate needles.* I felt the bed dip and opened my eyes to see Dave lean in to kiss my forehead.

"Tuppence, has anyone ever told you how much trouble you are?"

"Hmmm, some bloke named Tommy may have mentioned that in passing."

He shook his head. "I'm beginning to think your middle name is trouble—Tuppence Trouble Parker. And don't think all is forgiven because you solved a murder."

"Did I? Which one? I still don't know who killed Scarlett, but I think Oliver admitted he—oh no, where is he?"

Dave glanced over his shoulder, and I realized Jake Nancarrow was standing in the doorway. It was Jake who answered my question. "Leta, I'm afraid he didn't make it. But I think that was the way he wanted it."

Belle bustled in with a cup of tea. "Okay, that's enough for now. She's in no condition to hear all this. Leta, let's get some tea down you and then see about a shower."

I was toweling my hair dry when Wendy appeared. "Between you and Rhys, I almost had a heart attack, but you both seem to be recovering—at least physically. May I help you with your hair?"

As I sat on the vanity stool, she blew my hair dry. When I was somewhat presentable, she waited while I searched for something comfortable to put on. "Despite being abducted and drugged, how do you feel?"

"Like I just came out of surgery, but I suppose this too shall pass."

"Does it help to know we were right about Oliver Fletcher?"

"Were we? You mean he killed Scarlett too?"

"Yes, but we had the motive wrong. She put two and two together. She figured out he killed Emily and told him that she was going to turn him in. I guess no matter how much she'd begun to hate Emily, she didn't think she deserved to die."

"So that's why the two murders were so dissimilar. Scarlett's murder wasn't planned." An image of Rhys sipping cognac flashed into my brain, and I shuddered. "But he *did* plan to kill Rhys. Oh my goodness, Wendy. It was like watching a horror movie. Did Rhys tell you Oliver quoted Elizabeth Barrett Browning?"

My friend paled. "Yes, and I'm not sure whether Rhys will get through this. It's one thing to lose your best friend. It's another to hear her death was part of an elaborate revenge plot. The man got his wish. Rhys is in pain."

"Thank goodness he misjudged the dose he gave Rhys—or was it that the cavalry arrived in time? And that's something I haven't heard yet. Who found us and how?"

Wendy scrubbed her face with her hands. "I forget. You haven't read the letter. He never intended to *kill* Rhys. He wanted him to suffer. As he put in his letter, death was too good for him. He wanted Rhys to think he would die, and he wanted him to wish he had."

Wrapping my arms around myself, I looked at my friend. "Wendy, I'm sorry I misjudged Rhys. Did he tell you how Oliver got him to drink the cognac?"

She gave me a puzzled look. "Just that he invited him to his room so he could apologize about how badly he'd treated him and insisted they drink a toast to Emily. And he put morphine in the drink, just as he'd done with Emily's."

When I explained that Rhys had chosen to drink the dose he thought was intended to kill me, her eyes flooded with tears. "How could anyone be so cruel? He made Rhys think you would die unless he sacrificed himself?"

"Yes. And Rhys chose to save me."

She whispered, "That part wasn't in the letter. And I'm sure Rhys would never have told me."

We found Jake and Dave in the living room. Dave hopped up to usher me to the couch as Jake offered Wendy a glass of wine. Unfortunately, after being dosed with morphine, wine was off my list of approved beverages for a few days.

Curling my legs beneath me, I cleared my throat. "Can you fill me in, please? How did you find us? And what was in the letter Wendy mentioned?"

Dave started. "It was like following a trail of breadcrumbs. When I walked into the room, I heard Christie screeching from the bedroom. I knew you wouldn't have locked her in there and left her."

"You're right. I would have paid for that."

"When I opened the bedroom door, it barely registered with me that you weren't in there with her before she streaked past me. She was determined to get out to the hallway and then Dickens started barking, and I had no idea what was going on with them—still don't."

I knew what was going on with them. Christie must have told Dickens who took me, but they couldn't get Dave to understand them. Christie jumped in my lap and put her paw on my face. "He doesn't listen very well, you know."

"So, did the three of you set out to find me?"

"Yes, I couldn't get through the door without them, and Christie even beat Dickens into the hall. I was following them and trying to call you at the same time, and of course, my call went to voicemail. Christie darted up and down crying and Dickens raced up and down after her. I was trying not to over-react. I hoped you'd gone down the hall to see Belle and Ellie, except they hadn't seen you. The odd thing was that Dickens and Christie took one look in their room and took off down the hall again. That's when I started to *really* worry."

Dickens barked. "We didn't know where the man was, Leta, but then we found him."

"I didn't stop to think, and I couldn't take the time to put Christie back in the room, so we three hit the elevator. It's almost as though they knew Oliver Fletcher had you because when we saw him leaving the lobby, they both ran up to him and raised Cain. I swear, Leta, I think Christie tried to bite his ankle."

"Did you ask him if he'd seen me?"

"I did, and his polite response was that 'he hadn't but was sure you'd turn up.' We jogged down the hall to the workroom, but the only one there was Gilbert. He was reading up on the afternoon conference he was going to facilitate, and he hadn't seen you either. Wendy had gone off to run errands for Rhys, something about books and posters."

Wendy interjected. "Rhys sent me to the bookshop to pick up more copies of *Gaudy Night*, and I also had to find a print shop to produce some posters for the Saturday night event."

Dave ran his hand through his hair. "So, Gilbert was no use, and I knew you couldn't be with Wendy. I thought Daisy was my next best option, but would you believe she was conducting a tour of the area for a potential client and had taken them to Greenway? I *had* to do something, so I left Christie with Gilbert while Dickens and I searched outdoors, all around the grounds. I kept asking where you were like he was some kind of bloodhound."

Dickens was indignant. "Do I look like a bloodhound?"

"I was at my wit's end, and then I had the bright idea that maybe I'd missed you when I walked back from lunch. Maybe you were on the beach, or worse, maybe you were in a changing hut. Honestly, I wanted to believe you'd had a brainstorm and gone off to investigate something. You know, like maybe you went to the Imperial Hotel to ask questions about Daisy—not that you were in real trouble."

Dickens barked. "We went to the beach, Leta!"

"The whole time we searched, random images from our room surfaced in my brain—things I wasn't conscious of as I left—two teacups on the table, and your red hat on the counter. Why? Did that mean you had a visitor? If so, who?"

It was Wendy's turn. "He was coming in from the pool area as I was coming in the front door lugging books. I could tell he was frantic."

"Some detective I am. It never occurred to me to check with Rhys. But that's the first thing Wendy did. She knew he was holed up in his room working."

"And that's when you figured out Rhys and I were together?"

Wendy looked apologetic. "Not right away. I called Rhys, but his phone went straight to voicemail. Even then, we only wanted to know if he'd seen you. It didn't occur to either of us that you were together."

Dave started to pace. "Look at me. Going through it is making me frantic all over again."

"When we couldn't get Rhys, Dave helped me carry the books to the workroom, and before I knew it, he and Gilbert were talking about enlisting the hotel staff to organize a search. Thank goodness, Daisy walked in before they got that far.

"She very calmly told us Rhys was probably with her uncle, that he'd insisted he needed to apologize to Rhys before he could leave for London. Don't ask me why, but that set off alarm bells for me."

Dave shook his head. "We still didn't know you were with Rhys, but Oliver wanting to speak with him after how he'd acted this week didn't sound right. Daisy said Rhys graciously agreed to call her uncle to set a time to meet—probably around three because there was a meeting with the catering staff planned for four."

Wendy was talking a mile a minute. "You were missing, and now we were concerned about Rhys, too. Daisy could tell we were worried, so she called her uncle. No answer. I called Rhys again. No answer. By then, even Daisy was anxious, so she offered to go with us to his room."

Jake interjected. "They were in full panic mode when I saw the three of them."

"I couldn't believe you were here, Jake. And just in the nick of time. Leta, he was waiting for an elevator, so Dave and I grabbed him, and we all piled in together—Dickens and Christie, too."

Christie licked her paw. "Well, we weren't going to stay behind."

Dave rubbed his face. "You were in Oliver Fletcher's room on *this* floor, Leta. It was one of the doors Dickens and Christie stopped at when they were racing around, but it didn't mean anything to me then." He looked at my dog. "Especially since there was a room service tray in the hall. Can you blame me for thinking that's what had attracted Dickens?"

Dickens barked. "That wasn't the only thing. It smelled like Leta had been there, but when we listened at the door, we didn't hear her, so we kept moving."

*Because I was unconscious.* "When you saw him in the lobby, Dave, it had to be right after he injected me the first time. He knew I wasn't going anywhere." I shuddered. "Oh, how I hate needles."

Jake took over. "We let Daisy knock on the door and call her uncle's name. The good news was that she had a passkey and could open the door for us. You never know about these situations, Leta, so I asked your friends to stand back while I entered the room."

Wagging his tail, Dickens barked. "But we beat you in."

Jake grinned. "You know, Dickens, you'll never be a police dog unless you learn to obey orders."

Christie piped up. "Oh, please, Dickens a police dog?"

"The last thing I remember is staring at a needle and thinking he was . . . he was going to kill me, too. He said he wouldn't hurt me, but . . ."

Dave sat by my side and pulled my head to his shoulder. "Ah, Leta. You had no way of knowing whether to believe him or not. He was playing it by ear at that point, but he explained in his scribbled note that he never planned to hurt you—beyond drugging you."

"So, what exactly happened? I heard him tell Rhys that he killed Emily, and Wendy says he killed Scarlett too. But why did he come to our door? Why did he abduct me?"

When Jake stood, I was reminded of the wrap-up he gave us in Tintagel. "It could be a plot for *Midsomer Murders*, where two to three people always die. You know he blamed Rhys for his grandson's suicide, and I understand he harassed the man every chance he had. He blamed Emily too, but not quite as much, and he allowed her and others to think he'd gotten beyond that. But he hadn't. He planned all along to kill her at the festival and to do it with liquid morphine. If he could implicate Rhys, all the better, and that's what made the night of Rhys's presentation the perfect scenario."

Dave looked at Wendy. "Remember when Wendy suggested someone had killed Marko, Emily, and Scarlett, and I laughed at the thought of a serial killer? In a way, she was right, except Marko wasn't a murder victim. Instead, his suicide was the reason for the elaborate plan."

With a nod, Jake continued. "Think about it. What better way to point the finger at Rhys than to kill his ex-wife after he gave a presentation on poisons? What made it more perfect for him was how Emily treated Scarlett that evening."

Wendy grimaced. "I still can't believe he fell for Scarlett's act, that he never saw her in any way responsible for Marko's suicide. Idiot."

"Well, Wendy, murderers aren't known for being rational. After Tuesday night, all he had to do was decide when to drug Rhys. Leta, do you know that part of the story?"

"That he never planned to kill him? Yes, Wendy told me. Instead, he tormented him." As I described how he quoted 'Let me count the ways I love you,' and how he made Rhys choose his life or mine, you could have heard a pin drop. "He taunted Rhys about Emily's death."

"Because," said Jake, "he wanted Rhys to live a long life—missing Emily *and* feeling responsible for her death."

By now I was shaking with the memory of what I'd heard and seen. "And we were oddly on track about him killing Scarlett. Except he didn't lash out in anger, did he?"

Jake pulled out a copy of the letter. "No, he didn't. It may not have been planned, but it was a necessary move. She was drunk. She told him she knew what he'd done, and he killed her. He had nothing to lose, because, in the end, he wanted to die, but not before he wreaked his revenge on Rhys."

Dave nodded at Wendy. "And, Wendy, you were on the right track there too. You suggested Oliver could be taking revenge on Emily, Scarlett, and Rhys. We danced all around the right scenario but didn't land on it."

I frowned. "And the notebooks? Why were they so important?"

Waving the letter, Jake continued. "He couldn't be sure exactly when Scarlett had twigged to the fact he killed Emily. If she'd figured it out on Wednesday, there was every possibility she'd written about it in her journal that night. Maybe it was only Thursday after being questioned by Felicity that it hit her, but he couldn't take that chance. It seems he truly was in shock after he killed her, or he would have searched for the notebooks immediately, but according to his scribbled addendum, he only thought of it this morning."

"And Rhys innocently told Daisy that I had them. The funny thing is that if he hadn't mentioned 'The Salerno Affair,' I wouldn't have connected the dots. He said he saw it in my face."

Jake read aloud. "Here's how he explains it.

*Proper preparation is critical. I hoped Leta would give me the notebooks, but I couldn't count on that. I never planned to harm her. I came prepared with morphine and slipped it into her tea, knowing that if she saw through my ploy, I'd have no choice but to take her away. She may recall my poker comment. If she hadn't given herself away, I would have left her on the couch feeling sleepy, and she'd have been none the wiser. As it is, once the morphine wears off, she'll be fine.*

"Did he tell you that bit about poker?"

Tears streamed down my face. "Yes, he did, right before the first injection."

Dave wiped my tears away. "I'm so sorry you had to go through that, sweetheart. If only I'd been here."

"Or if only I hadn't come back to the room by myself, but I never thought I'd be in danger in our room."

Jake shook his head. "I think he would have found his opportunity sooner or later. We're still piecing together his movements. And Felicity's been interviewing Rhys, so we may learn more. Do you feel up to telling us how he got you to his room? I'm sure you didn't go willingly."

I took them through what I could recall. "I had just hung up with Dave when he knocked on the door. He seemed disoriented, a frail elderly man who needed assistance. He must have been acting the entire time."

Closing my eyes, I thought back to the sequence of events. "He must have put something in my tea. I remember thinking

I'd added too much sugar, but the second cup tasted funny too. Oh! Is that why he wanted to see my hats?" I explained that part of the story. "Still, I wouldn't be wondering about it now if I hadn't gotten woozy. I could barely stand."

My memories of the black doctor's bag and the needle were vivid while other details were fuzzy. Dave told me I'd been held captive for nearly four hours. "There was talk of taking you to A&E, but Belle convinced the paramedics she could take care of you."

*Thank goodness for small favors.* "I feel like I've lived through the creepiest kind of horror movie. He may not have planned to hurt me, but I'm sure I'll have nightmares for a long time."

It took Wendy to lighten the mood. She winked at me. "Well, there's one good thing. At least this time, no one can say we took unnecessary risks. Heck, we hardly even spoke to Oliver Fletcher."

I knew the two men in the room weren't buying it when they rolled their eyes in unison.

# Chapter Twenty-Two

I KNOCKED ON RHYS'S door the next morning. He needed to know how grateful I was. In my mind, his ordeal had been so much worse than mine, and he wouldn't soon get over it—if he ever did. When he answered the door, he looked drained.

"May I come in?"

"Please do." He grasped my hand in both of his. "Bloody hell, what we went through."

As he made tea, we talked about how we felt physically, skirting carefully around our emotional condition. I broke the ice.

"Rhys, I didn't hear everything, but I heard enough to know he put you through hell." He held up his hand as if to ward off my words, but I ignored him. "No matter what he said about Emily, about you, I want you to hear this from me. I will never, ever be able to repay you for the sacrifice you were willing to make for me. Rhys Ford, you are a good man."

"But, Leta . . ."

"Rhys, look at me. Don't say it. When he presented the options, you thought only one of us would live, and you were willing to die in my place. Nothing will ever change what you did."

He closed his eyes and shook his head. "Leta, thank you for that."

We sat in silence for a few moments. "Were you able to hear the story he read to me? The one Scarlett wrote about Emily, about me?"

I spoke softly. "No, but I read it before he took the notebooks. I can't believe he made you listen to that. I knew Scarlett was bad news, but that story, those words? Bad news doesn't begin to describe it. "

"Oliver wasn't clear, Leta, about how it started, but I think he recognized something in her and encouraged it. She must have confided in him about the scandal and her regrets."

"What I don't understand, Rhys, is how he could bond with the girl who quite possibly broke his grandson's heart."

"I can't say much, since Marko was my patient, but it's no secret to say he had lots of relationships and they never seemed of much consequence to him. Oliver probably knew that. My supposition is that Scarlett and Oliver fed off each other. I guess we'll never know."

"Svengali to her Scarlett O'Hara?"

"Perhaps. But in the end, she turned on him. The one decent thing he did was apologize to you."

"Huh? For drugging me?"

"No, for creating the circumstances that led to your arrest. I'm told he left a letter at the front desk for Felicity telling her you were innocent."

*A small kernel of goodness?* "And he could be kind. He liked dogs. What happened to him? Was he always evil deep down?"

"No, Leta. I think most of us at our core are decent people, though there are evil people out there. Oliver was grieving, and he was dying. And he was self-medicating. All of that took a toll."

I clutched my teacup. "What now, Rhys?"

He stared into his cup of tea before looking up. "We go on. Emily planned tonight's event as the pièce de resistance—the grand finale that would ensure the GALA festival was a standout affair. I'm not going to let her down."

Squeezing his hand, I repeated myself. "You're a good man, Rhys Ford."

Dave and I spent a quiet day together, with our friends dropping by the room to see how I was faring. I kept telling them I didn't feel much different than I had the few times I'd had outpatient surgery. There was nothing wrong with me that a nap or two wouldn't take care of, and I fully intended to make it to the final dinner that night.

I laughed at the expression on Sue's face when Wendy commented that getting dressed up that night would cure whatever ailed me. "She'll be good as new once she slips on her velvet dress and pearls."

Dave chimed in. "Sue, you'd be amazed at how her eyes light up when she hears the words 'black-tie affair.' Almost as much as they do when she thinks about shopping."

"Hey, I've hardly shopped on this trip."

"You know, you're right. You've shown remarkable re-straint—only a bagful of books from The Quill, gifts from the booths, and two hats. Tsk-tsk."

Jake was the last visitor of the day. He'd been busy combining sightseeing with police business. After spending the morning with Felicity tying up loose ends, he took the opportunity to explore the promenade and a few of the stops on the Agatha Christie Mile.

"How are you today, Detective Parker?"

"Oh, hanging in there. And how is Felicity? How's she dealing with you inserting yourself into her investigation?"

He shrugged. "Since she's been using me as a sounding board, she couldn't get too upset. Except she did point out that she never invited me to assist in person." He handed me an envelope. "I'm playing delivery boy for her."

It was a short handwritten note. "Well, that's nice. She says she's glad I'm okay. Maybe if I read between the lines, I'll find an apology."

"Leta, we don't apologize for arresting people. Between you and me, though, she didn't feel she had a choice, and the fact that she liked you made it that much harder for her."

"Well, it helps to hear that. I take it she won't be here tonight."

"No. She's taking me to dinner. She was clear about that. She did mention something about a little black dress and Kinsey Millhone though. Any idea what that meant?"

Dave chuckled. "Jake, we need to introduce you to American detective fiction. You'll think Leta and Wendy are little angels once you meet Kinsey."

Reading, snoozing, and gentle banter passed the time until the dinner hour drew near. As Wendy had predicted, preparations for the fancy dress ball perked me up. I smiled as I sat the fascinator atop my head. The tiny velvet headpiece with its single black peacock feather and short veil was the crowning touch.

Dave came up behind me and wrapped his arms around my waist. "Perfect in every way, Leta Parker."

As Dave and I exited the elevator, I felt a mixture of curiosity and sorrow. Curiosity about what Emily had planned for her guests and sorrow that she wasn't here to see it.

The banquet room was a sight to behold. A banner spanned the stage above the podium, the words "The Detection Club" written on it. All but one wall were hung with black curtains, and the fourth featured a series of posters. Displayed as centerpieces on the black-clothed tables were skulls holding flickering candles. By each plate, a miniature black skull echoed the large one.

Belle and Ellie were seated at a table with Sue, and Wendy was returning from the bar with wine. She placed two glasses in front of the senior members of the Little Old Ladies' Detective Agency and turned as we approached. "You're just in time. Sue and I were about to check out the posters."

With Wendy leading the way, we toured the room. The display included pictures of Detection Club presidents mixed with reproductions of the ten commandments from the Fair Play rules of detection. Gilbert joined us along the way and complimented Wendy on the selection. I'd forgotten that one of her Friday errands had been to work with the print shop. A stop by the bar was a must before we returned to our table, though Dave was quick to point out that wine was still off-limits for me.

Rhys greeted us. "Good evening. Tell me, what do you think of the setting?"

Our delight in the Detection Club touches brought a smile to his face. "Marvelous. Will you save me a seat? We'll be kicking off the evening soon."

The conversation tapered off when Rhys approached the podium and quieted the room. It was likely that only those of us who knew what he'd been through could detect his weariness. Attired in a black tux, he looked calm and confident.

"Welcome, ladies and gentlemen. Tonight concludes the Poison Pens Literary Festival, brought to you by the organization Emily Paget-Ford founded two years ago. It was always Emily's dream that the Golden Age Literary Association—or the GALAs, as she called the group—would hold a festival. She hoped this would be the first of many." He paused. "By now, most of you are aware that Emily passed away Tuesday evening."

He was right, but there were still a few gasps around the room.

"Many of you have expressed your condolences. Some asked why the GALAs chose to carry on with the event. The answer is simple. Emily wouldn't have had it any other way. She would never have forgiven us if we failed to see it through. So, please join me in a toast to Emily." He held up his glass. "Here's to her dream come true."

He went on to thank the guest speakers, the GALA members who had worked tirelessly behind the scenes, and the staff of The Grand Hotel. "Now, one never wants to stand between dinner guests and their meal, so I'll be brief. Tonight, we bring you a taste of the Detection Club—food first and then a ceremony. Cheers!"

When he returned to our table, I could tell that his master of ceremonies mask was beginning to slip. His food remained untouched, and he only occasionally engaged in the conversation. My heart ached for him.

He returned to the podium as dessert was being served. "Harken with me back to 1930, when G.K. Chesterton presided over the Detection Club. Close your eyes and imagine yourselves surrounded by Golden Age authors. Yes, close your eyes while we conjure up the period that produced some of the best mystery writers we know."

My eyes popped open when I heard a familiar voice. "I say, what are we doing here?" It was Gilbert onstage with Rhys. "Are we initiating this group en masse?" He scanned the room. "Quite unusual, but if we must." He was the spitting image of G.K. Chesterton, right down to the cape, crumpled hat, and cigar hanging from his mouth. How fitting that the two men shared the same first name.

Gilbert cleared his throat. "Please place your hand on the small skull in front of you. When you take this oath, you will be following in the footsteps of celebrated authors like Agatha Christie, Dorothy Sayers, Ngaio Marsh, and many others."

*Do you promise that your detectives shall well and truly detect the crimes presented to them using those wits which it may please you to bestow upon them and not placing reliance on nor making use of Divine Revelation, Feminine Intuition, Mumbo Jumbo, Jiggery-Pokery, Coincidence, or Act of God?*

The guests responded solemnly. Some said I do. Others simply uttered "yes." Gilbert— or G.K. Chesterton—winked at our host. "This is quite a serious crowd, isn't it? Well, my work is done. Shall we carry on?"

Rhys gave a nod, and Gilbert lifted his glass towards the audience. "Cheers." Around the room, glasses clinked, and murmurs of "cheers" and "well done" could be heard.

Gilbert joined us as Rhys worked his way around the room, playing his role as host. *What a yeoman's effort.* When he made it to our table, he pulled out his chair and collapsed into it. He gazed around the table as if in a daze, and it wasn't long before Wendy whispered in his ear, and they left together.

It was supposed to be a festive dinner, but as the evening came to a close, I couldn't shake the sadness I felt. Perhaps it was too soon after the events of the week for me to feel any other way.

Dave and I were both quiet as we prepared for bed, and I sensed his mood was the same as mine. Even Dickens and Christie were subdued.

When he climbed into bed, he didn't immediately turn out the light. He lay still for a moment before his hand found mine. "Leta, you don't know how glad I am that you're safe."

"Shhh, I know, and I'm sorry for what you went through."

"No, that's only part of it. It's everything that's gone on this week. So much loss, so much sorrow. It brings home how quickly life can change." He turned to me. "You know that better than I do because you lost Henry."

"That's true." I touched his cheek. "But then life changed again, and I found you."

"And I'm so glad you did."

When he kissed me and turned out the light, I snuggled against his back and breathed a sigh of contentment. All was once again right with my world.

**Book VIII**

The village is merry and bright. Until a flurry of disappearing dogs puts a damper on the holiday season.
Can the little old ladies bring them home for the holidays?

Read **Candy Canes, Canines & Crime** to find out. Available on Amazon https://amzn.to/3Q8SwIL

*What was Leta's life like before she retired to the Cotswolds?*

How did Dickens & Christie become part of the family? Find out in **Paws, Claws & Mischief,** the prequel to the Dickens & Christie mystery series.

Sign up for my newsletter to get your complimentary copy TO-DAY! https://bit.ly/Pennnewsletter

*Don't miss out on the Dickens & Christie prequel.*

# Psst ... Please take a minute

Dear Reader,

Writers put their hearts and souls into every book. Nothing makes it more worthwhile than reader reviews. Yes, authors appreciate reviews that provide helpful insights.

If you enjoyed this book, Kathy would love it if you could find the time to leave a good, honest review ... because after everything is said and done, authors write to bring enjoyment to their readers.

Thank you,
Dickens

# Books, Authors, and Series mentioned in Pets, Pens & Murder

## Books and Short Stories

- *Hangman's Holiday* (Dorothy Sayers)

- *Dorothy and Agatha* (Gaylord Larsen)

- *Master Lists for Writers* (Bryn Donovan)

- *Deadly Doses* (Serita Deborah Stevens)

- *Strong Poison* (Dorothy Sayers)

- *A Study in Scarlet* (Arthur Conan Doyle)

- *The Brazilian Cat* (Arthur Conan Doyle)

- *The Black Cat* (Edgar Allan Poe)

## Agatha Christie Mysteries

- *Appointment with Death*

- *Murder in Mesopotamia*

- *Death on the Nile*

- *Death Comes to an End*

- *Destination Unknown*

- *They Came to Baghdad*

- *Sparkling Cyanide*

- *And Then There Were None*

- *A Pocketful of Rye*

- *Third Girl*

- *Cat Among the Pigeons*

## Authors

- Agatha Christie

- Dorothy Sayers

- Arthur Conan Doyle

- J.M. Barrie

- Sophie Hannah

- Anthony Horowitz

- Mary Westamacott

- Edgar Allan Poe

- A.A. Milne

- Margery Allingham

- Ngaio Marsh

## Series
- Wesley Peterson (Kate Ellis)

- Joe Plantaganet (Kate Ellis)

- Tommy and Tuppence (Agatha Christie)

- Sherlock Holmes (Arthur Conan Doyle)

- Kinsey Milhone (Sue Grafton)

- Agatha Raisin (M.C. Beaton)

- Father Brown (G.K. Chesterton)

- Albert Campion (Margery Allingham)

# Acknowledgement

Thank you to Kate Ellis, award-winning author of the Wesley Peterson and Joe Plantagenet detective series, for graciously permitting me to put words in her mouth as a guest speaker at a literary festival.

# About the Author

A corporate escapee, Kathy Manos Penn went from crafting change communications to plotting page-turners. She adheres to the adage to "write what you know" and populates her cozy mysteries with well-read, witty senior women, a sassy cat, and a loyal dog. The murders and talking pets, however, exist only in her imagination.

Years ago, when she stumbled onto a side job as a columnist, she saw the opportunity as an entertaining diversion from the corporate grind. Little did she know that her serendipitous foray into writing would lead to a cozy mystery series—much less a

2020 Readers' Favorite Gold Award in the Mystery-Sleuth genre for *Bells, Tails & Murder*, Book I in the series.

Picture her sitting serenely at her desk, surrounded by the four-legged office assistants who inspire the personalities of Dickens & Christie. How does she describe her life? "I'm living a dream I never knew I had."

To learn more about Kathy *and* get a free download of the Dickens & Christie prequel, **sign up** for her newsletter, https://bit.ly/Pennnewsletter .

For book news and pics, follow Kathy on

—Facebook https://www.facebook.com/KathyManosPennAuthor/and

—Instagram https://www.instagram.com/kathymanospennauthor/.

# Also By Kathy Manos Penn

Bells, Tails & Murder

Pumpkins, Paws & Murder

Whiskers, Wreaths & Murder

Collectors, Cats & Murder

Castles, Catnip & Murder

Bicycles, Barking & Murder

Pets, Pens & Murder

Candy Canes, Canines & Crime (2022)

Made in the USA
Monee, IL
07 October 2022

15397399R00173

# The Jumping Boy

Here is the jumping boy, the boy
who jumps as I speak.

He is at home on the king's highway,
in call of the tall house, its blind
gable end, the trees – I know this place.

The road, on broad contourings drawn out of sight,
stops – wherever – but not at Lyonnesse,
though from Lyonnesse I shall bring you,

through grimed orchards, across gorse-hummocked
old common land everywhere given back
to the future of memory.


2

He leaps because he has serious
joy in leaping. The girl's

eyes no way allowed for, or else
she is close in covert and we
are to know that, not knowing how.

I'll bet she worships his plebeian
bullet head, Hermes' winged
plimsolls, the crinkled toy tin hat

held on by elastic. He is winning
a momentous and just war
with gravity.

3

This may be levitation. I
could do that. Give my remembrance
to his new body. These episodes occur.


4

Jump away, jumping boy; the boy I was
shouts go.

## Offertorium: December 2002

For rain-sprigged yew trees, blockish as they guard
admonitory sparse berries, atrorubent
stone holt of darkness, no, of claustral light:

for late distortions lodged by first mistakes;
for all departing, as our selves, from time;
for random justice held with things half-known,

with restitution if things come to that.

# The Storm
### (after Eugenio Montale, 'La Bufera')

The storm that batters the magnolia's
impermeable leaves, the long-drawn drum roll
of Martian thunder with its hail

(crystal acoustics trembling in your night's lair
disturb you while the gold transfumed
from the mahoganies, the pages' rims
of de luxe books, still burns, a sugar grain
under your eyelid's shell)

lightning that makes stark-white the trees,
the walls, suspending them –
interminable instant – marbled manna
and cataclysm – deep in you sculpted,
borne now as condemnation: this binds you
closer to me, strange sister, than any love.
So, the harsh buskings, bashing of castanets
and tambourines around the spoilers' ditch,
fandango's foot-rap and over all
some gesture still to be defined . . .
                                    As when
you turned away and casting with a hand
that cloudy mass of hair from off your forehead

gave me a sign and stepped into the dark.

## Broken Hierarchies

When to depict rain – heavy rain – it stands
in dense verticals diagonally lashed,
chalk-white yet with the chalk translucent;

the roadway sprouts a thousand flowerets,
storm-paddies instantly reaped, replenished,
and again cut down:

the holding burden of a wistaria
drape amid drape, the sodden
copia of all things flashing and drying:

first here after the storm these butterflies
fixed on each jinking run,
probing, priming, then leaping back,

a babble of silent tongues;
and the flint church also choiring
into dazzle

. . .

like Appalachian music, those
aureate stark sounds
plucked or bowed, a wild patience

replete with loss,
the twankled dulcimer,
scrawny rich fiddle gnawing;

a man's low voice that looms out of the drone:
the humming bird that is not
of these climes; and the great

wanderers like the albatross;
the ocean, ranging-in, laying itself
down on our alien shore.